HONEY, I'M HOME!

Stavros stumbled over a shoe and almost fell. That forced him to notice what a mess the place was. Leaving the apartment in such disarray was not like Andrea, but Stavros did not think anything of it until he saw that his icons were missing. He swore and dashed into the bedroom.

The drawer under the bed was open. So was the little strongbox inside. Stavros turned on his computer. He could not access any of his files. They were not there to access—they were gone.

He had not thought he could be more afraid.

By Harry Turtledove
Published by Ballantine Books:

The Videssos Cycle:

Harry Turtledove

NONINTERFERENCE

A Del Rey Book

BALLANTINE BOOKS • NEW YORK

A Del Rey Book
Published by Ballantine Books

Library of Congress Catalog Card Number: 87-91663

ISBN 0-345-34338-7

Manufactured in the United States of America

First Edition: January 1988

For the people who helped me make it
happen and make it better:
Stan and Russ and Owen and Shelly
and Shelley and Tina

FEDERACY
STANDARD
YEAR 1186

I

Sun, stench, racket: market day at Helmand.

The sun was a G-0 star, not much different from Sol. Asked to generate a name for it, the computer called it Bilbeis. It blazed from the blue cloisonné dome of the sky. Beyond the Margush river and the canals that drew its waters for the croplands of Helmand and the other river valley towns, the land was a desert, baked brown and bare.

The stench went with city life. The twelve or fifteen thousand inhabitants of Helmand had no better notion of sanitation than throwing their rubbish, chamber pots and all, into the narrow, winding streets. After a few years, the floors of their dwellings would be thirty or forty centimeters below street level. Then it was time to knock down the whole house and build a new mud-brick structure on the rubble. Helmand perched on a hill of its own making, a good fifteen meters above the Margush.

As for the racket, expect nothing else when large numbers of people gather to trade, as the folk of Helmand did once a nineday. And they *were* people. Only by such details as hair and skin color, beard pattern, and shape of features could they be told at a glance from Terrans. There were more subtle internal differences, but David Ware and Julian Crouzet had no trouble passing as foreigners from a distant land.

The two Survey Service anthropologists strolled through the marketplace. They paused gratefully in the long shadow of a temple for the time it took to drink a cup of thin, sour wine.

In their boots, denim coveralls, and caps, they attracted some attention from the people swarming around them, but not much. The city dwellers were already typical urban sophisticates, though Helmand and the other towns of the Margush valley represented the first civilization on Bilbeis IV.

Most of the stares came from peasants, in from the fields

3

with produce or livestock to trade for the things they could not make themselves. Here a farmer weighed out grain to pay for a new bronze sickle blade, there another quarreled with a potter over how much dried fruit he would have to give for a large storage jar. The latter man finally threw up his arms in disgust and stomped off to find a better deal.

David Ware had been taping the argument with a camera set in a heavy silver ring. "You think that one's unhappy," Crouzet murmured, "look at the trader over there."

The fellow at whom he nodded was from the Raidan foothills west of the Margush. He let his gray-green mustachios grow barbarously long and wore a knee-length tunic of gaudy green and saffron stripes. "You try to cheat me, you son of a pimp!" he shouted in nasally accented Helmandi, shaking his fist at the fat stonecutter who sat cross-legged in front of his stall.

"I do not," the stonecutter said calmly. "Seventy *diktals* of grain is all your obsidian is worth—more than you would get from some."

The hillman was frantic with frustration. "You lie! See here—I have three beastloads of prime stone. In my grandfather's day, my animals would have killed themselves hauling back to my village the grain that stone brought. Seventy *diktals*—faugh! I could carry that myself."

"In your grandfather's day, we would have used the obsidian for sickles and scythes at harvest time, and for edging war swords. Bronze was hard to come by then, and even dearer than stone. Now that we have plenty, we find it more useful. So what good is your obsidian? Oh, I can make some of it into trinkets, I suppose, but it is no precious stone like turquoise or emerald. The jewelry would be cheap and move slowly."

Ware turned away with a half-amused, half-cynical snort. "Even in a Bronze Age society, changing technology throws people out of work."

"That's true at any level of culture," Crouzet said. "I will admit, though, the pace has picked up in Helmand under Queen Sabium."

"I should say so." Ware's craggy face, normally rather dour, was lit now with enthusiasm. "She's one in a million."

His companion nodded. As if summoned by the mention of their ruler, a platoon of musicians marched into the square down the one real thoroughfare Helmand boasted: the road from the palace. They raised seashell trumpets to their lips and blew a discordant blast. The two Terrans winced. The market-day hubbub died away.

"Bow your heads!" a herald cried. "Forth comes Sabium, vicegerent of Illil the goddess of the moons and queen of Helmand." Actually, the word the herald used literally meant "lady king"; Helmandi had no exact equivalent for "queen," as Sabium was the only female ruler the town had ever known.

Fifteen years before, she had been principal wife of the last king. When he died, his firstborn son was a babe in arms, and Sabium administered affairs as regent. The town prospered as never before under her leadership. A few years later, the child-king died, too. Sabium ruled on, now in her own right, and did so well that no one thought to challenge her.

"I wonder what brings her out," Crouzet said, his eyes on the dirt. "She's missed the last couple of market days."

Ware nodded. "I didn't think she looked well, either, when she was here."

The royal bodyguard preceded the queen into the square. The troopers carried bronze-headed spears and maces with wicked spikes. They used their big leather shields to push people out of the way and clear a path to the raised brick platform in the center of the marketplace.

A retinue of Helmand's nobles followed. The hems of their long woolen robes dragged in the dust; their wide sleeves flapped languidly as they walked. Not for them the bright colors that delighted the semisavage obsidian seller: like the bodyguards and most Helmandis, they preferred white or sober shades of brown, gray, and blue. But gold and silver gleamed on their arms, around their necks, and in ear and nose rings.

A sedan chair borne by twelve husky servants brought up the rear of the procession. David Ware whistled softly when he saw it from the corner of his eye. "I'll bet she is sick, then!" he exclaimed. "She always walked here before."

"We'll know soon enough," Crouzet said calmly. He was a big moon-faced man; his phlegmatic nature made him a good foil for Ware, who sometimes went off half-cocked.

Skillfully keeping the sedan chair level, the porters carried it to the top of the platform, set it down, and scurried down the stairs. The white-robed priest of Illil who had accompanied them stayed behind. The shell-trumpets blared again. The priest drew back the silk curtain that screened the interior of the sedan chair from view.

"Behold the queen!" the herald shouted.

The crowd in the marketplace raised their heads. Ware lifted his arm as if to scratch, so he could record Sabium's emergence.

When he saw her, he tried to suppress his involuntary gasp of surprise and dismay but could not. It hardly mattered. The same sound came from Crouzet beside him and from the throats of everyone close enough to Sabium to see how ill she truly was.

A month before, Ware thought, she had been a handsome woman, even without making allowances for the differences between Terran and Helmandi standards of good looks. Her grayish-pink skin, light blue hair that receded at the temples, and downy cheeks seemed no more strange, after one was used to them, than Crouzet's blackness or his own knobby-kneed, gangly build. Even the false mustache she wore to appear more fully a king somehow lent her face dignity instead of making her ridiculous.

Her strength of character was responsible for that, of course. It shone through her violet eyes like sun through stained glass, animating her aquiline features. One could hear it in her clear contralto, see it in the brisk pace with which her stocky body moved. No wonder the whole city loved her.

Now she got out of the sedan chair with infinite care, as if every motion hurt. She had to lean on the priest's arm for a moment. Her body seemed shrunken within the heavy, elaborately fringed robe of state, shot all through with golden thread. She held the royal crown—a massy silver circlet encrusted with river pearls and other stones that glowed softly, like moonlight—in her hands instead of wearing it. Her face was more gray than pink.

"My God, she's dying!" Ware blurted.

"Yes, and heaven help Helmand after she goes," Crouzet agreed. The one thing Sabium had not done was provide for a successor. Probably, Ware thought, she was too proud to admit to herself that her body had betrayed her.

She could still force it to obey her for a time, though, and she carried on with the ceremony as if nothing were wrong.

Her voice rang through the square: "Shumukin, son of Galzu, ascend to join me!"

A small, lithe man climbed the steps and went on his knees in front of the queen. Sabium declared, "For the beauty of your new hymn to Illil, I reward you with half a *diktal* of refined gold and the title of *ludlul*." The rank was of the lesser nobility; Shumukin went down on his belly in gratitude. The trumpeters at the edge of the square struck up a new tune, presumably Shumukin's hymn. The crowd applauded. Shumukin rose, smiling shyly, and stepped to one side.

There was a visible pause while Sabium gathered herself. The priest spoke to her, too softly for the Terrans to hear. She waved him aside and called out, "M'gishen, son of Nadin, ascend and join me!"

This time the Helmandi was old and stout. He leaned on a stick going up the stairs. The priest held the cane as he clumsily got to his knees. Sabium said, "For sharing with all of Helmand what you have learned, I reward you with three *diktals* of refined gold and the rank of *shaushludlul*." That was a higher title than the one Shumukin had earned. M'gishen prostrated himself before the queen.

Sabium bent to bid him rise and could not hide a wince of pain. "Tell the people of what you found."

Shifting from foot to foot like a nervous schoolboy, M'gishen obeyed. His thin, reedy voice did not carry well. He had to start over two or three times before the calls of "Louder!" stopped coming from the back of the marketplace.

"Everybody knows what a taper is, of course," he said. "You take a wick and dip it in hot tallow. Well, if you dip it again and again and again, more and more tallow clings, y' see. When you light it then, it gives off a real glow like an oil lamp, not just a tiny little flame. Lasts as long as a lamp, too, maybe longer. Eh, well, that's what my new thing is." He reclaimed his stick and limped down the steps.

"Rewards await anyone who learns something new and useful and passes on his knowledge or who shows himself a worthy poet or sculptor or painter," Sabium said. "I set aside the first morning of every nineday to judge such things, and hope to see many of you then."

"Amazingly sophisticated attitude to find in such a primitive society," Crouzet remarked.

"I'm sorry, what was that?" David Ware had been watching

the priest of Illil help Sabium back into the sedan chair. The
process was slow and agonizing; he saw her bite down hard on
her lower lip to distract herself from the other, greater torment. It was a relief when the silk draperies gave her back her
privacy.

Crouzet repeated himself. "Oh, yes, absolutely," Ware
agreed. "For this sort of culture it's better than a patent system; the bureaucracy to run anything like that won't exist here
for hundreds of years. But the up-front reward encourages
people to put ideas into the public domain instead of hanging
on to them as family secrets."

"To say nothing of spurring invention." Crouzet's eyes followed the servitors bearing Sabium back to the palace. "What
do you think the odds are of whoever comes after her keeping
up what she's started?"

Ware laughed without humor. "What's the old saying? Two
chances—slim and none."

"I'm afraid you're right. Sometimes the rule of noninterference is a shame." Survey Service personnel on worlds
without spaceflight were observers only, doing nothing to
meddle in local affairs.

When Ware did not reply at once, Crouzet turned to look at
him. His colleague's face was a mask of furious concentration. Crouzet was no telepath, but he did not need to be to
know what the other Terran was thinking. Alarm replaced the
black man's usual amused detachment. "For God's sake,
David! There's never justification for breaking the noninterference rule!"

"The hell there isn't," David Ware said.

Lucrezia Spini played the tape of Queen Sabium in the
marketplace for the fourth time. "Yes, it might be a malignancy," the biologist said. "If I had to make a guess just from
seeing this and from the speed of the illness's advance, I'd say
it could well be. But making a real diagnosis on this kind of
evidence is pure guesswork. There are so many ways to fall
sick, and on a world like this we'll only learn a tiny fraction of
them."

"What can you do to pin it down more closely?" Ware
asked. A flier had brought him and Crouzet back to the *Leeuwenhoek* the night before. They had summoned the machine to
a field several kilometers outside Helmand. It was silent; the

local fear of demons who dwelt in darkness made the chance of being observed vanishingly small. The *Leeuwenhoek* itself had landed in the northern desert, safe from detection.

Spini rubbed her chin as she thought; had she been a man, she would have been the type to grow a beard for the sake of plucking at it. At last she said, "I suppose I could sneak a small infrared sensor onto the roof of the queen's bedchamber and do a body scan. If there are tumors, they'll show up warmer than the surrounding normal body areas."

"Would you?" Ware tried to hold the eagerness from his voice. He had kept quiet about his gut reaction back in the marketplace. If Sabium was suffering from some exotic local disease, she would die, and that was all there was to it. If, on the other hand, she had cancer . . . Time enough to worry about that when he knew.

"Why not? Either way, I'll learn something." When the anthropologist kept hovering over her, she laughed at him. "I don't have the answers yet, you know. I have to program the sensor, camouflage it, and send it out. Come back in three days and I may be able to give you something."

Ware had plenty to keep him busy while he waited but could not help fretting. What if Sabium died while they were investigating? She had seemed so feeble. Ware also noticed Julian Crouzet giving him suspicious looks every so often. He pretended not to.

When the appointed day came, he fairly pounced on Lucrezia Spini, barking, "Well?"

She put a hand on his arm. "Easy, David, easy. Anyone would think you were in love with her."

He blinked. That had not occurred to him. He was honest enough with himself to take a long look at the idea. After a few seconds he said, "You know, I might be, if she came from a civilization comparable to ours. As is, I admire her tremendously. She's kindly but firm enough to rule, she boosts this culture in ways it couldn't expect for centuries yet, she's three times as smart as any of the local kings—and she carries on like a trouper in spite of what she's got. Whatever it is, she deserves better."

"No need to preach. I'm convinced." Spini laughed, but Ware could tell his earnestness had impressed her. She fed a cassette into the monitor in front of her. "This will interest you."

The screen lit in an abstract pattern of greens, blues, reds, and yellows: an infrared portrait of Sabium's boudoir. "Ignore these," Spini said, pointing to several brilliant spots of light. "They're lamps, so of course they show up brightly. Here, now—"

Yes, the pattern at the bottom might have been a reclining figure. "Lucky the Helmandis sleep nude," the biologist remarked. "In this climate it's no wonder, I suppose. Clothes would have confused the picture, though. Look here, and here, and especially here—" Her finger moved to one area after another that glowed yellow or even orange. "Hot spots."

"That's her belly?" Ware asked harshly.

Spini nodded. "Full of tumor. A classical diagnosis. Too bad, if what you say about her is true. If she were a Terran, I wouldn't give her more than another month, tops, with that much metastatic cancer in there."

"Just how different biologically are the locals, Lucrezia?" Ware hoped he sounded casual.

He must have, for she answered readily. "Not very. When you were in Helmand, you ate the food, drank the beer. Some of the desert herbs here synthesize chemicals that look promising as pharmaceuticals."

"How interesting," the anthropologist said.

"No," Senior Coordinator Chunder Sen said flatly. With his round brown face and fringe of white hair, he usually reminded David Ware of a kindly grandfather. Now he sounded downright stern—something Ware would not have imagined possible—as he declared, "The rule of noninterference must be inviolable."

Heads nodded in agreement all around the table in the *Leeuwenhoek*'s mess, which doubled as the assembly chamber. It was the only compartment that could hold the ship's twenty-person complement at once. Julian Crouzet had taken pains to sit as far from Ware as he could, as if to avoid any association with what his colleague was proposing.

"So this is what you were leading up to," Lucrezia Spini exclaimed. It sounded like an accusation.

The anthropologist nodded impatiently. "Of course it is. We ought to cure Queen Sabium, as I said when I asked for this meeting. It could be done, couldn't it?"

"Technically speaking, I don't see why not. I already told

you that the natives' metabolism isn't much different from ours. With the interferons and other immunological amplifiers we have, we could stimulate her body to throw off the malignancy. But I don't think we should. Noninterference has been Federacy policy from the word go, and rightly. Where would we be if more advanced races had tinkered with Terra when we were just a single primitive world?"

"Maybe better off; who knows?" Ware saw at once he had been too flip. He backed off. "What's the reasoning behind the rule of noninterference, anyway?"

"Oh, really now, David," Jemala Gürsel snorted. The meteorologist went on: "There's no point to treating us like so many children. Everyone knows that." She shook a finger at Ware in annoyance.

"Let's get it out in the open and look at it," he persisted.

"Very well." That was Chunder Sen, sounding resigned. As a bureaucrat, he was vulnerable to proper procedure. "Julian, do the honors, will you?"

"Gladly," the other anthropologist said, "since a chance comment of mine seems to have touched David off in the first place. There are many sound reasons behind noninterference, but the most telling one is the one Lucrezia gave—less advanced cultures deserve to develop in their own ways. We have no right to meddle with them."

"That's exactly what I thought you'd say," Ware told him, "and it sounds very noble, but it doesn't bear much relation to reality. Truth is, we interfere every time we come into contact with a local."

"Nonsense!" Crouzet snapped, and that was one of the milder reactions. Coordinator Chunder Sen, a devout Hindu, could not have looked more pained if he had suddenly discovered he'd been eating beef the last six weeks.

Ware did not mind. He felt filled with a sudden crazy confidence, like a gambler who knows the next card will make his straight, the next roll will be a seven. "It isn't nonsense," he insisted. "The physicists have known for a couple of thousand years that the act of observation affects what's being observed."

"Don't throw old Heisenberg at us out of context," said Moshe Sharett, the chief engineer. "He's only relevant at the atomic level. For large-scale phenomena, the observer effect is negligible."

"Who says Helmand's a large-scale phenomenon? Fifteen thousand people or so strikes me as being awfully different from the sextillions of atoms chemists and physicists play with."

Sharett scratched at an ear. Several other people frowned thoughtfully. Julian Crouzet, though, said, "I defy you to show me how walking through the streets of Helmand could twist the culture out of shape."

"Even that might. Suppose we bumped into someone and made him late for an important meeting, so a decision was taken that he would have changed if he'd been there. But walking about isn't all we do, you know. Remember that scrawny vendor we bought wine from? The grain we gave him could well have kept him and his whole family from starving. We might have changed a thousand years of bloodlines if a child that would have died grows up to breed."

"Oh, come now," Courzet said. "If we hadn't bought from him, someone else would."

"Would they? Not many people did, or his ribs wouldn't have shown so clearly. Julian, I'm afraid we did him a good turn, whether we wanted to or not. Let's give ourselves up."

Crouzet threw his hands in the air. "Spare me your sarcasm. What if we did? It's a long way from going in and healing Queen Sabium."

"Of course it is," Ware said at once, "but the difference is one of degree, not of kind—that's the point I'm trying to make. It's interference either way. For once, let it have a purpose. Here; I'm going to show two tapes and then I'm done."

He walked over to the big vision screen that took up most of one wall. The first tape was the one he and Crouzet had made of Sabium in the marketplace. "Give us a running translation for those who don't know Helmandi, will you, Jorge?" he said. "You're smoother than I am."

Jorge Morales, the ship's linguist, was a self-important little man. He jumped a bit but did as Ware asked him. The anthropologist nodded to himself. After two minutes of translating, Morales would think any attack on the tape was an attack on him personally.

But there were no attacks. Sabium's courage impressed the company of the *Leeuwenhoek* even more than her wisdom. In the dead silence that filled the mess hall, Ware inserted the other tape. "This has two parts," he said. "The first one is from a spy camera I had planted in the palace bedroom the other day."

Seen from above, attendants bustled around Sabium. One offered food and drink, most of which she declined. Others helped her take off the stifling royal robes; she accepted that attention with relief, as she did the cloth soaked in cool water that a serving maid pressed to her forehead.

Some of the water ran down her face and got into her false mustaches, which began to come off. She said something that made her attendants laugh. "What was that?" Moshe Sharett asked.

"Something to the effect that that was one thing her husband hadn't had to put up with," Morales replied. Several of the people watching the screen grinned; not all of them were those Ware expected to back him.

After a while the servants bowed their way out, leaving Sabium alone in the chamber, a small, tired woman wearing only a thin shift that covered her to midthigh. Much of the flesh had melted from her legs and arms, but the fabric of the shift stretched tight across her swollen belly, as if she were pregnant.

If she had not known how ill she was that day in the marketplace, she did now. She pressed herself here and there and flinched more than once in the self-examination. When she was done, she shrugged and spoke, though she did not think anyone was there to hear her. This time, Ware did the translating himself: "'Another day gone. Now to do the best I can with the ones I have left.'"

Sabium rose, stripped off the shift with an involuntary grunt of pain, and blew out the lamps. The leather thongs supporting the mattress creaked as the bedchamber went dark.

The second piece of tape was the infrared sequence Lucrezia Spini had taken: a death sentence in bright, cheerful false colors.

"Which is the greater distortion?" Ware asked softly. "To let such a queen as that die before her time, knowing that nothing she had worked for would survive her, or for her to live out her natural span? That's the choice before us now." He sat down.

Had Coordinator Chunder Sen been a military man instead of an administrator, he would never have let it come to a vote. But he was confident of the outcome. The rule of interference was as much an article of faith to him as his belief in Brahma, Shiva, and Vishnu. He could not imagine anyone else having a different opinion.

To his amazement, he lost, twelve votes to eight.

Ware turned curiously to Julian Crouzet as they walked through the streets of Helmand toward the palace. "Just why are you coming along if you disagree so strongly with what I'm doing?"

"Frankly, to keep an eye on you."

"I'm not going to give Sabium the secret of the stardrive, Julian. For one thing, I don't know it myself."

"Thank God for small favors."

Ware glared at him but let it go; they were coming up to the entrance of the palace.

The arched doorway was twice the height of a man. Most of the palace was built of the same sun-dried mud brick as the rest of Helmand, but in the wall that held the doorway expensive fired bricks had been used lavishly for show. Their fronts were enameled in bright colors, like giant mosaic tesserae. Here a predator was shown leaping on a herd animal, there a hunter's arrow brought down a flying creature. The entrance itself was flanked by a pair of apotropaic gods.

A steward—a low-ranking one, from his unadorned robe and plain white conical hat—approached the two Terrans, asking, "What do you foreigners wish?"

With Crouzet standing by in silent disapproval, Ware launched into the cover story that had been hammered out aboard the *Leeuwenhoek*: "As you can see, we are from a far country. We have done well for ourselves here in Helmand, and we would like to give your splendid city a gift in return. Forgive me if I speak now of intimate matters, but is it not true that your queen is unwell?"

The steward's eyes narrowed. "What if it is?"

"We saw her on her last trip to the marketplace, I and my friend," Ware said, including Crouzet whether he liked it or not. "If her illness is as it appears, it is one for which our people have a cure."

"As what charlatan does not?" the steward said scornfully. "And for your so-called cure, no doubt, you will want all the silver and half the grain in the city—payable in advance."

The Helmandis were very human indeed, Ware thought. He said, "No, it is a gift, as I told you. We will heal your queen if we can, and ask nothing for it. Indeed, we will refuse whatever you may offer."

The toplofty steward clearly was taken aback. "Come with me," he said after a few seconds, and led the Terrans into the palace. Away from the entrance, only torches lit the rush-strewn narrow halls, which smelled of burning fat, stale sweat, and ordure.

Several functionaries, each more important than the one before, grilled the anthropologists. The last barrier before Sabium was the priest of Illil who had helped her on the platform. "Do you swear by all your gods that your remedy will cure?" he demanded.

"No," Ware said at once. The natives' metabolism was almost identical to Terrans', but not quite—and there were always individual idiosyncrasies. "If it fails, it will not harm her," he added.

"Well, what is there to lose?" the priest muttered under his breath. Ware did not think he was supposed to hear. Then the local did speak directly to him. "Stay here. I shall take your words to the queen, to let her decide." Spearmen stood aside to let the priest pass but never stopped watching the Terrans.

The wait could not have been more than ten minutes, but it stretched till it seemed like hours. At last the priest of Illil returned. "This way," he said brusquely. Ware gave a sigh of relief and followed, Crouzet at his side.

Something small and nasty buzzed down onto Ware's neck, bit him, and flew away before he could swat it. Lucrezia Spini said the local pests weren't exactly insects. Close enough for government work, though, Ware thought, rubbing.

Braziers of incense smoked in the small chamber where Sabium received the Terrans, but the sweet, resinous smoke could not quite cover the sickroom odor of the place. The queen reclined on a low couch with a headrest; a rug embroidered with river flowers covered her legs. The walls of the chamber were whitewashed to help reflect torchlight.

Sabium had grown even thinner, Ware thought as he and Crouzet went on their knees before her. Only her eyes, smudged below with great dark circles, showed life. They glowed, enormous, in a face now skeletally lean.

"Rise," Sabium said. She studied the Terrans with an interest still undimmed by illness, commenting, "I remember noticing the two of you in the marketplace once or twice. What distant land do you come from that grows men of your colors?"

"It is near the great western ocean, Your Majesty," Ware replied. The Helmandis knew nothing about that part of the continent.

Sabium asked more questions; a scribe took down the answers the anthropologists gave. Only when a spasm of pain wracked her so that her hands twisted and her lips went white beneath her false mustache did she say, "Tupsharru"—she nodded toward the priest of Illil—"tells me your city is skilled in medicine." For all the emotion that showed in her voice, she might have been speaking of the weather.

"Yes, Your Majesty," Ware said eagerly. He drew a stout syringe from the pouch he wore on his belt. He showed her the point, warning, "I will have to prick your arm to give you the medicine. It may hurt you some."

She astonished him by laughing. "What is the sting of a needle against the beast of fire in my middle? Come forward, and fear not; if I were to harm the physicians who failed to cure me, none would be left in Helmand."

She did not flinch when he made the injection, and held her arm motionless until the entire dose had been administered. As she watched the medicine enter her, he could see her grasping the principle of the syringe. "Ah, the needle is hollow, like the sting of the *gurash*," she murmured. "That idea might prove valuable in other ways as well."

Ware could feel the weight of Crouzet's sardonic glance on his back but did not turn around.

"That's all?" Sabium asked when he put away the hypodermic. He knew what was puzzling her: in Helmand, witchcraft and medicine were hard to tell apart, and drugs and elaborate charms went hand in hand.

He shrugged. "Yes, Your Majesty. To us, that our remedies work is more important than the spectacle involved in using them." She dipped her head thoughtfully, then returned to her questions about the Terrans' fictive homeland.

Before long, yawns began punctuating the interrogation. Lucrezia Spini had warned that drowsiness was a common side effect of the drugs, and so Ware was more encouraged than not to see Sabium sleepy—it was a first sign she was reacting as Terrans did. Tupsharru, though, started up in alarm when his queen dozed off in the middle of a sentence.

The priest searched Ware with his eyes as the anthropologist explained that there was no danger. "Then no doubt you will not object to staying here in the palace until Her Majesty returns to herself," Tupsharru said coldly.

"No doubt," Ware replied, and hoped he meant it.

Although it only had a slit window and was therefore very stuffy, the room in which the Terrans were confined was well appointed, and their evening meal fit for a noble: bread, salt fish, boiled leguminous plants, candied fruit, and a wine hardly less sweet. The squad of soldiers outside the barred door, however, did nothing to improve the appetite.

Most of a day went by before the door opened again; Crouzet beat Ware out of a week's pay at dice. They were still crouched over the plastic cubes when Tupsharru burst into the chamber, half a dozen spearmen at his back.

Ware grabbed for the stunner by his belt pouch, but there was no need. The priest of Illil went to one knee before him, as if in salute to a great lord. "She wakes without torment, for the first time in the gods know how many ninedays!" he said exultantly. "And she is hungry, as she has not been for even longer!"

"Well, David, you seem to have pulled it off," Julian Crouzet said, his voice sober. "I hope you're pleased."

Ware hardly heard him; he was too busy trying to be polite declining the gifts Tupsharru wanted to shower on him. At last he did take a couple of fine small bronzes, one a statuette of Illil with a moon in either hand, the other a portrait bust of Sabium that managed to capture something of her character in spite of being almost as rigidly formulaic as the image of the god.

"It would have been out of character for traders to turn down everything," he told Crouzet a little defensively as the two Terrans made their way back to the city gate. They had had to argue Tupsharru out of an honor guard.

"No doubt you're right," Crouzet said, and lapsed back into silence.

"You still think I was wrong, don't you?"

"Yes," Crouzet answered promptly. Ware thought he was going to leave it at that, but he went on with a sigh, "For better or worse, it's over, and there's nothing I can do about it anymore. Maybe it will all turn out for the best in the long run; who knows?"

"Julian, listen to me: in the long run, it won't matter at all. No matter what we say, noninterference just isn't that important on a preindustrial world, except as a policy to prevent exploitation. The same discoveries always get made, if not now, then in a few centuries."

"That's not what you were claiming back at the ship," Crouzet remarked.

"You're right, but I wouldn't have got anywhere taking that tack. Think about it, though. By the time the next survey ship comes to Bilbeis IV, in fifteen hundred years or so, who'll remember anything about Queen Sabium? The crew will, sure, because they'll have copies of the tapes we made here, but what about the locals? Maybe a priest or two will know of her name, if the Margush valley civilization survives—maybe not, too. So what, either way?"

Crouzet looked him in the eye. "You, my friend, are talking through your hat. What's more, you know it. You don't have the slightest idea what the effect of this interference is going to be, any more than anyone else does."

"Don't I?" Ware snapped. He sounded very tired. "Whatever it is, it won't be much. This society is as tradition-bound as any other early civilization. If Sabium gets too far out in front of her people, they won't follow her anymore, and that'll be that. Or the priests will say her changes offend the gods, and overthrow her. That'll solve your problem, too. You tell me, damn it—am I right or not?"

Crouzet considered. "Maybe," was all he would let himself say.

To Ware, it was like a concession. "There, you see? What I set out to do was to save a good woman from a lot of anguish and a nasty death, and that's what I did—that's *all* I did. Where's the evil in it? That's what I want to know."

They walked on a while in silence, but it was not an angry silence anymore. Then Crouzet sadly said, "Oh, David, David, David," and put his arm around the other anthropologist's shoulder. "Justify it any way you like. When we get home, the review board will crucify you all the same, not least for playing on everyone's emotions so shamelessly."

"Let them," Ware said. "For my money, it's worth it." The walls of Helmand loomed ahead, close now. He began to whistle.

FEDERACY
STANDARD
YEAR 2686

II

Bilbeis IV hung in the stereo tank: a blue globe, streaked with the white and gray of clouds. Like any terrestrial world seen from space, it was heart-stoppingly beautiful. The crew of the Survey Service ship *Jêng Ho* eyed it with the same affection they would have given a nest of scorpions at a picnic grounds.

"Why did it have to be us?" Atanasio Pedroza said to no one in particular. In spite of his name, the biologist was big and blond; long ago, his home planet had been settled by Guatemalans and by Afrikaner refugees fleeing the fall of South Africa.

"There's a technical term for the reason," Magda Kodaly said. Despite the anthropologist's cynical turn of mind, Pedroza looked at her expectantly. "It's called the short straw," she amplified.

"Oh, come now," Irfan Kawar said. His specialty was geology, so he was able to take a more dispassionate view of Bilbeis IV. "Odds are, David Ware's interference made no difference at all in the planet's cultural development, just as he said it wouldn't."

"Interference?" Magda snorted. Her green eyes glinted dangerously. "There's a technical term for that, too: fuckup, I think it is. Ware got less than he deserved, if you ask me." The Survey Service had cashiered David Ware, of course, as soon as Central learned what he had done. Now every new class of recruits had his folly drilled into it as the worst of bad examples.

Magda rose from her chair and stretched, deliberately turning her back on the image of Bilbeis IV. She was conscious of Pedroza's eyes following her, and suppressed a sigh. The *Jêng Ho* was cramped enough to make politeness essential, but he wanted her and she did not want him.

23

Maybe, she thought hopefully, he would be too busy to pester her anymore once they landed.

Hideko Narahara punched a button. The engineering officer said, "Observation satellites away."

"Good," Kawar said. "I for one won't be sorry to have new data to work with."

"How much can a planet change in fifteen hundred years?" Pedroza asked rhetorically.

Kawar answered him. "A good deal. For one thing, there was a fair amount of glaciation when the last survey ship was here. They didn't stay long enough to find whether the ice was advancing or retreating. The answer will mean something to your biology, Atanasio, and also to Magda's area: changes in climate and sea level have to affect the locals' culture."

"I suppose so." Pedroza did not sound as though he meant it. He really wanted to believe every discipline had its own cubbyhole and operated in isolation from all the others. That struck Magda as intellectual apartheid; it was one reason she did not find the biologist appealing in spite of his blond good looks.

She started out of the control room. "Where are you going?" Pedroza asked. "Would you care for company?"

"No, thank you, Atanasio," she said, swallowing that sigh again. "I'm heading north back to my cabin to review Margushi irregular verbs."

Pedroza's clear, fair skin showed his flush. All he said, though, was, "It seems a waste of time, when odds are no one speaks the language anymore."

"They may still write it," she said, "or use tongues descended from it. Anyway, until we have some fresh information, it's the best I can do." She left quickly, before he came up with a different suggestion.

Magda was glad she liked working with Irfan Kawar. Over the next several days, she and the geologist from New Palestine spent a lot of time together, using the satellite photos to remap Bilbeis IV.

He made another comparison between the old coastline and the new. "Not much change, I'm afraid," he said, running his hand over the balding crown of his head. He smiled. "One always hopes for drama."

"Of course, if you want anyone to read your data card."

He cocked an eyebrow at her. "This once, I think you would be just as happy with obscurity."

"Between you and me, I won't say you're wrong."

"Be careful, my dear. Such sentiments could get you burned at the stake in the quad of any university in the Federacy."

Magda snorted. "God deliver me from that kind of academic. I delivered myself, by getting into fieldwork as fast as I could once I had my degree."

She bent over the photomosaic map of Bilbeis IV's main continent. The settlement pattern was peculiar. Not surprisingly, the Margush valley was still the most densely populated area. Several other river systems also had good-sized cities, which they hadn't before. And it was reasonable for towns to have arisen along the eastern coast, where only a narrow sea separated the main continent from a lesser neighbor.

But the western coastline also boasted some large towns. That was strange. High, rugged mountains separated it from the rest of the continent, and the ocean to the west stretched for several thousand empty kilometers. The data they had showed no minerals to draw settlers.

"Puzzling." Magda must have said that aloud, for Irfan Kawar gave a questioning grunt. She explained.

"Maybe it is an independent civilization," the geologist suggested.

Magda brushed auburn curls back from her face. "I hope so. Comparing it to the one that diffused out of the Margush would tell us a lot." She scribbled a note to herself. "I have to talk to Hideko. I need high-resolution photos of a western town to compare to some east of the mountains."

"I hate interrupting the mapping program I've set up," the engineering officer said when Magda called, "but I'll see what I can do." Coming from Hideko, that was better than Pedroza's solemn vow of aid.

All the same, the picture series was not done till late afternoon, ship's time. Magda popped a shot of a west-coast town, one from the Margush valley, and one from another valley into a viewer.

She whistled softly. That all three cities were built around large central squares was not surprising. The neat grid pattern of the surrounding streets was. And it was stretching the odds to find the same sort of hexagonal building in a prominent place in each square.

"Coincidence?" Pedroza asked in the galley when she mentioned what she'd found.

"Anything is possible," Magda shrugged, "but that's not very likely. Six-sided buildings aren't common anywhere. It's easier to imagine, say, a common cult than to think them separate developments. The other parts of the towns seem similar, too, and they shouldn't. What would attract people from the Margush valley culture out to that godforsaken coast?"

"Special timber, maybe, or some kind of fur or flavoring or drug?" Pedroza was not a fool—unfortunately, Magda thought. He would have been easier to dislike if he was. The suggestions were all plausible.

She gestured in frustration. "I wish there were more variation."

"Variety is the life of spice," Pedroza agreed with a look that was not quite a leer, and Magda decided he was not so hard to dislike after all.

Her distaste plainly showed. There were several seconds of uncomfortable silence before Norma Anderssen said, "We'll find all the variety we need, I'm sure, when we land." The linguist was pretty, fair as Pedroza, and even-tempered enough to put up with his machismo. Why hadn't he settled on her to bother? Magda thought unhappily.

She supposed that would have been too easy. Sighing, she took a long pull at the vodka and soda in front of her. It did not help much.

After a good deal of wrangling, the *Jêng Ho* made planetfall west of the mountain chain. To Magda's surprise—and to her annoyance—the person who agreed most vociferously with her was Pedroza. She was eager to investigate those anomalous western cities, he to see how much difference there was between the plants and animals east and west of the range.

Norma, on the other hand, complained. "So far from the site of the last survey, any linguistic work I do is going to be worthless."

Irfan Kawar echoed her. "The most detailed information I have is on the Margush valley and the desert to the north. I could really get a good picture of how they've changed over time—and here we are, six thousand kilometers away. Not that new data aren't welcome, you understand, but comparing new and old would yield more."

"I expect we'll get to the Margush eventually—" Magda began.

"Meanwhile, though, half the research staff might as well be twiddling their thumbs, for all they'll accomplish," Norma said. That she interrupted proved how upset she was.

"I don't think Captain Brusilov wants to get near the Margush any sooner than he has to," Magda said quietly.

"Ah," Kawar said with a slow nod. "That makes sense." Norma's eyes widened—she was too straightforward for that kind of explanation to have occurred to her.

Pedroza's specialty was the first to come in handy, disguising probes and sensors to look like local flying pests so the natives would not notice them. The resulting pictures and sound tapes made the world vividly real in a way the old records could not.

Had the locals not been so human, Magda thought, the immunological amplifier would not have worked on the long-ago Queen Sabium in the first place. That would have saved everyone a lot of trouble—except, the anthropologist had to admit, Sabium herself.

Magda voraciously studied the incoming data: it gave her the basis for whatever fieldwork she would be able to do. She saw to her relief that Bilbeis IV—or at least this little chunk of it—was not as male-dominated as most pretechnological cultures. That so often hampered women in the field. Sometimes the only role available for them was courtesan, and Magda knew she lacked the clinical detachment necessary for that.

Hereabouts, though, the sensors showed women going freely through the streets, buying and selling, working at looms and potters' wheels and in jewelers' and bakers' shops on much the same terms as men. And when Magda saw a recording of a man handing over square silver coins to a woman and receiving in turn a scrawled receipt, the likeliest interpretation she could put on the scene was that it involved paying rent—which seemed to mean women could own property.

"Unusual," Norma Anderssen said when Magda remarked

on that: now she rather than Kawar worked most closely with
the anthropologist. The same tapes interested them both.

"Certainly a change from the last visit," Magda agreed.
"Then women hardly showed themselves in public. I daresay
it's the influence of this new cult the locals have."

As Magda had expected, the big hexagonal building in the
center of town was a temple. Fifteen hundred years ago, the
natives had worshiped a typical pantheon, with gods and goddesses in charge of the various aspects of nature. Now,
though, the dominant local religion centered on a mother goddess. Judging from the identical structures Magda had seen in
the orbital pictures, it was the dominant religion all over the
continent.

"Unusual," Norma said again. "Normally, from what I understand, mother-worshiping cultures aren't progressive technically. They tend to accept things as they are, don't they,
instead of seeking change?"

"Yes, usually," Magda said. That bothered her, too. The
natives used iron as well as bronze; their carts and wagons had
pivoted front axles; they used waterwheels to grind their grain.
They had come a long way in a relatively short time.

Magda pushed aside the thought of interference. She said,
"My best guess would be that the religion is fairly new and
that the technology we're seeing predates it."

"Maybe so. But why would a dynamic society shift to belief in a mother goddess?"

"I can think of several possibilities off the top of my head:
internal strife might have made the locals look away from this
world toward the next, for instance, or this cult might have
grown up in a land annexed by the dominant culture and then
spread through the big, politically unified area. That's what
happened with Christianity, after all. Maybe we'll find out.
What really interests me here is that everyone seems to be-
long."

The town had no temples but the central shrine. That was
not so strange—state-supported faiths, as this one plainly
was, tended to drive their rivals underground. But Magda had
not been able to find any rivals, any signs that other religions
existed at all. It puzzled her. Such perfect unity should have
been impossible on a world with no better mass communica-
tion methods than signboard and megaphone.

Yet it was there. Every household into which Pedroza's

disguised sensors had buzzed or crawled had an image of the local goddess prominently displayed. All were copies, good or bad, of the cult portrait in the hexagonal temple.

At first she suspected the ubiquitous images were in place only as an outward show of conformity. But no one ever came snooping to see if some house might not have a portrait on the wall. Not only that, the locals plainly believed in their goddess. It was not always showy, and so doubly convincing. A casual, friendly nod to an image as someone walked past said more than the rites at the temple.

Magda worked hard with Norma to pick up the local language. As she'd hoped, it was descended from the one the first Survey Service ship had learned. That helped a lot. These days, too, the natives wrote with a straightforward thirty-eight-character alphabet instead of the hodgepodge of syllabic signs, ideograms, and pictograms they'd used before. That helped even more.

Seeing the work she'd done on the way to Bilbeis IV paying off made it hard for Magda not to gloat at Pedroza. He had just started fighting with the language and was still a long way from the fluency he'd need for fieldwork in town. Magda wanted out of the *Jêng Ho* so badly she could taste it.

The sea breeze blew the stench from the city into the faces of Irfan Kawar and Magda as they hiked down from their hidden ship. The geologist coughed. "Plumbing often gets invented surprisingly late," Magda murmured.

"I knew I should have worn nose filters," Kawar said. "If I'd really wanted to experience the primitive at first hand, I'd've gone into anthropology the way you did."

She made a face at him. Their hiking boots scrunched over gravel. They were on their own, linked to their crewmates only by the little transceivers implanted behind their ears. Both wore khaki denim coveralls, standard Service issue. Traders in a variety of costumes plied their wares in the town's marketplace; one more drab style of clothing should not seem too out of place there.

The first native to spot them was a woman picking berries by the side of the path. She looked up warily, as if wondering whether to flee into the bushes. Magda and Irfan Kawar slowly approached, their hands clasped in front of them in the local greeting gesture.

"The peace of the eternal goddess on you," Magda said, hoping her accent was not too foul to understand.

She must have made herself clear, for the woman's eyes lit. "And on you," the woman replied. She stared at them with frank curiosity. Magda's red-brown curls and smooth cheeks, Kawar's swarthy skin and bald head, were unlike anything she knew. "What distant land are you from?" she asked.

"The far northwest," Kawar replied. The dominant culture had not reached that part of the continent, so the answer seemed safe enough.

The woman accepted it without blinking. Her next question, though, made the two Terrans look at each other in confusion for a moment. It sounded like, "What will you be doing in search?"

Magda was trying to twist the grammar to make the sentence mean "What are you searching for?" when she remembered that the literal meaning of Hotofras—the name of the town ahead—was "Search." She said, "We have jewels to sell or trade. Here, would you like to see?"

She unzipped a pocket and took out a handful of red, blue, and green stones: synthetic rubies, star sapphires, and emeralds from the ship's lab. "Our gems are very fine," she said cajolingly.

The woman's hand came out until she touched a sapphire with the tip of one finger. Then she jerked it away, as if scalded. "No matter how fair your stones, I must make do with beads and colored glass, I fear. My husband is but a candlemaker; we will never be rich."

Kawar chose a much smaller sapphire from Magda's palm and gave it to the woman. Her face was a study in confusion. "Do you seek to buy my body? This is the fee, many times over, did I wish to sell myself to you; but I do not."

"No," he assured her, smiling wryly—he was gay. "But surely you will tell many people of the foreigners who gave a jewel away. They will come to us without the wariness buyers should have, and we will make up the price of this stone many times over." His sly smile invited her to share in the scheme.

"Truly the goddess smiles on me today!" the woman exclaimed. She tucked the sapphire into a pouch that hung from her belt.

"Tell me of this goddess you people follow," Magda said. "When we use your language, we greet the folk we meet in her name, but in our far country we do not worship her our-selves."

The woman shook her head in disbelief. "How could any-one not worship the goddess? She lives forever and knows everything. I am only the poor wife of a candlemaker, and live far from her glory, but one day perhaps even I shall see her." Her face filled with awe at the thought.

"So say the priests of many goddesses," Kawar observed; the local tongue seemed to lack a masculine word for the divine. "How does anyone in this world know which goddess we shall meet in the next?"

"Careful," Magda warned in English-based Federacy Stan-dard. "That might be heresy."

The woman gaped at them, but not for that reason. "The next world!" she burst out. "Who speaks of the next world? If I sold this stone you gave me, I might make enough silver for the journey to the goddess's own home, far though it is."

"Selling a sapphire will not take you to heaven." Magda frowned, again wondering how well she was understanding the local language.

The woman set hands on hips, exasperated with these igno-rant strangers. "Your talk makes no sense! I do not need to die to see the goddess, only to travel to the Holy City where she dwells."

"The Holy City?" Kawar echoed.

The woman pointed westward, toward Hotofras. "If you seek to learn more of these things than I can tell you, you have only to speak to one of the upper priests or to the chief magis-trate. They have seen the goddess with their own eyes—how I envy them!"

"Perhaps we will do that," Magda said. She and Kawar were making ready to go when she remembered the roles they were playing. "And you, do not forget to speak of us and of the excellent gems we sell."

"I will not forget," the woman promised. "The peace of the eternal goddess on you." That served for good-bye as well as hello. The two Terrans returned it and walked on.

Magda snorted. "Nice setup they have here—the bigwigs talk directly to the goddess and tell everyone under them what to do. Who's going to argue?"

"Don't let your jaundiced point of view make you misread the facts," Kawar reproved. "From what the woman said, she could hope to visit the goddess herself. That would be the cult image the one in the temple here is based on, I suppose. Probably gorgeous, of gold and ivory—do they have ivory here? —and precious stones. That would be worth a long journey to see."

"So it would. I can't quite see, though, why she would refer to an image 'dwelling' in this Holy City of theirs. Maybe there's a line of high priestesses who assume the role of the goddess one after the other. Maybe—hell, what's the point in guessing before we know enough?"

A twinkle showed for a moment in Kawar's dark, liquid eyes. "Because it's fun, of course."

She grabbed his hand, liking him very much. Too damn bad he preferred men, she thought—no wonder he'd been amused at what the woman thought he wanted. But he certainly would be more enjoyable than the implacably serious Atanasio Pedroza. No, that didn't say enough of Irfan, Magda decided—almost anyone was more enjoyable than Pedroza. She sighed. If she'd wanted things to be simple, she should have stayed in her father's pastry shop.

The path from the mountain valley where the *Jêng Ho* lay hidden descended to meet the main road into Hotofras. The road was rammed earth, heavily graveled to make it of some use even in the rain. Coaches, carts, and wagons rattled along, drawn by the local draft animals, which looked something like zebras and something like camels. "Ugly, with stripes," Kawar put it.

Magda paid more attention to the coaches. Instead of subjecting their passengers to bone-crushing jounces, they had an arrangement of leather straps that cushioned riders from the worst jolts. "It's the first step toward springs," the anthropologist said.

"I think they have a good many more steps to go," Kawar said judiciously, watching a native flung against the side of the coach by the swaying motion the straps imparted. "That still looks bloody uncomfortable."

"Yes, yes, of course," Magda said. "But on Terra people took three times as long to come up with even this rotten a system."

Kawar groaned and put a hand to his kidneys.

Chuckling, Magda went on. "Yes, exactly. They've nipped a lot of aches and pains in the bud here."

"In the butt, you mean."

"That too." Magda made a face at the geologist.

The walls of Hotofras had been tall and strong once. Now they were ramshackle, as if often used to furnish building stone. Half the town lay outside their protection. To Magda that spoke of long years of peace, not what she would have expected from such an obviously energetic culture: that energy should have boiled over, and frequently.

Small boys in ragged smocks gaped at the Terrans. Adults ostentatiously ignored them, except for those who eyed Magda's exotic good looks. Even they were circumspect. Hotofras was a port that attracted all kinds of people—why get excited about one more set of strangers?

The innkeeper into whose establishment they walked found a reason—seeing a pair of foreigners, she tried to rent them a room at double the going rate. But Magda had viewed enough transactions of that sort to have a good idea of what she ought to pay, and her pungent sarcasm brought the woman back to reality with a bump.

"Was that really necessary?" Kawar asked as the chastened innkeeper led them upstairs to their room.

"It wouldn't be in character not to drive a sharp bargain." Magda shrugged. "Besides, everybody here enjoys haggling. If I'd've accepted that first outrageous price, she would have been almost disappointed to take my money . . . almost, but not quite."

The room was all right—cleaner, in fact, than Magda had expected. The cloth-covered mattress was supported by criss-crossing leather straps attached to a wooden bed frame.

Magda had noticed that arrangement before without thinking anything of it. But seen so soon after the coaches, it caught her eye. When she remarked on the similarity, the innkeeper said proudly, "Yes, it was a cousin of my father's who first thought to suspend coaches that way, and who earned the reward of the goddess for it."

"What is that?" Irfan Kawar asked. "The certainty of a happy life in the next world?"

The innkeeper stared at him. "You *are* from a far country, stranger, not to know of the goddess and her ways; I thought everyone did. No, Rumeli was summoned to the Holy City and rewarded with gold from the hands of the goddess herself.''

"Might we speak to such an illustrious personage?" Kawar asked. "Could you introduce us to him?"

"Er, no," the innkeeper said, suddenly less proud. "I fear he squandered the goddess's gift on wine and loose women and died three years ago of an apoplexy." Someone shouted for her from the taproom below; she left with embarrassed haste.

Amused, Kawar turned to Magda, but his grin faded before her grim expression. "What's wrong?"

"The reward-for-invention scheme, that's what. It should have died with Sabium; it was far ahead of its time. But here it is, still. And if that's not cultural contamination, I don't know what is. Damn, damn, damn! Won't the Purists love that?"

She felt like kicking something. Noninterference was the rule the Survey Service lived by. Humanity had learned from painful experience that ramming one culture's answers down another's throat was the wrong way to go about things. Given time and freedom from meddling, intelligent beings usually worked out what they needed—and if they didn't, whose business was it but their own?

The Purists, though, thought any contact with pretechnological worlds was contamination. They were very well meaning . . . especially if you asked one of them. Magda knew a know-nothing when she heard one, even when the talk, as it all too often was these days, was couched in terms of budget cutting instead of ideology.

"We're a good many hundred years too late to do anything about it now," Kawar said practically. He yawned, then patted his ample belly. "As for me, I'm going down to see what the food and beer are like, then coming back up here to sack out."

"Sensible," Magda had to admit; Irfan usually was. Now that she wasn't on the go anymore, she felt unfamiliar muscles starting to ache; exercise in the *Jêng Ho*'s little gym wasn't the same as hiking over ground sometimes rough. She looked around and started to laugh. "With only one bed, I'd sooner share it with you, Irfan, than with a lot of people I could think of; you'll just use it for sleeping."

He reached out and swatted her on the bottom. She leaped

in the air in surprise. "Who knows what strange perversions spending the night with you might tempt me into?"

She thought about it. "Maybe we'll find out."

Rather to her regret, the night passed uneventfully—except that Irfan snored. The sleepy man running the taproom grumbled when they asked him for hot porridge for breakfast the next morning; the locals ate at noon, sunset, and just before they went to sleep.

Action at the central bazaar was brisk by the time the Terrans arrived. Hucksters cried a hundred wares, from furs to roasted nuts to sailcloth. Almost as loudly, customers sneered at the quality of what they were offered. Magda and Kawar somehow managed to stake out a few square meters and took up a chant: "Rare jewels! Fine gems! Rare jewels! Fine gems!"

They quickly sold some saphires and emeralds; those went well with the natives' coloring. The rubies proved harder to move. The locals would admire them in Magda's hands, then put them against their own skins and wince at the effect. The repeated failures annoyed her, even though she and Kawar were just using their role for concealment. Whatever she did, she wanted to do well.

The Terrans' location let them watch the main temple entrance. Those huge metal doors, splendid with cloisonnéwork, were open day and night. Locals went in and out, both layfolk and priests. The latter were easy to recognize by their sober robes of white or light blue; most of the rest of the people preferred tunics, vests, and baggy troupers dyed in a rainbow of gaudy colors. There seemed to be about as many female priests as men.

As the morning wore on, Magda began to feel she and Kawar were being studied in turn by the priests. She expected curiosity from the locals, but these long, measuring stares were something else again. So were the conversations the priests started having behind their hands.

"Be ready to disappear in a hurry," Magda muttered to Kawar. "I have a feeling we're attracting undue attention somehow."

"Very well," he said gravely, interrupting his call for customers. "At your signal I shall grow a thick head of blue hair and turn pinkish gray all over."

She snorted. "You're incorrigible." Of itself, her hand patted the stunner in a front pocket of her coveralls. That, of course, was nonlethal and for emergencies only. There were stories of Survey Service personnel who let dreadful things happen to them rather than use an offplanet weapon. Magda admired that kind of altruism but did not intend to imitate it.

But when the priests made their approach, it proved peaceable enough. One white-robed woman threaded her way through the crowded bazaar toward the two Terrans. She waited until Magda was done haggling with a magnate in a particularly repulsive purple cloak, then bowed politely. "The peace of the eternal goddess on you, strangers."

"And on you, mistress," Magda and Kawar replied together.

"May we interest you in some stones, mistress, for yourself or for the goddess's temple?" Magda continued.

The priestess blinked, as if that had not occurred to her. "Perhaps you may, at that. But I have seen precious stones before, and I have never seen any folk with your aspect." She smiled; it made her look much younger and gave her an individuality she had lacked before. "Therefore, I am more interested in you. Will you tell me where you come from?"

The Terrans looked at each other. Finding no harm in the question, Kawar answered with the story they had prepared. "From the far northwest. Not many of our people travel as far south as your lands."

"Yes, I can believe that," the priestess said. Magda wondered if the woman's tone really was as dry as it seemed. But when the priestess went on, her questions were of the sort any newcomers might get, on how they had reached Hotofras, what they thought of it, what their homeland was like. She listened gravely to their answers.

At last the priestess said, "I thank the both of you for your patience. We always search out new knowledge of strangers who come to Hotofras."

The use of the verb reminded Magda of the place's unusual name. "If I may ask a question in return," she said, "why is this town called 'Search'?"

"Because it was founded to search out knowledge of strangers, of course," the priestess replied, smiling ever so slightly. She bowed to the Terrans and made her way back to the temple. Pausing outside the entrance, she spoke with a priest in a blue robe. He looked toward Magda and Kawar, scratched his head, and followed the priestess into the shrine.

"I wonder what all that's in aid of," Kawar said. "If we were going to get such a thorough grilling, it should have been at the gate coming in so we wouldn't have the chance to lose ourselves if we were ne'er-do-wells."

Magda shrugged. "I think that was a purely religious interrogation, not a security check. Maybe they have some sort of obligation toward strangers. That would fit a mother-goddess cult: shelter the homeless because in a way they're orphans, and so on."

"Makes sense," Kawar said. "But then, it should, you being the anthropologist and all." Ignoring the face Magda made at him, he went back to extolling the virtues of their jewels.

By evening, they had sold several more stones, two to buyers who had heard of them from the candlemaker's wife. Both ended up paying more than their other customers. "What do you know?" Kawar said, bemused. "I wasn't even lying."

"That's no way to advertise," Magda said. "Enough for one day. Let's go back to the inn. My feet are getting numb from standing in one place so long."

After a dinner of broiled many-legged river creatures with spicy gravy, the two Terrans went up to their rooms to transmit the data they had gathered and to plan what to do next. The latter did not take long: visiting the temple was the obvious next step.

They were walking toward the central square the next morning when they met a delegation of priests heading toward their lodging. Before Magda and Kawar quite grasped what was happening, the priests were all around them. One gave a hand signal. Suddenly the Terrans were grasped and held.

With a curse, Magda kicked out backward. The blow should have caught a male captor where it would do the most good—but the priest was not there when her foot lashed out. Whatever other arcane secrets the clergy of the mother goddess owned, they knew hand-to-hand combat.

Irfan Kawar did not try to break away. Instead he protested angrily. "By what right do you do this to us? We are but harmless traders!"

"If that is so, you will have our apology and a handsome reward," said the priest who had signaled. He turned to his companions. "Search them."

Magda tried again to break free, to no avail; the priests gripping her were strong and alert. She snarled as the locals' hands explored her body, though the examiners took no more liberties than the task required. A priest extracted the pouch of jewels from her hip pocket. "Are you robbers, then, in holy robes?" she demanded. Tears of fear and fury ran unheeded down her cheeks.

The priest opened the pouch, let bright stones cascade into his palm, and peered into the leather sack. When satisfied it was empty, he returned the gems to it. "By no means," he said quietly. "These lovelies are yours, and we shall give them back to you."

"What is the meaning of this outrage, then?" Kawar asked. "Do you always greet foreigners so? If you do, I wonder that you have so many ships tied up at your docks."

The priest in charge of the rest smiled thinly. "Foreigners of a certain sort interest us more than the rest: those who say they come from lands we know nothing of, and whose appearance bears them out. They interest us even more if they carry devices we cannot fathom." He hefted Magda's stunner.

"I will show you the use of that one, if you like," she said eagerly.

"Thank you, no," he replied with cool amusement. "It may be a weapon."

"Irfan! Magda! What's going on? Are you all right?" Norma Anderssen's voice sounded in their transceivers. All Norma and the people back at the *Jêng Ho* could do was listen and worry.

"What will you do with us?" Magda asked, as much to pass on information as for her own sake.

"Why, send you to the goddess, of course," the priest said.

Magda could not remember a ritual phrase of that sort in the local language. She wondered if it was a euphemism for human sacrifice. "To the next world?" she asked tensely.

The priest stared at her with the same puzzlement the candlemaker's wife had shown. "No, no," he said. "Do you think us barbarians? I meant only that you will be taken— under guard, lest you try to flee, but otherwise in comfort—to the Holy City, where the goddess dwells."

III

The leather straps that supported the body of the coach gave it a rolling motion like that of a small boat on the open sea. After four months of such travel, it had long since stopped bothering Magda or Kawar. Indeed, the solid ground seemed unstable when they got out to relieve themselves or to stop for the evening.

The Margush valley knew only two seasons: hot and hotter. Magda wiped sweat from her face. "This weather makes me wish we'd told the gang from the *Jêng Ho* to rescue us, after all."

"And miss a slow guided tour across the continent? You must be mad. The comparative planetologists will be playing with our data for the next five hundred years." Kawar twisted his wrist so the video unit hidden in his bracelet scanned a tributary joining the main current of the Margush.

"I suppose so," Magda said. "Still, do you want to know the real reason I turned down any try at spiriting us away?"

"Probably because you didn't want the fair Atanasio coming after you with stunner blazing."

"You've come to know me entirely too well."

"No wonder." Kawar patted her hand, then looked around at their escorts and shrugged. Thrown together on the long journey, it was not surprising they had turned to each other. In spite of Kawar's usual orientation, the background they shared made Magda a more attractive partner for him than the local priests.

She smiled back at him. She had known better lovers—though she did not say so—but also worse. He was gentle and tried hard to please her, which counted for a good deal. She did her best to return the favor; some of the variations he liked were interesting.

She stuck her head out the window of the coach. A city lay

39

ahead. Its walls were visible for a long distance across the floodplain of the Margush—like the other towns in the valley, it stood on a hill composed of a couple of thousand years of its own rubbish. "What's the name of that place?" she called up to the driver.

"That is Mawsil," the woman replied.

"We're getting to know where we are," Kawar said. He confidently spoke to the driver. "Helmand is the next city ahead?"

But her answer caught him by surprise. "No," she said, "the next city eastward is the Holy City, where the two of you, fortunate as you are, will meet the goddess."

Kawar scratched his head. "That has to be Helmand."

"So it does," Magda said grimly.

"More interference, you think?"

"I wish you'd convince me otherwise."

"Thankfully, the problem is not really mine—it's hard for geologists to interfere in a planet's life."

"Yes, but what happens when the Purists in the Assembly start yapping about terrible Terran cultural imperialism and cut the Survey Service budget in half? You'll find it even harder to interfere when you never get near another non-Federacy planet again."

"The Chairman can tell the Finance Committee that even if there was interference here, it turned out well," Kawar said. "This world argues for interference, not against it."

"Does not blowing your brains out at Russian roulette argue for playing it?" Magda retorted. "This is just as much fool luck as the other—once you spin the cylinder, you don't know what's going to happen till it's over. And when things go wrong, that's too bloody late, and somebody else has to clean up the mess. Us, in this case."

Magda also had a picture of the Survey Service Chairman going against doctrine in front of an Assembly committee. She kept it with her other fantasies, like guitar-playing woodpeckers and tap-dancing trees. The Chairman, a career bureaucrat named Paulina Koch, habitually wore gray only because there was no blander color.

They spent the night in a fine hostel in Mawsil, then pressed on to the Holy City with a fresh driver and a new set of priestly "escorts." As Magda had since entering the Margush valley, she questioned the newcomers about their faith. "How is a new goddess chosen when the old one dies?"

The leader of the escort was so startled, he almost fell off his mount. "The goddess does not die. If she died, how could she be a goddess?"

"Forgive me, please; I am only an ignorant foreigner," Magda said for the hundredth time. She tried another tack. "Does the earthly vessel holding the goddess's divinity die? If so, how is a new vessel chosen?"

"The goddess is the goddess," the priest said. Magda spread her hands and gave up. She'd gotten similar answers from others she'd questioned, but kept hoping that as she drew close to the Holy City she could penetrate the mummery surrounding the locals' deity. That she kept failing deterred her only a little.

Peasants labored in the lush green fields. They turned Archimedean screws to bring water from the Margush into the irrigation canals. Windmills also helped in that effort; Magda saw a crew repairing one. She pointed to them and asked the driver, "How long have your people known that device?"

The driver obviously had never thought in those terms. At last she said, "As long as anyone can remember."

"Not what one would call precise, but expressive," Kawar observed. Magda's agreement was strained.

The road, which paralleled the Margush, bent slightly south. Magda saw what had to be the Holy City ahead. "That's Helmand," she said flatly.

Irfan Kawar leaned out the window. "It's certainly in the same spot, isn't it?"

Traffic was heavy. Most of the travelers were pilgrims, seeking a glimpse of the goddess. But there were others. A woman propelled herself past the Terrans' coach on a contraption halfway between a scooter and a pedalless bicycle.

"I've never seen anything like that before," Magda said to one of the priests in the band of escorts.

"Nor have I," he said. "Doubtless she plans to present the invention to the goddess in hope of being rewarded for it."

"Doubtless," Magda agreed sourly. She was starting to wish none of the locals would ever have any more new thoughts; her reports would be a lot easier to write.

The Holy City was packed with people, beasts, and wagons. Because of the crush, the party took almost as long to find its hostel as they had traveling from Mawsil. Magda and Kawar gulped sour wine while one of their escorts went back out into the heat and crowd to report their arrival. "Poor devil," Kawar said, putting down his mug with a sigh of relief.

Magda leaned back in her chair. "Now that we're here, I expect we'll be able to relax a while. It'll take days for the word to pass up through the hierarchy—and more days, it looks like, for anyone to get through the jam to do anything about it."

"Good," Kawar said. "That will let me take a bath. I itch everywhere."

"Me too. God, I'd kill for a good cold shower."

"Don't speak of such things. I've been trying to forget they exist."

The tub was made of caulked wood. Servants hauled bucket after bucket of blood-warm river water to fill it; whatever else it boasted, the Holy City did not have much of a drainage system. The locals also knew nothing of soap—hard scrubbing and perfume made up some for the lack.

The Terrans flipped a coin to see who would get the tub first. Kawar won. The bathwater, already slightly turbid from the Margush, was even murkier after Magda unbelted the robe that had long since replaced her coveralls and started fighting the grime that coated her.

There was some sort of commotion down the hall. Magda was doing a good job of ignoring it until a squad of iron-corseleted troops burst into the bathroom. She yelped and grabbed at herself. The locals had no strong modesty taboos, but she did not care to be on display for them, either.

She shook her head to get the wet hair out of her face and glowered at the soldiers, as well as one can glower from a tub. "What are you armored louts doing here?" Her voice held thirty degrees of frost.

The squad leader did not leer at her; on the other hand, her hauteur failed to impress him. He said. "Dry and dress yourself as quickly as you may. The eternal goddess requires your presence."

He folded his arms and waited. Magda did not think he was trying to humiliate her, only to see she did not run. Nevertheless, it rankled. To make him fidget, she dallied as long as she could, until Irfan Kawar called anxiously from the hallway to make sure she was all right. She reassured him and moved faster.

Outside the hostel, a musician blew a harsh blast on a trumpet made from a seashell. "Clear a path!" she shouted. "Clear a path for the servants of the goddess!" *Taa-raaa!* "Clear a path!"

As nothing else had done, the discordant music melted the crowds. "The goddess *can* work miracles," Kawar said, nodding toward the empty roadway ahead. Despite his flip tone, he sounded worried; the summons was alarmingly abrupt.

Magda laughed, as much to keep up his spirits as for her own. She had her own reasons for concern, which she did not share with Kawar. The horn call was eerily like the royal flourish the *Leeuwenhoek* had recorded so long ago. The culture had changed so much in other ways that she wondered at such a strange piece of conservatism.

She had studied the *Leeuwenhoek*'s map of Helmand until she could have found her way around the town blindfolded. The Holy City's streets, though, were laid out in the same grid pattern that served most towns. It was nothing like the old maze. Nor was the building toward which the squad led the Terrans at all similar to the ancient royal palace. But Magda would have sworn it was in the same part of the city.

The soldiers hustled their charges along, so they had little chance to admire the goddess's residence. Magda kept her wrist camera busy, and made such notes as she could of the numerous artworks in their niches. A few were in the stiff, ornate style that had prevailed at the time of the first Survey Service visit. Others, newer, had a self-conscious, restrained excellence that reminded her of the work of Greece and Rome. The most recent sculpture and paintings were also fine work, but more lively and vibrant with motion.

While she was trying to examine the splendor of the palace, Kawar asked the guards, "What ceremony must we observe when we come before your goddess?"

"Why, everyone knows—" one of them began; then he paused, inspecting his charges. "No, I take it back; you may be from so far away, you do not. A bow before her will suffice. She is no mere king or chieftain, as I hear of in foreign lands, in need of being made great by ceremony. She is the goddess, and great by virtue of what she is."

The trumpeter blasted the fanfare one last time. The squad

leader murmured to an official who stood in the doorway of a large, brightly lit chamber. That worthy dipped his head, turned, and called, "Mistress, the strangers you summoned!"

A moment later, a priestess escorted out a plump, prosperous matron. The woman glared at these funny-looking foreigners as she passed. Magda felt a twinge of sympathy for her. Who knew how long she had waited for her audience, only to have it cut short?

At the doorman's nod, the guardsmen led the Terrans into the goddess' chamber. Despite what the trooper had said about her not needing to stand on ceremony, the room was richly furnished. And the throne on which the goddess sat gleamed with gold and precious stones.

As for the goddess herself, she wore a plain white robe like those of her higher-ranking priests, but a gold circlet rested on her forehead and confined her hair. Rather to Magda's surprise, she closely resembled the countless portraits of her. As in the better images, her eyes were arresting; Magda had the odd feeling she was completely transparent to her. It was a relief to bow.

"Rise; let me look at you," the goddess said. Her voice was a smooth contralto.

Irfan Kawar obediently straightened. Magda stayed bowed, rigid with shock. She had not recognized the face; a false mustache worn long ago to counterfeit those of kings was now gone. But she had heard that voice on endless hours of tape, and knew it again at once.

The goddess was Queen Sabium.

Magda must have said the name out loud, though afterward she did not remember doing so. Kawar did not understand yet; his eyes were questioning but not full of amazement—or horror.

Queen Sabium . . . the goddess . . . whoever she was . . . gasped. So did her servitors, who likely had never seen her disconcerted. Her guards growled and hefted their weapons, angry without thinking at anyone who dared disturb her.

"Hold!" she said, and the guards froze in their places. Magda heard that sonorous voice address her: "Stranger woman with the copper-colored hair, I pledge you will take no harm here. I ask it of you, I do not command it: look at me."

Trembling, Magda obeyed. At the same time, she came

back to herself enough to point her bracelet-camera at the goddess. It took only moments for stereophonic hell to break loose in the transceiver behind her ear as the people back at the *Jêng Ho* came to the same realization she had.

Norma Anderssen caught on first; she had used the tapes of Sabium as often as Magda. "That is the ruler from the *Leeuwenhoek*'s time," she said, her voice stumbling in disbelief.

Atanasio Pedroza was a split second behind her: "That is Sabium! How can she yet live?" He sounded as much indignant as astonished. After him came a swelling chorus of voices, until Babel rang in Magda's ear.

She reached up as if to scratch, pressed the transceiver to shut off reception, but let it keep sending to the *Jêng Ho*. Sudden silence fell inside her head. Out of the corner of her eye, she saw Kawar matching her gesture. Now the geologist had grasped the situation, or as much of it as anyone else. His mouth hung open in stunned surprise.

Magda was only peripherally aware of him. Through her own astonishment, she fought to focus her wits on the goddess. No, on Queen Sabium, she corrected herself, trying by the deliberate change of title to lessen the awe she felt. It did not help.

The goddess—the queen—waited. The byplay had lasted less than a minute. When Magda still did not speak, Sabium said, "The last person who called me by that name has been dust for more than a thousand years. There are days, there are weeks, when I do not remember I was born with it."

Any reply might have been wrong, disastrously wrong. Silence stretched. At last Sabium broke it. "In the very beginning of my days, I was ill, ill unto death."

Magda heard shocked intakes of breath from the locals. The goddess—it was impossible not to think of her as such— ignored them. She went on. "Two men from a far-off land— or so they said they were—cured me, where all hope had failed. Now *you* know my ancient, forgotten name. One of you"—she pointed toward Kawar—"is of the same sort as one of those. The other man then had skin like dark, polished wood. I had never imagined such a one, nor had I imagined any person with hair like metal."

Her finger turned toward Magda. "I ask you, then, if the two of you are of the people of those earlier strangers. Tell me, and know I will know if you lie."

She might, Magda thought, a little wildly. If she had some-how lived a millennium and a half, she must have learned to see through people as through glass. No wonder, then, her eyes had that piercing quality. The anthropologist found her-self unable to dissemble. "Yes."

Sabium's head bent very slowly. She turned to her retinue and gestured peremptorily. "Leave me. Yes, all of you; I would have speech with these strangers alone." Some of the locals were startled enough to protest, even to their goddess. She overrode them. "Go, and close the chamber doors behind you."

The locals went. The majordomo and other palace atten-dants scowled over their shoulders at the Terrans. Jealous of having their influence diluted, Magda thought, although what influence could mere mayfly mortals exert on their goddess?

The hinges of the chamber's doors squealed as they swung shut; they had not been used much or kept oiled. Magda was sure as many eyes as possible were pressed to the crack be-tween the portals.

Sabium did not seem to care. She descended from her throne and slowly and with immense dignity prostrated herself before the two Terrans. "Along with what was my name, death is a thing I seldom think of, not for me, not for years upon years upon years. But I would have died, I think, had your countrymen not saved me. Is it not so?"

"It is so," Magda muttered. Usually, doing fieldwork on a pretechnological world, she was conscious of the greater so-phistication the Federacy's long history gave her. Now, though, it felt obscenely wrong to have this being on her knees. "Please, your, uh, divinity, get up."

Irfan Kawar echoed her; she heard the embarrassment she felt in his voice as well.

"No," Sabium said, still with that same calm self-possession. "I am called a goddess, and I suppose I am, for I do not die. But your people must truly be gods, or gods of greater power than myself, for I received the gift of eternal life from you."

"Queen—goddess—Sabium—" Magda's tongue was fall-ing all over itself, and no wonder, because she had no idea what to say. Admitting the existence of space-traveling aliens violated every noninterference canon the Federacy had. But she could not see how letting Sabium think she was a god improved matters much.

"God damn David Ware to hell—this whole fucking mess is his fault," she said bitterly.

Sabium shook her head in incomprehension; Magda had spoken Federacy Basic, getting no relief from swearing in the local language. But Sabium understood the anger, if not the words. She said, "I have tried every day to deserve the gift your folk gave me, by ruling justly and seeing that my people live as well as they may. If I have not pleased you, spare them and punish me."

Magda winced. Suddenly she began to see why, fifteen hundred years before, Ware had thought this woman worth saving. She knew that was all he had intended. But what a mess his well-intentioned interference had left in its wake! It had twisted Bilbeis IV's whole historical and religious development out of shape.

While such dark thoughts filled her head, Irfan Kawar knelt and raised Queen Sabium. "You need have no fear of us," he told her. "We have not come to judge you." Magda winced again, this time in shame. The geologist was doing a better job than she was.

From outside the chamber came an anxious call: "Goddess, is all well?"

"Yes, of course; leave us be!"

"Let them in," Magda urged. "We can talk more whenever you want. They must fear for your safety, closeted alone with two such, uh, unusual strangers."

A ghost of amusement touched Sabium's lips. "Unusual indeed. Nevertheless, you speak rightly." She swept down the aisleway and flung open the doors. Some of her attendants almost fell over her as they rushed in. She said, "I will talk further with these"—it was her turn to hesitate—"people. Quarter them in the suite nearest me, Bagadat, so I may have speech with them whenever I wish."

"It shall be done," the majordomo said. He bowed to the Terrans. "If you will come with me."

Apparently, if his goddess accepted the foreigners, Bagadat would do the same . . . or, Magda thought, he might try to make them quietly disappear, to preserve his own position. No, probably not; not with an immortal looking over his shoulder. She shivered. That was true in the most literal sense of the word.

The suite Sabium had assigned to them was plainly one

reserved for high dignitaries. The furnishings were rich, the sofa and bed upholstered with cushions soft enough to sink into. The portrait bust of Sabium that sat on a table was very fine. Done in what Magda thought of as the classical style, it showed the goddess serenely at peace with herself and her world. She wore her hair long and straight; Magda hoped she would be able one of these days to use the style to date the piece.

At the moment, she had more urgent things to worry about. She plopped down on the couch with a groan, wishing she could hide under it instead. "Disaster!" she said. She waved her arms in a wild, all-encompassing gesture.

Irfan Kawar slowly shook his head, still stunned himself. "No one could have expected—this."

"Of course. But nobody knew *what* was going to happen, which if you ask me is a good reason for not doing anything."

As Pedroza had before, Kawar muttered, "Maybe it's coincidence."

"Oh, horseshit, Irfan; you don't believe that yourself." Magda knew her harshness hurt the geologist and was sorry, because he was a good man—but only somewhat, because she could not refuse to look facts in the face. She went on. "It was the stinking immunological amplifier, nothing else but. It just happened to work a wee bit better on Sabium than on us—a wee bit! I'm sure Atanasio will want to chop her into bloody bits to find out why."

That, unfortunately, reminded her she and Kawar had been out of touch with the *Jêng Ho* for several hours. She turned on the receiver part of her implant and promptly regretted it. Everyone back at the ship must have been going mad with frustration, and everyone started shouting hysterical advice at her at once.

She listened—or tried to—for only a couple of minutes, then switched off so violently, she hurt herself. "Idiots!" she snarled. "Halfway around the world from us and telling us what to do."

What with the turmoil in her own head, she had not noticed Kawar also turning on his receiver. He stood the din a few seconds longer before shutting it off again. He did hear one thing she'd missed: "They won't be halfway around the world for long—the *Jêng Ho* has been on the way here since the moment you recognized who the goddess was."

Magda only grunted. She liked the independence six thousand kilometers of distance gave her, but the move made sense. The action was here, with Hotofras abruptly a backwater.

Someone scratched at the door, which had a bar on the Terrans' side. Glad for the interruption, Magda raised the bar. Servants fetched in supper, bowed nervously, and left. The fare was similar to what nobles had eaten when the *Leeuwenhoek* was there: bread, boiled vegetables and roots, a stew of salt fish, with preserved fruit and sweet wine.

The Terrans had reached the tooth-picking stage when the scratching sound came again. Expecting more servants to fetch away the dirty dishes, Magda opened the door. Sabium stood there instead, alone.

"C-come in." Magda stepped aside, as wary as the palace servitors had been with her. She made no move to close the door, being unsure that was proper.

Sabium shut it. When she began to prostrate herself, Kawar stopped her. With an apologetic glance toward Magda, he said, "You do not need to humble yourself before us. Rather, we are in awe of you, hardly less than your own subjects. And why not? I am but forty-two years old, and my companion is—"

"Thirty-one," Magda supplied.

"I do not believe you," Sabium said. Then, studying them with that searching clarity of hers, she changed her mind. "No; I do. Say rather I do not understand."

Again Magda saw the quality in this woman that had led David Ware to find her worth saving. And he was dishonored dust these many centuries, and here she stood yet.

For a moment the anthropologist was tempted to tell Sabium everything, but she did not: she could not make herself believe one interference justified another. Instead, she said, "Queen ... goddess ... have you ever sent out couriers with messages they could not speak of, save to their own superiors who were to receive them?"

"Of course."

"Think of us in such a light, then. Much of what we know, we may not speak."

"You say you are messengers of the gods, then, not gods yourselves?"

"We are messengers." Magda let it go at that, relieved she

had not made a full confession. However brilliant and experienced Sabium was, it was in the context of her own culture. Asking her to assimilate the idea of the Federacy all at once was too much.

"That is marvel enough for me," Sabium said firmly. "My ships scoured the western coast, my artisans founded towns there in hopes of finding folk like unto those who had rescued me. And so they did, though long years after I proposed it."

"No wonder the city's name means 'search'!" Magda burst out. "All that time you were looking for Ware and Crouzet! They said they came from the west, didn't they?"

"If those were their names; I never knew them," Sabium said. "But yes, they said they were from the west. Here in this valley, we knew nothing of the west then. But though I never found a trace of my saviors, I never forgot them, either, or let my priests do so. If ever folk of strange aspect appeared, saying they were from a country of which we were ignorant, I wanted to meet with them, the more so if they had possessions unlike any of ours." She smiled. "And so you are here."

"So we are," Magda said, doing her best to hide her chagrin. Their "simple, foolproof" story could not have done a better job of advertising them to Sabium if they had concocted it for that very purpose.

She took a deep breath, forced herself to steadiness, and said, "We are glad to be here, for in you, Queen, we have found a greater marvel than any we know ourselves." She did not care whether Sabium was examining her for the truth in that—it was there.

"You are messengers, and you did not know of me?" Sabium paused. "I see it is so, though I do not see how. Well, if one tries to put it baldly, there is little to tell after the early years. You have said you know of my cure?"

At the Terrans' nods, Sabium continued. "Once I felt myself again, I went on as I always had, doing my best for Helmand. The years went by. People I had grown up with envied me at first, that I kept my looks while their hair whitened and their faces wrinkled. I remember I thought nothing of it, past the flattery a queen always hears."

She stared back into the distant past she alone remembered. "Then one day I noticed—it seemed very sudden at the time —that my servants were the grandchildren of those I had first known and seemed no younger than I. They did not envy me any longer. They felt awe instead . . . as did I, when I began to realize my span of days, whatever it was, truly was longer than the usual run."

"Did you not fear overthrow in war, even if sickness would not come for you?" Kawar asked.

"Oh, indeed, and that overthrow almost happened more than once, when I was young. But Helmand survived. Eventually we came to win more easily, through alliances with our enemies' neighbors or by fighting before our foes were ready. By then I had begun to see how such things were managed, for already I was wiser than any king who opposed me."

Sabium poured a cup of wine and sipped reflectively. "I do not say I am more clever than any mortal; time and again the brilliance of some woman or man bringing a new thing before me will leave me dumbfounded. But what wit I have draws on lifetime after lifetime of experience, against the few paltry years that are all others can gain. And what is wisdom but wit tempered by experience?

"I did not die; after a while I did not lose. And after a while my people looked as much to me as to the gods I had always known. Bit by bit they forgot the old gods, and only I recall I became a goddess by their favor."

She drank again. Magda had been looking for a chance to interrupt. "You spoke of people bringing new things to you. We know you encouraged them to do so long ago—you have kept it up all this time?"

"Why, of course," Sabium said in faint surprise. "All manner of worthy things have come from such inventors, to make the lives of my people and me easier and more pleasant. Weapons of war, too, at need, which also helped our triumph. But I own I prefer the tools of peace, or of thought."

She gestured enthusiastically. "Why, do you know, a woman last year had observations to show the world and the moving stars go around the sun, and not all of them around us. Other astronomers are still measuring away, to see if she is right. What a marvelous thing if it were so!"

"Marvelous," Magda echoed. She tried to ignore the look of consternation Irfan Kawar sent her way, but it wasn't easy. With a civilization less than two thousand years old, Bilbeis IV was right at the edge of the scientific revolution.

No planet Magda knew of came close to matching that— Earth was as progressive as any, but in 1200 B.C. people on

Earth were just getting around to finding out about iron. But then, no early culture on Earth or anywhere else she knew of had fostered invention for fifteen hundred years, either.

Sabium brightened. "Being messengers as you are, surely you would know the answer to our riddle. Is that why you have chosen to come now, to show us whether such a momentous change in the way we view the world is correct?"

"We're merely here to observe," Magda said.

The anthropologist had not had much hope Sabium would accept the lame evasion, but she did, and bowed her head as at a deserved rebuke. "Of course. What value to us if we are merely given knowledge without wrestling it from the fabric of the world for ourselves? You have great wisdom, to keep from interfering."

That made Magda want to laugh, or cry, or both at once. How would Sabium react if she ever learned that she herself was a product of interference? Would she say her greatness—which Magda could not deny—justified the meddling, or would she wish her world back to the slower but more proper course it would have taken had she died at her appointed time?

Magda did not know, and was afraid to ask.

Irfan Kawar had been thinking along a different line. He said to Sabium, "Perhaps you will have returned to us, then, the goods your priests confiscated at Hotofras? Some of them embody principles your people have not yet learned."

"Be it so," Sabium said at once. "When I leave you, I shall give the order to my servants."

"Keep the jewels, of course, as tribute to your own splendor," Magda said. She felt like kissing Kawar for his quick wits.

"I would not wish to impoverish you—" Sabium began.

"You do not," Magda said firmly.

Sabium acknowledged the gift with a dignity more than queenly. She departed a few minutes later, saying, "If it please you, I would speak with you again tomorrow. Though you may not speak of things I and mine do not yet know, surely there can be no harm in discussing the long-lost days. I never thought to meet anyone who knew of them but from my own tales, and to talk with such people is like seeing the reflection of a reflection of my own face. Sleep well now; use my servants as if they were your own." The door closed behind her.

"Whew!" Magda said when she and Kawar were alone

again. That seemed to sum things up as well as anything. Her clothes were soaked with sweat, and not just from the heat.

The palace attendants who returned the Terrans' property looked at them with wide eyes and bowed as they might have toward their goddess. At Magda's dismissal, they fled. She hardly noticed. She was too busy strapping on her stunner. After so many months of being a politely held prisoner, she reveled in the feeling of freedom it gave her.

The transceiver behind her ear let out a hoot loud enough to hurt. She had almost forgotten about the override signal; only Captain Brusilov had the authority to use it. His harsh voice echoed in her head and in Kawar's: "We are down, safe and undetected, in the desert country north of Helmand—I mean, the Holy City. Escape at once, using your stunners if you have to; you did well to get them back. Get far enough out of the city so a flier can pick you up without any of the locals seeing it."

"Hey, wait!" Magda protested. "Don't we get any say in this?"

"You know I have the right to tell you no, Dr. Kodaly," Brusilov said with cold formality. "I will, however, appeal to your reason before doing so. Would you not agree the situation we have encountered"—as polite a way to say "crisis" as Magda had ever heard—"calls for discussion and analysis with all experts present?"

She bit her lip and glanced toward Kawar to see if he would back her in defiance. It looked unlikely. She sighed. "Very well."

The escape itself proved preposterously easy. The Terrans used their stunners through the chamber door to knock out any guards outside. There proved to be two, lying slumped against the wall. Magda set an empty wine jar between them to explain their unconsciousness.

The torchlit hallways were almost empty so late at night. A couple of servants bowed low to the Terrans. No one tried to stop them; it did not occur to anyone that the goddess's honored guests would want to leave without her permission. And once out of the palace, Kawar and Magda became just another couple of strangers, a bit stranger than most, wandering the streets of the Holy City.

The only mishap came when Kawar turned his ankle descending the hill of rubble on which the city sat. He stumbled on, his arm around Magda's shoulder. The night was hot and sticky. The contact should have been uncomfortable, but it was a relief to them both. Kawar did not let go even after they reached flat, smooth ground.

When the Holy City was well behind them, Magda keyed her transceiver. "You may as well come get us," she said. "This spot is as good as any."

"Half an hour," Brusilov said. He was not one to waste words.

Magda sat in the dust with a sigh of relief. Kawar sprawled, panting, beside her. In the darkness, she took a while to recognize the expression on his face. It was more than exhaustion; it was fear.

"What's the matter?" she asked.

"We'll have to cover this up," he blurted.

She gaped at him. "What? Are you crazy?"

"Not me. You were the one talking about the damned Purists a couple of days ago. What better club than Bilbeis IV for beating the Survey Service over the head?"

Magda drew in a thoughtful breath. There was a good deal of truth in that. Still, she answered slowly, "Strikes me we deserve to get beaten over the head for this one. We've managed to twist the history of a whole planet out of shape. How do you go about justifying that? People have to know we screwed up, and how badly we screwed up. Maybe getting it out in the open will keep it from happening again."

"But under Sabium, the planet is better off and farther along than it would have been without her. Why not leave well enough alone?" Kawar said, returning to the argument he had raised before.

"It won't wash," Magda said. "A bit of interference I could overlook; that's the kind of stuff the Purists howl about, and it doesn't mean a thing. But this is too big to sweep under the rug: a whole powerful religion—powerful, hell! Real!—that never should have been here, and a goddess who wouldn't be either, if it weren't for us. I just shiver in my shoes to think how lucky we were here."

"Make up your mind. If what Ware did was as terrible as you're making out, how can we be lucky now?"

"How? Easy—suppose he'd been a rotten judge of character along with being an altruistic idiot. That Bilbeis IV is what it is, is all thanks to Sabium. You saw her. She happens to be just what Ware thought she was—a wise, kindly woman. What if she hadn't been? What if she'd used her immortality to burn anybody with green hair or to wipe out all the people who spoke with a lisp? Think what we'd be facing now."

"Ware didn't know he was giving her immortality," Kawar protested.

"Yes, and that's the point—when you interfere, you don't know what's going to happen afterward. What do you want, us using planets full of people as smart as we are for laboratories? Count me out."

"Well, what do *you* want? The Service to go down the drain, and us with it? Is that better?" He reached almost pleadingly to touch Magda's face, but his hand faltered and stopped before it reached her.

Through her own hurt, she answered, "I don't know. But if I have to go down, I'd rather do it for the truth than nailed to a lie. And as for the Service, it can take care of itself. Bureaucracies are tough beasts."

"Yes, and one reason is that they find scapegoats when things go wrong. Three guesses who they'll pick here. I'm serious, Magda—we can't let word of what's happened here get out. Too much rides on it. I think a lot of the crew will agree with me, too."

Magda grunted. She knew where she could find one certain ally—Atanasio Pedroza. His Afrikaner rectitude wouldn't let him be a part of anything underhanded.

She would rather have had a leg taken off without anesthetic. She liked Irfan Kawar; once or twice she had imagined she was in love with him. The thought of lining up against him with someone she loathed made her guts clench. But she realized how hard Kawar was trying not to see the scope of the interference on Bilbeis IV. She could not deliberately blind herself the same way.

The flier came down beside them, quiet as a dream. Magda climbed wearily to her feet. When she offered Irfan Kawar a hand, he ignored her and struggled up by himself.

She shrugged and turned away, but her nails bit into her palms. It was going to be a long trip home.

IV

"Thank you so much, Chairman Koch," Assemblyman Valleix said. He was a Purist; his voice dripped sarcasm.

"It is my duty and my pleasure, sir," replied the plump middle-aged woman who was Chairman of the Survey Service. Paulina Koch's own voice was studiedly neutral. She wore her habitual gray—the better to blend into the background, her detractors said.

Valleix returned to the attack. "Isn't it a fact, Madam Chairman, that the natives of Rugi II learned of the moldboard plow through an indiscreet remark by one of your Survey Service operatives? That strikes me as a serious breach."

Paulina Koch did not smile. One of her subordinates had leaked that report to the aide of another, less prominent Purist months ago. Now it was going to come home to roost.

She let him blather along, listening with half an ear.

"Under the best of circumstances, the Survey Service strikes me as a luxury the Federacy can ill afford in these days of budgetary constraints. Such debacles as Rugi II only make matters worse. I ask you again, Madam Chairman, isn't it a fact that the natives of that planet learned about the moldboard plow from Service personnel?"

"No, I am afraid that is not a fact, Assemblyman." That he showboated by repeating his question only made springing the trap sweeter, though she did not let her face show it.

His eyebrows shot up. "I suppose you have evidence to support such a startling assertion." By his tone, he did not suppose so at all.

"Yes, Assemblyman, here it is." She produced a data card. "This will show that the moldboard plow was in fact invented on an island off the main continent of Rugi II and that it spread there through normal trade contacts at around the time of the last Survey Service examination of the planet. That

56

accounts for its sudden appearance in areas where it had previously been unknown."

Valleix was a black man; had he been white, he would have blanched. He had tangled with Paulina Koch too often to suppose her data were anything but what she said they were. He was also painfully aware she had just made a fool of him throughout the Federacy. He cut his losses, nodding to the head of the subcommittee. "I request a day's recess to evaluate these documents."

"Granted. Madam Chairman, you will be available tomorrow?"

"Certainly, madam." Paulina Koch still did not smile or show any outward sign of triumph. She had been a bureaucrat too long for that. But having savaged one Assemblyman, she did not expect any problems from the others. The Survey Service's appropriation looked safe again.

Professor Fogelman breezed into the classroom fifteen minutes late, something he had done a lot in his undergraduate lecture course. Stavros Monemvasios was not surprised to find him acting the same way in his graduate seminar.

"Greetings, greetings, greetings." Fogelman peered around the room. The anthropology prof liked to show off. He started guessing students' home worlds by their looks and dress: "Iberia, Hyperion, Epirus, Saigon, Inshallah, Hyperion, Iowa—"

He came to Stavros and hesitated. "Alexander?"

Monemvasios grinned; Fogelman had made the same mistake in the undergrad course. "I'm from New Thessaly, sir." Unlike most men of his planet, he wore a beard.

"Damn!" The professor smacked his fist down on the lectern—he remembered, too. He got three of the last four people in the seminar right.

The one he missed was a girl from Earth—the University of Hyperion's anthro department drew students from all over the Federacy. "Earth! *Anyone* could come from Earth," Fogelman snorted, dismissing his error.

"Now for your first assignment," he said, and the students responded with predictable groans. "Even after you start doing your own fieldwork, comparative studies will require you to use Survey Service reports intelligently." He started tossing out data cards like a man dealing whist, one to each person in the classroom. "Fifteen-minute summaries of these next week. They're all fresh new reports—I just pulled them from the data net before I came. That's why I was late."

Stavros raised an eyebrow. Now he was surprised; Fogelman had never bothered with excuses before. He looked at the data card on his desk; it had no label. It could have been anything from a laundry list to the score for a symphony. He'd have to plug it into his computer to know for sure. No time for that now—he got sucked into argument and frantic note scrawling on just what the proper definition for "civilization" was.

The ringing bell took him by surprise. "See you all a week from now," Fogelman said. "I'm looking forward to the reports." A lot of profs would have been blowing smoke with that line, but he sounded as if he meant it. He grinned. "One of you has a real plum."

He was a good psychologist; Stavros was sure he wasn't the only student who hurried off to the dorm to see what world he'd drawn.

He brought the report up on the screen. The lead frame had a list of authors and a vid shot of the principal author. She was a redhead good-looking enough to make Stavros pause a moment before he started paying attention to the document itself. When he did, his jaw dropped. He whistled softly. "He wasn't kidding," breathed the young man from New Thessaly. "Bilbeis IV—"

Pleased with herself, Paulina Koch attacked the printouts in her IN basket with an energy alien to the dogged persistence that was her hallmark. She saw with relief that no red-flagged items were in there, and only a few with yellow warning tags. The Survey Service was orderly and efficient, as it should have been.

She disposed of the first two priority items in short order. One should never have had a flag; a deputy coordinator earned a black mark for not being able to make up his own mind.

The third paper with the yellow strip at the top made her frown. Why should she care in particular if the Survey Service ship *Jêng Ho* had come in to the Service base on Topanga from a routine survey of a world without space travel? Then she saw which world it was and punched for the full report.

The Survey Service had given itself a black eye on Bilbeis IV, no doubt about it. The Purists had been beating the Service over the head with David Ware's folly for fifteen hundred years. Fortunately, most interference canceled out in time, no matter how loud the Purists yapped. The odds were excellent that Bilbeis IV would be another case like that and could return to the obscurity it deserved.

The abstract came up on the screen. Paulina Koch read it. Disciplined as always, she started on the report itself. The phone buzzed several times while she was working through it. She was a trained speed-reader; the long document took her only about an hour and a half.

That was how long her career took to crumple, she thought when she was done. If Valleix howled for blood at the thought of giving a race a plow it had not had before, what would he say about giving a world a goddess? She knew the answer to that only too well: he would howl to shut down the Service. He'd have backing too, curse him, not just Purists but penny-pinchers of all stripes. She'd fought for years to keep that kind of unholy alliance from forming. Now it had a cause to coalesce around, one she knew would be strong enough to wreck the Service and her with it.

Even so, she thought she was in perfect command of herself until she tried to clear the report. She needed three stabs before she could hit the right button. At last the screen went blank and gray.

She also had to try several times before she got the extension she wanted.

"External Affairs," a deep voice said.

"Hovannis, will you come up here for a moment?" At least her voice gave away nothing, she told herself with lonely pride. Not that it mattered—not that anything would matter once the report came out. Still, rather than just yield to despair, she preferred to go on naturally as long as she could. "An interesting situation has arisen, one you'll want to see."

"On my way," Hovannis said briskly. The phone went dead. Hovannis was a capable man, Paulina Koch thought, well suited to running the Survey Service's External Affairs Bureau—Security, an organization less sensitive to public relations would have called it.

* * *

Stavros Monemvasios felt caffeine buzzing through his veins like current through wires. Excitement also energized him, perhaps more powerfully. Under both stimulants his exhaustion was rising, but he had no trouble shoving it down, though his clock told him the time was closer to sunrise than to midnight. He would be a zombie in class, but he did not care.

Fogelman couldn't have looked at the data cards before he dished them out. Stavros was certain of that. The report on Bilbeis IV was no plum; it was a bomb, waiting to go off and blow the Survey Service to smithereens.

Even as an undergrad, Stavros had learned about Bilbeis IV. It was the "don't" pounded into every would-be field-worker, and carried two lessons with it. Breaking the rule of noninterference not only improperly influenced primitive worlds, it also guaranteed—and earned—professional death for anyone foolish enough to try it.

Improperly influenced . . . "Ho, ho, ho!" Stavros muttered. His lips skinned back from his teeth in a humorless grin. He would have backed that phrase in any understatement contest anywhere.

That anthropologist had cured Queen—what was her name? Sabium, that was it—Queen Sabium's cancer, all right. He'd cured her so well that there she still was, very much alive, fifteen hundred years later. No wonder a whole continent and part of another worshiped her as the undying goddess.

Stavros wished it weren't so late. He wanted to call Fogelman and scream in his ear. He reached for his phone. The anthropology prof had given his grad students his home code, and he wouldn't mind getting out of bed for news like this.

Then Stavros put the phone down. Rousting Fogelman would be fun, but coming into class in a week, all cool and innocent, and stunning everyone at once sounded even better. He plucked at his beard, trying to compose a couple of innocent-sounding opening sentences for his presentation. He chuckled. That wouldn't be easy.

He wondered just how many heads would roll at the Survey Service because of the Bilbeis IV report. He was no Purist, but he didn't relish the idea of having a whole planet's development yanked out of shape by external influences. And the only way the Service kept its budget so nice and fat was by insisting that kind of thing never happened, never *could* happen. Now that it had, a lot of people would need to cover their asses in a hurry.

He caught himself yawning enormously. Caffeine or no, work on the presentation would have to wait till tomorrow.

Roupen Hovannis did not read as fast as his boss, but he did not have to wade through the whole report, either. Paulina Koch brought the relevant, damning sections up on the screen one at a time.

"Enough," Hovannis said, waving for her to stop. He was a big, dark stocky man with a large hooked nose, heavy eyebrows, and a permanent five o'clock shadow even though he shaved twice a day. The thuggish exterior added to his effectiveness; people underestimated his intelligence.

"Reactions?" Paulina Koch asked after Hovannis had sat silent for some time.

"We are in major trouble if and when this report gets out." Paulina Koch frowned; she preferred bureaucratic circumlocutions to plain speech. But at the moment Hovannis did not care; for one of the few times in his career, he was shaken. He went on. "PK"—no one called the Chairman by her first name, not more than once—"when the Purists see it, they'll scream for our blood, and I think they'll get it. The document is plenty to drive everyone cool or lukewarm to us into the Purist camp, and to make our friends look for a good place to hide."

"Very much my own assessment, Roupen." Hovannis glanced at Paulina Koch with surprised admiration; she might have been talking about the pricing policy for oxygen tanks. "What response do you recommend we make, then?" she asked.

His grin was frightening. "I wish the damned ship had crashed before that crew of traitors ever got the chance to file their report."

"That, unfortunately, is not relevant at this point in time."

"I suppose not," Hovannis said regretfully.

"Still," the Chairman said, "I do not relish the prospect of standing up before the Assembly and telling them of the blunder we have found."

"David Ware got his a long time ago."

"Too long ago, I fear, for it to matter. We are the ones available now to be punished for his mistake."

Hovannis grunted. "The report ought to disappear from the files."

"I thought of that also. I concluded it would yield us no lasting benefit. Eventually the crew of the *Jêng Ho* will simply refile: probably when they notice no outcry has erupted from the report."

"But then we'll be ready for them." Once Hovannis had an idea, he ran with it. "If they start raising a stink, they'll do it through channels at first. Computer foulup explains anything once, especially since odds are those bastards don't even realize the mess they've landed us in. Hell, they may even be naive enough to believe the file got erased by accident twice. Any which way, we'll have bought ourselves some time."

"Maybe even enough to see us through this session of the Assembly," Paulina Koch mused. "Maybe. And an old scandal, even if unearthed, will not do us nearly so much damage next time as a fresh one now." She took her time to think it over and then slowly nodded. "Very well, Roupen. The critical issue, you understand, is to make certain the deletion is either invisible or, if by some mischance it should be noticed, cannot be traced to your intervention."

Hovannis nodded. "Depend on it. I'll handle the erasure myself." His smile did not touch his eyes. "After all, we don't need more people thinking about Bilbeis IV than are already."

"No."

"May I use your terminal?" The question was only formal.

"No," Paulina Koch said again. Hovannis stopped in surprise, his stubby-fingered hands poised over the keyboard. She went on. "Please note, Roupen, I have not told you what to do, and I can truthfully state that under oath. Nor do I care to see you do anything."

The External Affairs Director's eyes lit in anger, but it faded as he thought things through. He gave a grudging nod. "Sensible, from your seat."

"Indeed."

"All right." Hovannis wet his lips. Paulina Koch was one of the few people who made him nervous, and not because she outranked him. He had to work to bring out his next words: "Remember, though, PK, if the wave rolls over me, I won't be the last one to drown."

"Who said anything of waves? All we aim to do is keep the water calm and quiet. Thank you for coming up, Roupen. Now I hope you will excuse me; I have other business to attend to."

Paulina Koch watched him go. Her brows drew together very slightly. A capable man, yes, and one who could prove dangerous—no one had had the nerve to warn her that way in a long time. But their interests here ran in the same direction. And the dismissal she'd given him would keep him in his place a while.

She set the matter of Bilbeis IV aside and turned to the printouts still cluttering her desk. She could not ignore all of them because of a single problem elsewhere; that would have been bad management. She had kept the Survey Service running smoothly for nineteen years; she wanted to keep her seat at least that much longer.

Hovannis's abrupt return startled her. "Yes?" she said coldly. What was he doing back here?

"It's gone from our files."

"I assumed so. I did not need to hear that, nor want to. If you are seeking to implicate me in what you have done, you may have succeeded, but I assure you that you will not enjoy your success much."

"I'm not stupid enough to think I would, PK."

"Well, then? I assume this visit does have some reason?"

Hovannis started to sink into a chair, hesitated, waited for the Chairman's nod, then finished sitting. "You know that survey ships' reports, like most other government reports, go into open access."

"How could I not know that? It helps the Purists meddle." Paulina Koch had been maneuvering behind the scenes for years to get Survey Service records shifted to restricted access. The Purists were only part of her political consideration. Too many things happened on primitive planets that the public could not be expected to understand. Bilbeis IV was a perfect example. The Chairman nodded slowly, as if to herself. "You are, I presume, about to tell me seventeen people on thirteen different planets have already made copies of the report. If so, we are finished, and nothing to be done about it."

"If that were so, I'd still be downstairs, working on my vita so I could start looking for another job." That was candid enough to surprise a smile out of Paulina Koch. Hovannis noted it with some relief; it would soften the bad news. "One copy was accessed, less than half an hour before I dumped the file."

"Tell me the rest."

"Accessor is Isaac Fogelman, home planet Hyperion."

"Have you checked on him? I've heard the name, I think."

"Not yet. You needed to know ASAP."

"Mmp." The grunt told Hovannis he was forgiven. "Let's see what the data store tells us about him," Paulina Koch said. "No, don't leave, Roupen; seeing who uses Survey Service information will not incriminate me unduly." She punched buttons and grunted again. "University of Hyperion, anthropology department."

"Bad," the External Affairs Director said. People who chose teaching over fieldwork had no real notion of what conditions were like away from their keyboards and terminals. Most of them were Purists, and most of the ones who weren't were sympathizers.

Studying the readout, he saw Fogelman was like the rest. Several of his publications criticized Survey Service field technique, though he himself had stayed on Hyperion the last fifteen years. He was also a member of the Noninterference Foundation, a private watchdog group that monitored the Service. If he wasn't an out-and-out Purist, he came too close for comfort. "Bad," Hovannis repeated.

"Yes," the Chairman said. "When he makes his dramatic revelation, he will have the credentials to be taken seriously."

"If his copy of the text was to vanish also—"

"No," Paulina Koch said. Then she reconsidered. With the Service on the line, what did one meddling professor matter? "Well, perhaps—if he never has the chance to accuse us of anything. In this area, any publicity is bad publicity: the less anyone outside the Service thinks of Bilbeis IV, the better."

Hovannis agreed with her completely. "I've done some checking. The Service has contacts with a discreet individual on Hyperion, one who, by luck, operates out of New Westwood, the university town."

"Yes, that is fortunate," the Chairman agreed.

Hovannis waited for a more definite order, then realized he would not get one. "It will be attended to," he said. Bureaucratic language sometimes had its advantages; he could truthfully deny under oath that he had ever said he would do any-thing.

The discreet individual had already made electronic hash of all the data cards in Fogelman's study. Trashing the professor's entire data storage system was about the craziest commission he'd ever had, but he got paid for results, not questions. Very well paid in this case, certainly enough to keep him incurious.

The screen of Fogelman's terminal came on, filling the study with pale gray light. The discreet individual got to work again. Fogelman's security precautions were more than suffi-cient to keep amateurs from getting into his files, but the dis-creet individual was no amateur. Besides, he had been briefed about likely key words and traps, which made the job go faster than it would have otherwise.

One thing the discreet individual had not been briefed about was Professor Fogelman's weak kidneys. As he usually did, Fogelman woke up in the middle of the night. The light downstairs bothered him. He sometimes left his computer up, but he thought he'd turned it off before he went to bed. Mut-tering to himself, he went down to check.

The discreet individual heard him coming, of course, and shot him through the head with a discreetly silenced weapon when he appeared in the study doorway. Fogelman lived alone; his neighbors would never notice the small noise he made falling. The discreet individual went back to what he had been doing.

When he was through, he efficiently ransacked the place —he had not been paid not to—and left through the same window he'd used to enter.

Unlike the luckless Fogelman, he had no trouble sleeping when he got home.

Stavros was the first one to the seminar room, which showed how eager he was to get on with his presentation. Cooling his heels outside while the group inside finished, he wondered if eagerness was cause enough to drum him out of the grad students' union. It probably was, he decided.

The session in the room broke up, and the students came out excitedly discussing something or other that wasn't anthropology and made very little sense to Stavros. He pushed through them and found a seat.

One by one, the other members of the seminar drifted in.
Some wanted to talk about their presentations. Others were
too nervous about speaking in public to care to put out their
conclusions more than once. Stavros kept quiet, too; he was
saving his ammunition for Fogelman.

He was no poker player, though. "You look like the cat that
ate the canary," the girl from Earth said. She was sitting
across from him.

"The what?" he said foolishly, not following the idiom.
What was her name? He'd only heard it at the meeting last
week. "You're Andrea Dubois, aren't you?"

She smiled, pleased he remembered. She was a big pink
blond girl and thus seemed strange to Stavros; most of New
Thessaly's population was Hellenic, as slim and dark as he
was. "How's this?" she said. "You look like someone sitting
there waiting for the Academic Medal to go on your chest."

"I think I did a good piece of work." He still didn't want to
talk about it, but she was pretty, obviously bright or she
wouldn't be here, and so he didn't want the conversation to
end either. "You speak beautiful Basic—you sound like the
instruction tapes I learned from."

"Thanks." She smiled again. "I wish I could take more
credit for it, but I just happen to come from Perth, and everyone in Australia talks this way. At home we call it English."

"I'm jealous."

"It's not as big an advantage as you think," Andrea said.
"Because I use Basic all the time and never had to learn another language, I'll probably have more trouble than you in
picking up alien languages."

"Well, maybe," Stavros said dubiously.

Without heat, they argued about it for a while until Andrea
looked at her watch and said in some surprise, "Professor
Fogelman is very late."

"He makes a habit of it." Stavros chuckled. But when Fogelman did not show up after another ten minutes, he began to
wonder himself.

The door opened. But it was not Fogelman who came into
the seminar room—it was one of the administrative aides
from the anthropology department. The fellow looked shaken;
his voice wobbled as he said, "May I have your attention,
please?"

The class quieted. He went on, "I'm extremely sorry to

have to tell you that Professor Fogelman died last night. His body has just been found at his home."

The seminar group exclaimed in shock and dismay. Stavros crossed himself. He had grown agnostic since coming to the university, but childhood habits still returned in times of stress. "What did he die of?" someone called.

The aide looked unhappier yet. "Professor Fogelman appears to have been murdered, apparently in the course of a robbery. Police investigations are continuing."

The second round of gasps and groans was louder and longer than the first. Stavros was too stunned even to join in. Fogelman had been too full of vigor—to say nothing of being too much a fixture on campus—to imagine him dead.

Andrea apparently accepted the idea more quickly, but then, Stavros didn't think she'd done her undergrad work on Hyperion, so she'd seen Fogelman only once or twice. "What does this do to our enrollment in the seminar?" she asked.

"Professor Richardson has agreed to take over the course," the aide said. Andrea looked relieved. Odds were the girl from Earth didn't know Richardson either, Stavros thought. Richardson specialized in physical anthropology, and thought the cultural half of the discipline a waste of time.

"Get ready for fifteen weeks of potsherds and middens," Stavros whispered to Andrea.

The aide left. The grad students trailed after him, still struggling to accept what they'd heard. "If I'd known he was going to get himself killed, I wouldn't have worked so hard," one said.

"Nice pragmatic fellow," Andrea said, rolling her eyes.

"We both know how he feels," Stavros said. "A lot of the time, I'd agree with him. Not now, though."

"No?" Andrea gave him a curious look. "You *are* carrying something big there, aren't you?"

Stavros hesitated. Sometimes professors ended up publishing work graduate students did. Sometimes other grad students pulled the same stunt. He sometimes thought anybody who wasn't a little paranoid had no business in grad school. But Andrea was right—he did have a blockbuster in his briefcase, and he felt he'd explode if he didn't show it to someone.

"Do you really want to see it?" he said. "Let's go over to the Bistro. What they do to *dolmades* is a crying shame, but they're cheap and close."

It was Andrea's turn to pause, but after a moment she laughed and said, "All right, you've got me curious. And what are dol-whatevers?"

"Grape leaves stuffed with lamb and rice. They're an ancient dish; the recipe goes back to Greece, the Earth region the settlers from New Thessaly came from. The cooks at the Bistro don't season them right, though."

"How long has New Thessaly been settled?" she asked.

He shrugged. "A couple of thousand years. Why?"

"Just that I'd be surprised if your people didn't use native spices in their cooking. Everybody does. For all you know, these *dolmades* may be more like the originals than the ones you're used to are."

That almost made him angry, as if she had somehow maligned his home planet. A few seconds of reflection showed she was right, but that did not help much. "Come on," he said gruffly.

Again, he didn't quite know how to take the appreciative noises she made over the Bistro's *dolmades*. After a couple of glasses of red wine, he worried less. He fiddled with his briefcase. "Are you ready yet?" he asked.

"Eager, eager, eager," she teased, but good-naturedly. "Yes, show me your great mystery, now that I'm not distracted by starvation."

He got out the hard copy of his paper, and ordered *baklava* —not even he could fault the way the Bistro made *baklava*. Andrea paid him the highest compliment of all: she left hers untouched while she read.

She looked up after a couple of pages. "You're sure you're not exaggerating this?"

"It's all straight from the report. If anything, summarizing it cuts the impact because so much of the documentation and supporting detail boils away."

She gave an absent nod; she was reading again. When she was done, she knocked back the wine in her glass with a single gulp. "You weren't kidding," she said quietly. "What are you going to do now?"

He shook his head. "I just don't know. I was going to ask Fogelman, but now—what a mess this is."

He felt the inadequacy of the words, but Andrea understood what he meant. "If I were you, I'd be careful about showing this to a lot of people, at least ones you don't know you can trust."

"Don't be silly," Stavros started to say. He stopped. Knowing something important *could* be dangerous; New Thessaly's politics had proved that more than once. He touched her hand. "I'm not sorry you saw it."

"Good."

"Unfortunate the professor had to go downstairs at such an inopportune time," Paulina Koch remarked.

"Yes, very," Hovannis said. "Especially for him."

"No danger of any of that being traced to us?"

Hovannis snorted. "Not a chance. The deal went through an intermediary; our friend doesn't have any idea who he was working for. He didn't even know exactly what he was supposed to do—just to scramble the computer system was all the instructions he ever got. They may catch him; Hyperion has a fair constabulary. It won't do them any good."

"All right. That suffices, I suppose; you've already told me more than I ought to know."

"I apologize for the need," Hovannis said. The External Affairs Director left. Paulina Koch was very good at putting data in compartments. That was one reason she made such an effective Survey Service Chairman. She began raising the walls around the compartment that held the Bilbeis IV affair. Eventually, she was sure, those walls would be too high to see over, and she would forget whatever was behind them.

If Stavros hadn't taken off his headphones to change disks on the music player, he never would have heard the knock on the door. He rushed to open it, expecting Andrea. She had been over once to see the Survey Service report on Bilbeis IV and again the next day just to talk. Stavros hoped for something more.

"Hello!" he said enthusiastically—too enthusiastically, for standing in the hallway was not Andrea but a middle-aged oriental man whose face was vaguely familiar. Stavros's tongue stumbled over itself. "Er—yes?"

"I'm Van Shui Pong," the man said, "from Hyperion Newsnet." He dug out a holo ID, but Stavros did not need it. He had seen the other now and then on the screen.

He stepped aside. "Come in, Mr. Pong. What could Hyperion Newsnet possibly want with me?" If anyone is less newsworthy than an anthropology grad student, he thought, whoever it is probably hasn't been born yet.

"It's Mr. Van," the newsman said with the air of someone who had said it a great many times. He had a round, good-natured face, but his eyes were disconcertingly keen when he turned them on Stavros. "You were one of Professor Isaac Fogelman's students, weren't you?"

The polite smile vanished from Stavros's face. "Yes. What of it?" Fogelman's murder hadn't even made the news.

"Very possibly, nothing," Van admitted. "There was something in the constabulary report strange enough to make me do a little checking on my own, though."

"What's that?" Stavros recovered his manners again. "Here, I'm sorry; sit down." He waved to the less disreputable of the two chairs in the dorm room.

"Thank you. As I say, it may well be nothing. Still, I find it strange that a burglar would take the time to dump an entire computer memory. Suppressing the internal surveillance program is normal, but this went far beyond that. There's no doubt it was done deliberately; all of Fogelman's data cards were blanked, too." The newsman rose in sudden concern. "Are you all right, Mr. Monemvasios?"

"Yes," Stavros said, but the word rang hollow in his own ears. He sat down himself, heavily. For the first time in his life, he knew what fear felt like.

Van saw his agitation. "You know something of this, or can guess?" he asked eagerly.

Stavros hesitated. Andrea's warning abruptly seemed much better advice than when she'd given it. Telling Van about the data card leaning against his computer could land him in genuine trouble that keeping quiet would avoid. But if Fogelman had been killed to make sure the report on Bilbeis IV never surfaced, then staying silent would only let the killers, whoever they were, get what they wanted. But, Stavros thought hopefully, most likely there was no connection between the burglary and the report but the long arm of coincidence. The Federacy was a big place; anything could happen, and probably would, somewhere.

Stavros got up. "You'd better see this and tell me what you think." Van followed him to the computer console. He put in the data card. The screen lit. No going back now, he thought. He did not feel the way he imagined investigators were supposed to feel. He just felt nervous.

Van Shui Pong went through the abstract of the report and got a couple of chapters into the body before he hit the pause button. When he looked over to Stavros, all the good humor had fallen from his features. "I take it you believe this document to be genuine," he said at last.

"Of course it's genuine," Stavros said indignantly. "I told you, Professor Fogelman gave it to me. His fingerprints must still be on the data card, if you doubt that."

"Not what I meant." Van held up a hand. "I am no anthropologist. Is this an authentic Survey Service document? The Service is an influential arm of the Federacy, and not forgiving to anyone with the gall to call it to account. I'd hate to have my career blighted for no good reason."

"Here—look at these, then." Stavros secured the data card with the Bilbeis IV report and took out a couple of others.

Van went through them as carefully as he had the first one, perhaps more so. "If it is a forgery, it's masterfully done," he conceded. "All right, I'm willing to spend the money to check one step further. To spend the newsnet's money, anyway—I'll have to go back to my office to use the accessor there. Do you want to come along?"

Nothing could have held Stavros back. He grabbed a cap. "Let's go." Accessors to link in with computer systems planets away were uncommon and exorbitantly expensive. Of course the university had one, and the local government, and Fogelman had doubtless used the anthro department budget, not his own, to get up-to-date data cards for his seminar. The newsnet setup might well be the only other one on Hyperion.

Stavros had never been to the newsnet office before. It reminded him of the way the university got the week before exams: both had the same air of intense concentration and near panic aimed at getting something important done on time.

"Better be good," somebody called as Van sat down in front of the accessor, "or they'll make you pay for it out of your own pocket."

"Funny, Flavius, funny." The newsman punched buttons,

paused in thought, punched again. He gave Stavros an apologetic glance. "I haven't used this gadget in a while."

Despite the caveat, he did not take long to make the connection with the Survey Service archives. BILBEIS IV, MOST RECENT SURVEY REPORT, he typed.

SURVEY SERVICE REPORT—BILBEIS IV—FEDERACY STANDARD YEAR 1186 appeared at the top of the screen.

Stavros paid no attention to the text below. "That's not right! That's the old report—the one that tells how what's-his-name got this whole mess started."

Van typed, MORE RECENT REPORTS?

NO MORE RECENT REPORTS. The reply was immediate and uncompromising. Van looked at Stavros, who wanted to hide under his chair. He wondered where Fogelman had come by the data card, if not from the Survey Service. He could not imagine the professor manufacturing such a document or how he would go about it even if he wanted to. The video perfectly matched the first report's pictures and supported the text it accompanied.

"It's crazy," Stavros said. Van Shui Pong did not answer. Grasping at straws, the grad student suggested, "Ask when the next report from Bilbeis IV is due. The place must be up for resurvey—fifteen hundred years is the standard interval for pretechnological worlds."

Shrugging, Van typed in the question. NEXT REPORT EXPECTED WITH RETURN OF SURVEY SHIP *JÊNG HO*, was the response. Van shrugged again. "Your data card has that much right, at any rate."

"Well, when is the *Jêng Ho* coming back?" Stavros asked. Van entered that question, too. They both waited impatiently, hoping the reply would do something to clear up their confusion.

The screen stayed blank for some time. "Must be going through a different data base," Van said. The words were barely out of his mouth when the answer came: SURVEY SHIP *JÊNG HO* SCHEDULED TO RETURN FEDERACY STANDARD YEAR 2687:139.

"What's the current FSY date?" Stavros asked. The Federacy Standard Year, based on Earth's, had 365 days of 86,400 seconds each. It gave thousands of planets, each with its own natural period, a common way to reckon time. Like Hyperion, though, most of them used local time for everything but Federacy elections and other matters of offworld importance. Stavros hadn't worried about FSY dating in months.

Van dealt with it more often; as a newsman, he used FSY datelines to see how recent stories set away from Hyperion were. But he did not have the FSY date at the tip of his tongue either. He fiddled with his watch, frowned, cleared it, tried again. "I knew I had to get this thing fixed," he muttered. "It says it's already FSY 2687:157."

"That's crazy," Stavros agreed. "Ask somebody else."

Van did, loudly. "It's 157," three people yelled back, one of them adding, "for another three hours, anyway."

"But that makes no sense," Stavros said. "If the *Jêng Ho* was due back from Bilbeis IV eighteen days ago, the crew must have filed its report already. Why isn't it on-line for accessing?"

"I'm beginning to think they did file," Van said, and he was not talking loudly at all now. "If the report you have is the real one, and it's missing from the Survey Service files, and your professor had all his data—to say nothing of himself— erased just after he pulled it out, what does that suggest to you?"

Stavros thought about it. "Trouble."

"To me, too." But Van sounded as though he enjoyed the prospect.

V

"You appear to have made a mistake, Roupen," Paulina Koch said.

"So I do," Hovannis replied stolidly.

"Is that all you have to say?" The Survey Service Chairman seldom let anger into her voice, but this was an exception. The first tape she'd just played from Hovannis was of some muckraker's story from the Hyperion Newsnet. It quoted at length from the Bilbeis IV report Hovannis had been so sure he'd squelched and then went on to scream cover-up. The second tape worried her more. She had just gotten that one. The story on it was much like the one from Hyperion, but it came from Fezzan, a dozen light-years away.

"What do you want me to do, jump off the top of the Survey Service tower?" Hovannis was finding that Paulina Koch no longer intimidated him as much as she once had. They were in the same starship now, even if it had sprung a leak. The thing to do was patch it, not argue. "I scrubbed the report, but I missed the notice of the *Jêng Ho*'s return date. The snoop spotted it and drew the right conclusions, that's all."

"I've been called into the Assembly for more questioning tomorrow," the Chairman said.

"And?" Hovannis waited for her to tell him she was throwing him out the air lock. If she tried, he had no intention of going alone.

"And I will deny everything, of course," she replied. "The initial report was bad enough. It would have cost us embarrassment, funding, and influence. Now we have suppressed evidence and involved ourselves in various other unsavory activities. If those are discovered, we stand to lose more than influence."

Hovannis gave her an admiring glance. "The whole thing is

74

a forgery, then?" She had balls if she thought she could bring that off.

"From top to bottom. We have no record of any such report, so it could never have entered our files in the first place. Obviously, then, it must be a fabrication. How will the Assembly prove otherwise, from the computer records?"

"No way, of course." The External Affairs Director had already corrected his blunder; the *Jêng Ho* was now due to arrive any time, at least in the Survey Service data bank. He amended, "That's just from the computer records, though. If they start summoning the *Jêng Ho*'s crew, everything is out to lunch."

Paulina Koch smiled a wintry smile. "Not necessarily. They will take a while to think of that, and we already have."

"Yes, I see what you mean," Hovannis said. If and when he tackled that job, he planned to handle it so indirectly that no trace would ever lead back to him. He went on. "I just hope they don't decide to make another visit to Bilbeis IV and check things out firsthand."

He saw he had actually managed to amuse the Chairman. "I assure you, I shall not waste my time worrying about *that*," she said. "The controversy at the moment is over the report, after all, not the planet, and I intend to keep it focused there. Besides, can you imagine the cost?"

Hovannis nodded. Bureaucrats thought that way. Data cards and money were more real to them than barbarous worlds. He returned to more immediate concerns. "We ought to check out where Mr. Van Shui Pong is getting his information now that Fogelman's data base is gone."

"You really think it is?" Paulina Koch asked. "I'm beginning to wonder."

"I've used that person before, for one thing and another. He's reliable."

"If you're so sure, Fogelman must have passed it onto someone before your friend visited him. Not to this Van busybody, or we would have had him yapping at us sooner. To whom, then?" It was not really a question; the Chairman was thinking out loud. "To one of his students, perhaps, for a class project."

"Sensible," Hovannis said. "Fogelman pulled a lot of recent survey reports, not just the one on Bilbeis IV. We can check out why he wanted them without too much trouble.

Then we start narrowing things down, and then, well, I suppose another visit from that discreet individual."

"Yes, overall that bears the potential for greatest benefit to the Service. With the focus of the infection removed, the hubbub should die down in fairly short order. Tend to it, Roupen; I have to prepare my testimony."

Tend to it, Roupen, Hovannis thought sourly as he left the Chairman's office. He would; his neck was on the block, too. But afterward, Paulina Koch would owe him a debt. He intended to collect.

Magda was in the shower when the phone chimed. She swore and stayed under the warm needle spray, hoping whoever was on the other end of the line would give up and go away.

Whoever it was had stubbornness to go with an exquisitely misplaced sense of timing. The chime kept ringing. Muttering under her breath, Magda turned off the shower, pulled her hair back from her face so it would not drip in her eyes, and shrugged on the robe she had hanging by the stall. Let this idiot figure out what he'd interrupted, she thought—maybe he'd be embarrassed enough to hang up in a hurry.

The minute she clicked on the screen and saw she was face to face with Atanasio Pedroza, she knew she had made a mistake. She had turned aside the biologist's advances all through the mission of the *Jêng Ho*, but he had not given up even after the ship had come back to the base on Topanga.

Now he did not look embarrassed; he looked as though he was picturing her wet naked body under the robe. She pulled it together so it covered more of her, but that proved wrong too, because it drew his attention to her breasts. The guardsmen who'd caught her in the bath on Bilbeis IV had been more polite.

"Hello, Atanasio," she said, sighing. "What is it?"

"Hmm? I'm sorry, Magda, I was too busy admiring." Even his voice had a leer in it, the anthropologist thought with distaste. He somehow never failed to set Magda's teeth on edge.

"*Will* you come to the point?" she snapped; patience had never been one of her long suits. She was also getting cold.

He looked hurt. "After we fought that report through together, I thought we might be able to get along better in other ways, too."

"Don't get your hopes up." To give Pedroza his due, he had fought hard for an honest report. He had rigid standards of right and wrong and the courage of his convictions. It was his personality outside those convictions that made Magda dislike him. "Just because we were able to work together once, Atanasio, doesn't mean I want to go to bed with you."

"I don't give up easily."

She grimaced. She knew that was true. Professionally, it was an asset; here, it was more a pain in the ass. He went on. "Soon I'll have a chance to try changing your mind under more pleasant circumstances than this semiconscious excuse for a planet offers."

Magda rather liked Topanga's relaxed pace, but that had nothing to do with the sharpness of her question. "What do you mean?"

"The whole crew has won a round trip to Carson Planet. Once a month here, they throw the names of all the incoming ships into the computer, and the *Jêng Ho* came out. Captain Brusilov delegated the arrangements to me."

That last sentence killed the pleasure the previous two had given Magda. She had been to Carson Planet before, and had enjoyed it. The place specialized not in industry or agriculture but in no-holds-barred fun: "Everything in Excess" was the local motto. Not surprisingly, it was one of the richer worlds in this part of the Federacy. However—

"I suppose you booked the two of us into the same cubicle on the flight out," she said. She had intended it as sarcasm, but Pedroza refused to meet her eyes. "You bastard, you didn't!"

"As a matter of fact, no," he said, flushing, but before she could be mollified he admitted, "You *are* in the one next to mine, and they do connect."

"You have your nerve. After the *Jêng Ho*, I'm not overjoyed being on the same planet with you, let alone the same starship—and being in the next cubicle is way, way too close. I'll stay here, thanks. Have yourself a good time."

"Everyone else I've gotten hold of is eager to go. We even got a credit advance to gamble with."

"I—don't—care," she said between clenched teeth. "Now, will you get off the damn phone and let me finish my shower?"

"I'll send the tickets and such over to you, in case you change your mind." He blanked the screen.

"Not bloody likely," she muttered. She took off her robe, flung it against the wall, and got back under the water. It did not wash away her foul mood, which was not helped by finding that Pedroza was as good as his word: a ticket for a tour ship, a reservation at one of the better Carson Planet hotels, and notification of her credit advance were sitting in the fax slot. She scowled at them, wishing Pedroza were less stubborn, or at least that he would find someone else to pursue.

She dressed in a hurry and took a shuttle to the Survey Service field office. She could have done her business by phone, but she was too irked to stay in her apartment. Besides, she was also annoyed at the field office people, and snarling at them in person gave more satisfaction than fuming by phone.

"Any word on that report yet?" she snapped without preamble as she walked in. The report on Bilbeis IV had gone in to Survey Service Central days ago, but none of the explosions Magda expected was going off yet.

"Let me check," the clerk sighed. He fiddled with his terminal so slowly that Magda wanted to leap over the partition separating them and do it for him. He seemed oblivious to her impatience. After what could not possibly have been a year and a half, he looked up and said, "Central says the report never reached their files. Must be some computer trouble in the system somewhere."

"Oh, damnation," she said, loud enough to make people all over the office turn their heads her way. "Have you ever had trouble with the FTL link to that data base before?"

"No," the clerk said. "Of course, there's always a first time. I think you'll have to resubmit." He sounded almost pleased at the prospect. Fieldwork attracted adventurers; Survey Service offices drew routineers. The two groups often clashed.

Magda was not about to give the petty bureaucrat any more satisfaction than he'd already gotten. "All right," she said, so sweetly that he looked at her with sudden suspicion. "Of course, at the same time I expect you'll submit a notice of trouble in the system. Give me your supervisor's name, so I can notify him or her that it's coming."

The clerk grumbled at the prospect of work he couldn't do

on automatic pilot, but Magda had him, and he knew it. He reluctantly coughed up his boss's name.

"Thank you very much," Magda purred. "I'll be back tomorrow with that data card." She kicked herself for not having brought it with her, but she really had thought the glitch was at her end, not in the computer network. Still, she was not altogether displeased as she rode back to her place. Not only did she know now where the trouble lay, she had also won the little duel with that officebound bungler.

Her roommate was home when she opened the door. She and Marie Roux had been friends during fieldwork training half a dozen years ago and then, as was the way of such things, had not seen each other since, though they had kept in touch with tapes. Finding each other on Topanga at the same time, they overrode the computer's temporary housing assignment to be together and talk about old times.

"Hi, Magda," Magda said.

"Hi, Marie," Marie said. They both laughed. They had been the only two redheads in their training group, and the instructors—and even some of the other recruits—had mixed up their names so often they started doing it themselves.

"I wish I *were* Magda," Marie said. "My ship couldn't win an overhaul, let alone the travel pool. Carson Planet—mmmm! I'm jealous." She waved at the goodies Atanasio Pedroza had sent.

"Do you want to go?" Magda asked. "Be my guest."

"What? Don't be ridiculous, Magda. That trip is worth plenty, and besides, you'll have a good time."

"No I won't, because I wouldn't go if they paid me a bonus." Magda explained about Pedroza's unwelcome attentions, finishing, "So you see, Marie, that cabin will just be empty if you don't use it."

"You're serious, aren't you?" Marie said wonderingly. "I really would like to go, but—"

"But what? I told you already—go ahead, do it. You're not taking anything away from me, because I like Topanga without dear Atanasio about a hundred times better than Carson Planet—let alone the"—she checked the ticket—"*Clark County*—with him."

"But—" Marie began again, but Magda knew she was wavering when she shifted her approach. "Even if I did try to go, that prize is for the crew of the *Jêng Ho*. What do I do when somebody asks me what I'm doing there?"

"So long as it's not Atanasio, tell 'em the truth. They all know about him and me. For that matter, you can tell him, too. I have, often enough. He just doesn't listen."

"That's not what I meant. What do I do when they check my ID at the air lock?"

"Odds are they won't." Magda frowned, though, because they could, and she knew it. "Hmm, tell you what—take my spare credit card."

"I couldn't do that!"

"Why not? We've known each other a long time now; you're not going to steal me blind. You'll need it anyway, to tap into the line of credit that goes with the trip. All your other expenses are paid; you shouldn't need to dip into my account. If it makes you feel better, you can leave your spare behind as a hostage."

"I'd insist on that at the very least. Damn it, I'm so tempted now, but it still won't work. When your credit card goes into the computer, the screen will display your picture."

"Hi, Magda," Magda said again.

"I don't think we look alike," Marie said.

"Well, I don't either, but most people certainly seem to. After all these centuries of stirring genes around, redheads are so uncommon that hardly anybody looks past our hair. You're going to gamble *on* Carson Planet, for heaven's sake; are you afraid to gamble a little to get there?"

Marie threw her hands in the air. "All right. I give up. Thank you!" She hugged Magda. "I still think you're crazy, but when do I leave? Do I have time to pack?"

"Here, give me that ticket. I didn't even look." Magda quickly checked it. "You're all right. You're not due out till tomorrow morning."

"Plenty of time," Marie agreed. "One thing the Survey Service does teach you is how to live out of suitcases." She went over to the closet and with practiced efficiency started filling one. Her only hesitation came when she happened on something thin and filmy. She giggled and put it in.

Magda's back was turned. "What's funny?"

Marie displayed what she'd packed. "I was just thinking I might end up liking this Atanasio what's-his-name better than you do."

"Maybe," Magda said. She let it go at that; Marie was her friend. What she was thinking was, Better you than me.

Stavros thumbed the remote unit; the holo screen came to life. "What's on?" Andrea asked. They were studying together. They both found Professor Richardson about as exciting as watching a shrub grow, and broken bits of pots did not much interest either of them, but Richardson expected her students to work.

"The news," Stavros answered.

That was plenty to make Andrea put down her notes. Hyperion Newsnet had been flailing away at the Survey Service for a couple of weeks now, with as yet no reply. The long silence from the immense government bureau made Stavros think of someone sticking a pin in a dinosaur. First the beast had to notice you were there at all, and then it would take a while longer to figure out what to do.

Of course, if it did decide to flick its tail, it was apt to squash you flat . . .

The lead story was local—an ore boat had capsized on some river over on the western continent, killing four sailors and losing a big cargo of rare-earth metals. "In offplanet news," the newswoman began, and Stavros tensed, but the item was about the crash of a starship full of gamblers trying to land at Carson Planet. "Three hundred seventeen people are known dead; the complete toll will not be known until the rubble has been cleared from what was until recently a spaceport terminal building."

"Four people here count for more than hundreds somewhere else," Stavros said scornfully.

"Isn't it the same on your world?" Andrea asked. "It is on Earth. Somebody here may know one of the ore haulers, or know someone who does. That makes that story more important in New Westwood than one that happens worlds away."

Stavros had not thought of it that way. Indeed, he had not thought much about it at all. He just knew he was impatient for some kind of response from the Survey Service, and frustrated because there was none. "I suppose you have a point. You know—"

He stopped. Van Shui Pong was on the screen. "In the continuing Survey Service scandal," Van declared, "Chairman

Paulina Koch has at last issued a statement." Stavros's whoop drowned out Van's introduction of the Chairman.

"She looks so ordinary," Andrea said. Dowdy is a better word, Stavros thought. Paulina Koch reminded him of a gray dumpling. The suit she wore did not flatter her figure. The curtains behind her podium were bright blue, but she contrived to fade into the background nonetheless.

She was saying, "The Survey Service regrets the delay in response to these allegations, but did not believe they could possibly be taken seriously by anyone aware of the Service's long and successful record of integrity both within the Federacy and in its dealings with people at a pre-Federacy stage of culture. The Service must deny both the charges leveled in respect to activities conducted on the pre-Federacy world Bilbeis IV and those even wilder accusations relating to removal of data from storage. They are baseless, without foundation, and insusceptible to proof."

"What about the report on Bilbeis IV, then?" a newsman interrupted.

She gave him a chilly look. "The report that purports to be about Bilbeis IV, you mean. It is a forgery, and not a very clever forgery at that. Were I here to guess instead of telling you the facts as I know them, I might give you more than a fair idea of the perpetrators of the hoax."

Stavros grunted. He could predict where that line would lead the reporters. "Who?" three of them yelled together.

"Who else but the Purists?" the Chairman replied. "For almost as long as the Survey Service has existed, they have tried to curtail and even halt legitimate scientific inquiry. In the past, I did not question their motives, no matter how strongly I disagreed with their conclusions. When they stoop to tactics such as this, however, I can no longer sit idly by."

"Turn that off," Andrea said in disgust. "She's got them all eating out of her hand. Why won't they *see*?"

Stavros was reaching for the control when a newswoman called to Paulina Koch, "You haven't said anything about the Survey Service computer showing the *Jêng Ho* due back on 139 when it was already 157." The grad student decided to keep watching a while longer.

"Computer error is such a common excuse in a certain type of fiction that I am aware it is difficult to accept in fact," the Chairman said calmly, "but if it didn't occur, it would never have become such a cliché. An investigation into the nature of the error is now ongoing and will be published when complete. Any required modifications in hardware or software will of course be implemented."

At that, Stavros did turn off the holo, jabbing the switch with ferocity directed away from the image of Paulina Koch. She might as well have been coated with some fluorinated resin; nothing stuck to her. "No one even asked about professor Fogelman," he said bitterly.

"What good would it do?" Andrea said. "I can figure out what she'd say already: that Fogelman's death was just a coincidence, and how can anyone possibly tell what was in his data store, as it has unfortunately suffered erasure—she'd never come right out and say anything as plain as 'been erased.'"

"You're right about that." At another time, he would have found her observation wryly amusing; now he was too angry to rise to the bait.

"I wish we could get hold of the *Jêng Ho*'s crew directly," she said, "instead of waiting for whatever the Survey Service decides to claim is their report."

Stavros sprang to his feet, rushed over to her, and gave her a hug. "Let's try! Van ought to know how to contact them without going through the Survey accessing system. They can't be in on this scheme of the Chairman's, or they never would have filed that report in the first place."

Andrea did not pull back right away. She looked Stavros in the eye—they were about of a height. "Good idea. Call Van."

"He doesn't like me to at night. He's usually busy working up his stories for the newscasts. I'll do it in the morning. No—you do it. You've earned the chance to be in on this."

"All right, I will." To Stavros's surprise, she added, "Thank you."

"Are you sure I'm doing you a favor? You were the one who told me this might get dangerous."

"It's already dangerous if we're right about Fogelman. But if we are, the Survey Service has already done a lot worse than cultural interference."

"Yes. We can't prove that, though."

Andrea clucked her tongue in annoyance. "We can't prove any of this, not when the chairman denies the report on Bilbeis IV is genuine. That's why we need to reach the people who wrote it; they can give her the lie. As a matter of fact, I'm surprised they haven't started squawking before this."

"So am I. It worries me."

"Me too, but I can't do anything about it now. What I can do—and you too—is get ready for the next quiz Richardson is going to drop on us. We ought to get those scrapers and tureens from Cappalli III up on the screen. Them, we can do something about right this minute."

Stavros laughed. "There's practicality for you." He fiddled with the controls. The screen lit, this time full of implements of bone and baked clay. "These are from the small continent in the northern hemisphere—what's its name?"

"Maximilian."

"That's right. I don't know what you're worrying about. You know the material a lot better than I do."

"I want to do a good job."

Even an anthropology grad student can examine only so many artifacts before the brain begins to numb. Andrea and Stavros reached that point at about the same time. She was the one who finally said, "Enough!" and turned off the text.

"What now?" Stavros asked.

"Let's check the entertainment menu. After all that, I need something mindless." She found a costume drama. Some of the costumes were hardly any costume at all. "Like that?" she asked ironically, noticing Stavros's sudden interest in the screen.

"More interesting than ladles and vials," he retorted. "Seriously, though, I was shocked silly the first time I saw bare breasts on the holo. They don't show that kind of thing on New Thessaly; the church is strong there."

"Were you?" Andrea raised an eyebrow. They watched the show sitting close together, as they had been while they were studying. When it was done, Stavros thought Andrea would leave. Instead, she leaned back in her chair and stretched lazily.

He slid an arm around her shoulder. She moved closer to him. "What else have you learned on Hyperion?" she asked.

"Shall we find out?"

Some time later, she leaned up on one elbow in his narrow bed. "You picked up all that in the last few years here?"

He sat up himself, offended. "Good God, no! After all, Andrea, I'm twenty-nine years old."

He watched the flush rise under her fair skin as she blinked in confusion. "But you said—"

"I said I didn't watch that kind of thing on New Thessaly. I didn't; my planet holds to keeping what it reckons private matters private. That doesn't mean we don't do them, though."

She laughed out loud. "You don't need to sound so defensive. I'm glad, that's all."

"Hmm. Prove it." Stavros tried to make his voice gruff, but he was laughing, too.

She poked him in the ribs. "How am I supposed to do that?"

"Think of something."

She did.

The discreet individual was not altogether pleased with the way things were going. It was not any failure to turn a profit that disturbed him. His fees, especially lately, were keeping him in a state of luxury that satisfied even his exacting standards.

Rather, his problem was figuring out a quiet way to earn this latest commission he had received. The woman who proposed it to him was the same person who had given him his last big job. She was so vague about this one that he was sure she was only an intermediary, and probably not the first in a chain.

Despite such precautions, he suspected he could make a good guess about where the chain's other end lay. He tried not to make the guess, even in his own mind. Some things, he felt instinctively, were better left uncontemplated.

The problem had two parts. Neither was easy, and the second, rare in his line of work, required him to draw his own conclusion and act on it. Bugging the comm lines into Hyperion Newsnet had been tough enough, but he was used to doing that. Now he had to decide just where Van Shui Pong was getting information he shouldn't have.

The discreet individual punched for the latest set of playbacks. A burst of static made him scowl. The next several conversations were garbled. The newsnet had most of the latest confidentiality protectors.

Not all of them, though. After a while, his electronics outdueled the opposing defense systems and he was able to eavesdrop again.

He had done some discreet checking on Van's contacts and had found that two in particular had connections of interest to his carefully unthought-about employer. He had not been able to decide which of them knew more; they both knew too much.

He wondered whether it mattered. Dealing with one ought to teach the other to stop meddling. He was not wasteful: no point to getting rid of both of them unless he found himself without another choice.

In spite of his income, one luxury he could not afford was impatience. He wished he could; Van Shui Pong talked with a lot of people, most of them dull and most of them absolutely unconnected with this business.

At last Van got another call from one of the pair the discreet individual was interested in. After he finished listening to the taped conversation, he nodded thoughtfully. These people were doing their best to be difficult. In the abstract, he could almost wish their best to be good enough.

He was not, however, given to thinking in the abstract.

"He'll check," Andrea said with satisfaction as she switched off the phone. "He says it may take a while to work around the Survey Service network to get in touch with the *Jêng Ho*'s crew, but he thinks he can do it. He was boasting about his connections when he got a call on another line and had to give me a quick good-bye."

"All right," Stavros said. "I hope those connections come through."

"So do I. Reporters always boast about connections, whether they have them or not."

Stavros's long, dark face wore a frown well. Not for the first time, he had the feeling of being in over his head. Actually, he'd had that feeling from the moment he'd seen the report on Bilbeis IV. Running into it when thinking about a woman he cared for, though, was different from facing it when confronting a large, powerful, hostile organization.

He wondered how Andrea came to speak of reporters with casual familiarity. Van excepted, he had never dealt with one in his life. New Thessaly was not that kind of place. Gossip there was as incessant as anywhere else, but it was local and amateur, not industrialized.

Andrea was getting to know him well enough to guess some of the things behind his silence. She said, "Don't worry. We'll just do the best we can as long as we can, with us and with Bilbeis IV."

That was advice he might have heard on his home planet, and it was down-to-earth enough to shake him out of his apprehension. "Fair enough," he said. "I suppose that also applies to the quiz this afternoon."

"I wish you hadn't brought it up." She made a face at him. "I was just at the point of letting myself believe I could take it without doing any more studying. Now I suppose I'll have to get back to it."

"I know *I* need more work. You're good company." He turned on the computer. They sat down together. He looked at her sidelong. "Maybe you should pick out another spectacle instead."

"Ha! Not with that damn quiz waiting for me—no, don't pout, this is what you deserve for reminding me of it."

"All right." Stavros did get down to studying, disappointed but not really displeased. No matter what she knew about reporters, Andrea also knew what came first. That counted for more.

"Thank you for inviting me here today," Paulina Koch said. "It is always a privilege to provide information to this distinguished Assembly subcommittee."

"Thank you for agreeing to appear before us on such short notice, Chairman Koch," Assemblyman Valleix replied.

—*Here you are, snooping again.* —*Damn straight, and maybe we'll nail you this time, too.* The Chairman knew the real meaning of the opening amenities perfectly well. So did Valleix. The Purist was a blockhead but not, she thought, that big a blockhead.

He asked, "Have you any opening statement you care to read into the record?"

"Perhaps it would be better merely to respond to questions." Paulina Koch smoothed an imaginary wrinkle from the collar of her gray tunic.

"Very well. I will make the first question as general as I can, then, and ask how you respond to the allegations raised on Hyperion and other planets concerning Survey Service cultural interference on the pretechnological world Bilbeis IV."

"To that, sir, I have only the reply I already gave in public: that the report which—as you properly said—is *alleged* to deal with Bilbeis IV is not a product of Survey Service personnel and was produced to denigrate and cast doubt on the numerous successful activities of the Service."

Assemblyman Valleix nervously licked his lips. He remembered the last trap the Survey Service Chairman had set for him. If she blew him out of the water again here, not only would he look like a fool with elections coming up, but no one would dare tackle the Survey Service again for the next generation and a half.

His voice wobbled as he asked, "Have you conducted a thorough investigation through Service records to ascertain the truth of the statement you have just made?"

"Indeed we have, sir. Nothing in our data files gives any support whatever to the wild claims first raised on Hyperion and then copied by sensation seekers elsewhere. From that, one must conclude the supposed report to be fraudulent. The Survey Service is also conducting an investigation on Hyperion to attempt to discover the source of these scurrilous rumors."

"Yes, I can well believe that," Valleix said dryly. Paulina Koch sat quietly, waiting for his next question. If she heard his sarcasm—and he was certain she did—she never let on. "Perhaps computer specialists from outside the Service will have more luck accessing relevant documents than your own people."

"I hope they do," Paulina Koch said. "Our records are of course at their disposal." She was the perfect witness, polite, attentive; every fact Valleix wanted was at her fingertips.

He fought down the impulse to sigh. If anything ever had been in the Survey Service files, it was not there now, or the Chairman would never risk its being exposed. Still, he was slightly heartened. She had not flattened him by, say, producing a report on Bilbeis IV that showed everything normal there. Maybe she could not. "There remains the discrepancy between the arrival date of the *Jêng Ho* as first taken from Survey Service records by ah"—he paused to check his tickler screen—"by Hyperion Newsnet and that later offered as correct by your organization. Such alteration would seem to support the charge that information is being suppressed."

"Not, I would hope, sir, in the absence of any and all other data. Electronics are fallible, as has been made evident on several painful occasions in the history of the Federacy."

"That is true, Chairman Koch. Sometimes I think we rely too much on electronics. You would not take it amiss, then, if we were to summon some of the crew members of the *Jêng Ho* from, ah"—he glanced down at the note screen again —"Topanga, so they can testify as to what they witnessed on Bilbeis IV? Surely their ship will be in by this time."

"I would think so, sir. Of course I have no objection to such an action. Do whatever you can to uncover the truth here. That is also what we are trying to do, for the sake of our own good name. The wild claims this report makes are wholly inconsistent with the principles upon which we are conducting our operation."

"Thank you, Madam Chairman. I shall instruct the clerk of the subcommittee to issue and serve the appropriate subpoenas." This time Assemblyman Valleix did sigh. If the Chairman was so eager to let the crew people appear, odds were they'd back her up. Valleix turned to the head of the subcommittee. "I have no further questions of the witness at this time."

"Very well. Assemblywoman O'Kelly, you may proceed."

The clerk she had dealt with the day before looked up sourly from his tea as Magda came in. He grew even more unhappy when she walked around to his side of the desk. She took a data card out of her holdall and handed it to him. "I just want to make sure you don't have any trouble copying the document to the data base," she said innocently.

"I'm sure there will be no problem." He looked as if he wanted to erase her card but didn't quite dare. Instead, he put it in his terminal, punched two buttons, waited for a light to go from red to green, and handed it back to her. "It's in the system."

"Good. I hope that wasn't too difficult for you." Now the clerk looked as though he wished he had scrubbed the data card. She tossed him a note handwritten on a memo form. "This outlines the foulup and your part in it. Take it to your supervisor and be careful with it till she gets it—it's the only copy." Of course the memo would end up in the nearest trash can, but getting the report on Bilbeis IV to the attention of the Survey Service—and the public beyond the Service— counted for more than making a functionary's life miserable, however much fun the latter was.

After that, as had happened after the first time the *Jêng Ho*'s crew sent in the report, she had nothing to do but sit around and wait for the roof to blow off Survey Service Central. Even if a new assignment came through, she wouldn't be able to do anything about it until the rest of the crew got back from Carson Planet. But if she had to vegetate, Topanga was a nice place to do it. The climate was warmer and drier than she cared for. The locals had adapted. They never hurried; they made a point of taking things easy and viewed life with a relaxed detachment Magda envied without wanting to emulate.

She also did not care for the way they baked themselves under the sun. She preferred pale skin to bronze, and also preferred not to have to undergo skin cancer therapy every so often. The locals took that annoyance in stride, as they did everything else.

Thinking about the Topangans' indifference to malignancy brought Magda back inevitably to Queen Sabium. Had David Ware not meddled with her fate, she would have been a millennium and a half dead, and Bilbeis IV would be like any other pretechnological world.

Having met Sabium, though, Magda could understand his interference, if not condone it. Sabium was—something else. With time on her hands, Magda began a monograph detailing the effect of her reign. The work progressed only by fits and starts; Topanga's easygoing style proved infectious. Eventually Magda realized with a guilty start that a couple of weeks had gone by without her checking on what was happening with the report she had refiled. She went down to the field office to see what was up.

The clerk was friendlier than he had been the last time she had come in. Amazing what giving him something to throw away could do. He didn't even seem unwilling to check on the status of the report. "There shouldn't be anything wrong," he said reassuringly as he punched buttons. "Survey Service Central is a busy place, you know, and sometimes these things take a while to get a reaction."

"This one will get a reaction," Magda said.

The clerk's look said that Magda thought her little concerns were a lot more important in the grand scheme of things than they really were. She glared at him. Then the screen on his terminal lit. His brown face went smug as he glanced over to it—here he was, handing down the word from on high, Magda thought scornfully. His smugness abruptly shattered. "What the—" he said, startled into a purely human reaction.

Magda walked around to see the screen for herself. He didn't scowl at her the way he had before when she took such liberties. REPORT FROM SURVEY SERVICE SHIP *JÊNG HO*: NOT IN FILES, she read.

"That's crazy," she muttered. She turned on the clerk. "You must have screwed up the transmission again, uh, Pandit." She had to read his name backward through the clear plastic plate on his desk; she'd never bothered noticing what it was before.

"I did not," he said angrily. "What are you doing, saying things like that? You hovered over me like some miserable vulture, and you didn't complain then."

"So I didn't," she admitted, taken aback by his hot response. "Well, what has gone wrong, then?"

"How should I know? Whatever it is, as far as Survey Service Central can tell, you and your whole crew are still in space. You'll have to retransmit one more time."

"Wonderful. The whole damn crew *is* in space, except for me. Captain Brusilov will nail my hide to the wall when he gets back, too. He'll have as much trouble believing back-to-back computer failures as I do."

"What else could it be?" said the clerk—Pandit, Magda reminded herself. She could not stay irritated at him; he sounded as puzzled as she was.

She said, "For all I know, the people at Central are scrubbing the damn thing on purpose every time it comes in." Pandit's expression said what he thought of that. Magda didn't believe it either. A little paranoia was all well and good, but letting it run wild was something else again. She sighed. "I suppose I'll have to bring it in again, won't I?"

"Unless you'd sooner save yourself the trip and just send me a copy through your computer."

"Not after all the trouble we've gone through already. I

want to watch you again while you make the transmission to Survey Service Central."

"Whatever you say." It wasn't Pandit's problem.

"I'll see you tomorrow."

Magda went back to the apartment and made another half-hearted lunge at her monograph. Before long, she was looking for an excuse to quit. She turned on the news. She did not watch often; most of the time on Topanga it was comfortable chatter and not much else. Not this afternoon. A rubble-strewn crater filled the screen; disaster crews struggled frantically amid the debris.

The newswoman was saying, "—almost certainly dead, of course, are the 317 passengers of the ill-fated starship. The toll is expected to rise far higher as the ruins of the crowded terminal building yield their grim secrets. Here is a list of deaths confirmed by credit card recovery—"

"Vultures," Magda muttered. She reached out to switch off the screen.

"—in the crash of the *Clark County*," the newswoman finished.

Magda's hand froze in the air. The rest of her also felt as if it had turned to ice.

Credit cards were nearly indestructible; men and women, sadly, not. Every so often, another name Magda knew would come up, setting her crying again. Irfan Kawar . . . Norma Anderssen . . . Captain Brusilov would never nail Magda's hide to the wall now. She even had tears for Atanasio Pedroza.

Then she saw her own name.

VI

Stavros opened the door and stepped back in surprise. "Hello! Come in."

"Thank you." Van Shui Pong had not phoned ahead. For that matter, he had not been back to the dormitory since the day he had first introduced himself. He nodded to Andrea, who was eating a candied orange. "Perhaps you and Stavros would like to go for a walk with me. The campus is a pleasant place; I don't get here often enough."

"A walk?" Stavros echoed foolishly. "It's close to midnight."

Van only waited. Andrea stood up and threw on her cloak. Muttering, Stavros got his cap and mantle out of the closet and closed the neck clasp. He and Andrea followed Van to the elevator.

The night was just this side of chilly. The air had a cool green smell, different from the way it smelled during the day. A few lights glowed in distant labs and offices. Still, the path the three walked was to the eye merely a pale snake coiling across dark lawns.

After a while, Van stopped. Stavros could hear the silence between the trills of Terran insects and Hyperion's own small night creatures. Van said, "I've finally managed to track down the crew of the *Jêng Ho.*"

"Have you? That's wonderful!" Stavros exclaimed. "Will they back their report?"

Andrea, though, found another question. "Why did you bring us out here to tell us that?" Even before Van answered, that dampened Stavros's first rush of excitement.

The reporter nodded somberly. "You begin to understand. Here I can hope, at least, that we are not overheard. I don't dare be so optimistic about your rooms anymore, Stavros."

The grad student took a moment to find a name for what he

heard in Van's voice. "You're afraid."

"Yes, I am. You see, the *Jêng Ho*'s crew was aboard the *Clark County*." When neither Stavros nor Andrea reacted, the newsman snorted in irritation. "Why do we go to so much trouble getting out the news when no one pays any attention to us? The *Clark County* is the ship that crashed on Carson Planet not so long ago. Something over three hundred people died, including all of the crewmembers of the *Jêng Ho*."

"That proves the Survey Service is lying in its teeth," Stavros burst out. "If the *Jêng Ho* didn't get back till the day Paulina Koch claimed, how could the crew have gone on their junket and had that accident?"

"If it was an accident," Andrea said slowly.

Stavros felt the air rush out of him as if he had been kicked in the belly. "That makes too much sense for me to like," he said at last.

"And for me, too," Van said. "I was going to point it out to you people if you didn't come up with it for yourselves. Too many coincidences add up to scaring me a lot—if we keep pushing at this thing, I have a bad feeling we'll end up the same way your Professor Fogelman and twenty Survey Service crewfolk ended up. I'm sorry, but I've had enough. I wish you well if you want to go on, but you'll have to do it without me. My phone won't accept your calls anymore; if I hadn't been afraid it was tapped, I'd have called you to tell you this. As is, we have a decent chance of talking in private here. Now I've talked, and now I'm going to leave."

"But, but—" Stavros sputtered to a halt and tried again. "But now we can prove the Service really is trying to suppress the report on Bilbeis IV. They lied about when the *Jêng Ho* came back, which meant the report I have is genuine. It can't mean anything else."

"No, it means one thing more, Stavros. It means the Service isn't just trying to suppress that report—they're doing it. Ask Fogelman, ask the *Jêng Ho*'s crew, ask three hundred other people on the *Clark County* if you doubt me . . . and if you can. I don't need to ask them: I get the message loud and clear."

Andrea said, "How can you back away from this, knowing what you know?" She did not sound angry; if she had, Van would never have answered her. She only sounded bewildered.

The newsman's reply came slowly and grudgingly. "I thought about all this. I've done nothing but think about it the last couple of days. I've lived with my ideals a good many years now. I've always believed in them, but I've found that if I have to choose between keeping my ideals and keeping alive, I'd sooner live. If I go on, I don't think I will, and if you go on, I don't think you will either."

"But—" Stavros had been saying that ever since they got out into the quiet dark. He felt stupid, but nothing better came to mind.

"No more buts." Van thumped him on the shoulder, reached to take Andrea's hand, but dropped his own when she drew back from him. He grimaced. "Good-bye, then." He strode quickly away.

Stavros stared after him, still trying hard not to believe any of what he'd heard. It sank in despite his best efforts. Van's fear was too real to ignore. So was the *Clark County*. "Three hundred some odd people dead," Stavros whispered. "They are playing for keeps."

"Three hundred some odd innocent people dead, on top of Bilbeis IV itself," Andrea said. "Can we let the Survey Service come away untouched after that?"

"Can we stop them?" Stavros did not feel anything like a hero. The longer he stood outside in the blackness, the better he understood Van Shui Pong.

"We have to," Andrea said indignantly.

"Yes, I suppose we do." Giving up would mean not calling the Survey Service to account for what it did on a good many thousand pre-Federacy worlds, to say nothing of leaving Paulina Koch in charge of that immense and powerful bureaucracy. But Stavros remembered Andrea's warning after she first saw the report on Bilbeis IV. Then he'd had to hesitate before he even took her seriously. Now she was proving only too good a prophet.

His shiver had nothing to do with the chill of the night.

"The problem appears to be contained within manageable limits," Paulina Koch remarked.

"Yes," Hovannis said. "The loss of the *Clark County* was a great tragedy."

"So it was." The Chairman did not ask her External Affairs Director any questions about that. Whatever he knew, he knew. She hoped it was nothing, but she did not want to find out.

Certainly, the Assembly probe had crashed with the *Clark County*. No one was in a position to contradict Survey Service testimony after that. A few people, Paulina Koch's informants said, made snide comments about the crash's convenience. No one made them to her face or on the record.

"Is there anything more?" she asked Hovannis.

"Nothing to speak of, PK. Hyperion Newsnet is finally calming down, as you may have noticed. I understand some small fuss or other is still going on there, but I expect that will fade out, too."

"All right." Paulina Koch dismissed Hovannis. She wondered how long she would be able to dismiss him and be sure he would obey. He knew too much, had done too much to help her cement her own position. One day, she thought, she might have to make certain he would stay silent. That carried its own risks. Roupen Hovannis was no one's innocent. Data could point an accusing finger even after a man was gone.

The Chairman's lips creased in a bitter smile. If she had not known of the power dead men carried, Bilbeis IV would have taught her all about it. That damned anthropologist had been dead more than fourteen hundred years, but the trouble his meddling had caused looked to be as immortal as the queen whose cancer he'd cured.

The smile disappeared. Paulina Koch drilled herself never to reveal too much. Behind the impassive mask she cultivated, though, her mind was still racing. More and more she thought she should have let the report on Bilbeis IV go public and simply taken whatever heat descended on her and on the Service because of it.

Too late for that. If it had not been too late from the moment the report vanished from the Service file, it had become so with the death of—what was his name?—Fogelman. She had managed to make herself believe that was necessary to protect the Survey Service for which she had worked so long and hard.

About the *Clark County* she did not want to think at all. Most of the people aboard the *Clark County* had never heard of Bilbeis IV. Well, they never would now, that was certain. And now she was not just protecting the Service but herself as well. Rehabilitation—she shuddered at a euphemism grimmer than any in the Survey Service lexicon—would be the least she could hope for if the truth came. No way but forward, then.

"But that's insane!" Magda yelled. She was tired of having people turn around to stare at her and even more tired of being in positions where she made them turn around to stare. More quietly, she went on, "Here I am in front of you, Mr. Peters."

"Yes, Ms., umm—" The credit manager's voice trailed away. He'd done that before, as if he wouldn't have to admit Magda was alive if he didn't speak her name. Peters reminded her of Paulina Koch, though he and the Survey Service Chairman looked nothing alike. Both of them had the same air of being not quite human, only projections of the organizations they represented.

"Mr. Peters, do I look dead?" she demanded.

"No," he admitted, not sounding pleased about it.

"Then why can't I make this stinking piece of plastic work? The red light goes on every time I try to use it. I've explained about how Marie was carrying my card when she went aboard the *Clark County*."

"So you have. Unfortunately, you have not explained why no card authorized to Marie Roux has been unearthed on Carson Planet. If that card appears, it will facilitate the substantiation of your account and the restoration of your credit. Until then, I lack the authority to make that restoration, as the cancellation of your account was not originally implemented here. All I can do is pass on the discrepancy notice to our headquarters and allow them to make the determination."

"Where *are* your headquarters?" Magda asked dangerously.

"Why, on the capital world, of course."

"You officious idiot!" Magda shouted. Everyone in the office who hadn't been looking at her before was now. She was past caring. "Here I am, and you can't even tell I'm not dead? Make any check you want on me, for heaven's sake. If the ID doesn't match what's on my card, put me away and throw out the stinking key."

"I was going to suggest that in any case. It will bolster your account in the report I submit."

That was as far as he would go. Gradually Magda realized that he was not out to give her a hard time but that he would not stick his neck out one millimeter for her either. "How long will your miserable report take to go through?"

"I can't be sure. A couple of weeks perhaps, if the medical data are as you say. I'll hold off filing till I have them from you."

"A couple of weeks?" Magda echoed in dismay. "What am I supposed to do in the meantime, starve?"

She had meant it as a rhetorical question, but Peters took it literally. "If I might make a recommendation—"

"Please." By then Magda was ready to listen, seeing no way anything Peters said could make things worse.

"Well, then, I would suggest you use this Marie Roux's card, which is active, as your own while your credit identity is being reconfirmed. When that happens, or when her own death is established as fact, charges accrued can be transferred back to your account."

Magda knew he was trying to be helpful. She even knew he was giving her good advice. That didn't make it any easier to take. She had practically frog-marched Marie onto the *Clark County* in her place; if anyone but Pedroza had told her about the trip, she knew, she would have gone, and gone eagerly. But she hadn't, and Marie was dead instead of her. The thought of using her friend's card made her feel even worse than she did already—she hadn't felt like a ghoul before. And worse still, she knew she would do it. She left the credit office in a hurry.

The doctor who ran the medical checks on her that afternoon gave her a quizzical look. "You're paying me with *this* credit card so I can confirm you're the rightful user of *that* one?"

"Believe me," she told him, "it doesn't make any more sense to me than it does to you. Just rush those results over to Credit Superintendent Peters." She gave him the access code.

She went back to her apartment and for the most part stayed there. She lived as frugally as she could, not wanting to use any more of Marie's credit than necessary. She watched the screen more in ten days than she had in years—and discovered why she hadn't bothered. She did not watch the news.

Every morning she tried her own credit card. Every morning the system rejected it. She used the thesaurus program on her computer to generate page-long curses to call down on Peters's head.

The monograph got short shrift; Magda lacked the heart to work on it. She also kept delaying taking the report on Bilbeis

IV back to the field office. Finally she made herself do it. She had no better monument to offer the crew of the *Jêng Ho*.

Riding the shuttle felt strange—she had grown too used to being cooped up. Pandit the clerk raised an eyebrow when she walked into the office. "You were so intent on transmitting this, and then you never came back. May I ask what happened?"

"I died," she said. "Ask your computer if you don't believe me."

His eyes widened as he made the connection. "The *Clark County*—"

"Exactly. I was supposed to be on it." Briefly, not naming names, she explained how she had stayed behind, and finished, "So if I had been on that ship, odds are this would have stayed shelved for good. Make sure Central gets it this time, will you, Pandit?"

"I don't know what went wrong the first two times." He sounded genuinely aggrieved; like Peters, he did not care for anything that upset his routine. Unlike the case of the credit representative, though, getting that routine back implied helping Magda, not frustrating her. He loaded the data card into his terminal and squirted its information across the light-years.

"Come in, Roupen. Do please sit down." Paulina Koch flicked an imaginary speck of lint from her gray blouse. Her slacks were a darker shade of gray, almost charcoal; that was as much extravagance as she allowed herself as far as clothes went. Anyone who thought of the Survey Service Chairman in a negligee—in itself an unlikely notion—would have imagined her in a gray one.

"What's up, PK?" Hovannis rumbled. Paulina Koch handed him a printout. His always dour features grew harsher still as he scanned it. "We've already scrubbed this twice," he observed. "If we do it again, whoever keeps filing the damned thing will really start wondering what's going on."

"It's already gone," the Chairman said, "though I leave to you the details of making the erasure invisible. We've involved ourselves too deeply in denying the authenticity of the report to have it linger in public files even for a moment."

"That's true," Hovannis agreed. They both knew what an understatement it was.

Paulina Koch hesitated before going on, as if searching for

words. At last she said, "After the tragic loss of the *Clark County*, I had not expected to see this document surface again."

"Neither had I," Hovannis answered. They said no more than that; the subject was much too touchy to go into deeply.

"We have to be more thorough," the Chairman said.

"I'll look into it," Hovannis said.

Paulina Koch was checking another printout. She nodded to herself. "As I thought: the entire complement of the *Jêng Ho* is listed as having been aboard the *Clark County*."

"I'll look into it," Hovannis repeated.

"Very well. Thank you for coming up." The Chairman's eyes had returned to her screen before Hovannis was out of her office.

VII

"Thank you." Andrea switched off the phone and savagely flung it against the back of one of Stavros's chairs. "Oh, that bastard!"

"Another one?" Stavros sighed. Both of them had grown very familiar with a stock set of responses over the last few days.

"She might as well have been a recording," Andrea said glumly. " 'I am sorry. You may even be right, but people are bored with Bilbeis IV, and what you have is not exciting enough to make them sit up and take notice again.' At least she didn't tell me it wasn't sexy enough to get on the news, the way some of them have."

"Trouble is, they're right. How do you make people care about eighteen days? You can't show them a picture of eighteen missing days the way you can of eighteen missing starships."

"But when they show the Survey Service is lying—"

"The way it looks, not everyone cares about that," Stavros said. "Do you know what one of the people I talked to told me? Something to the effect that of course government agencies lie, and the job of the news team was to catch them lying at something interesting. Without the *Jêng Ho*'s crew, we just can't do that."

Andrea set her hands on her hips. "You'd think the crash of the *Clark County* would wake them up."

"I know, I know." Stavros banged his fist against his thigh in frustration. "Trouble is, we shouted murder at the Survey Service over Professor Fogelman and weren't able to make it stick. Now it doesn't matter how loud we yell it, because no one's willing to pay attention anymore."

"Does that mean you want to give up?" Andrea asked.

"No, of course not." Stavros hoped he sounded indignant. He very much wanted the Service brought to account for all it had done. He was no longer confident that would happen, but he wanted it all the same. And even more, he wanted not to lose Andrea. If he quarreled with her over this, he was sure he would. So, suppressing his misgivings, he went on. "We'll keep trying."

"All right, then. Who's next on our list?"

He recalled it on the computer. *"The Unvarnished Truth."*

"I've seen their output once or twice." Andrea looked unhappy. "Have we really sunk so low?" She retrieved the phone from where it leaned drunkenly against a wall and punched buttons. "Hello, this is Andrea Dubois. Could you please put me through to your managing editor? Yes, I'll wait . . . Hello? This is Andrea Dubois. I have important new information on the Bilbeis IV scandal—"

The discreet individual wanted to take those two idealistic idiots off to one side and pound some sense into them. Newsmen were notorious fools, but Van Shui Pong got the message once it was shouted loud enough. He might not have been able to put together two and two, but he could add one and three hundred-odd. Hyperion Newsnet was very quiet these days.

Sometimes the discreet individual thought about picking up some extra money blackmailing the Survey Service—after so long on the job, he could not escape realizing who was paying him. The Service would give him what he wanted, he thought; he had already shown he could keep his mouth shut.

But he kept on taking his fees and not pushing for more. The *Clark County* told him a story, too: he decided he did not want the Survey Service reminded of how much he knew. Sometimes being discreet and seeming slightly stupid looked a lot alike.

He wished the graduate students could understand that, and understand he was just the cutting edge of what they were up against. It wasn't going to happen, though. All their training went against it. They had to seem smart in class, so they thought they had to be smart all the time.

That, he knew, wasn't so smart itself.

* * *

One evening a week, Stavros had a class Andrea did not. Though his Basic was more than fluent and he also wrote it well, he kept working to improve. Being with Andrea so much showed him how much better he could do, and so he endured the composition course for the sake of the tricks it taught him. Andrea felt the class was helping his writing.

That night the instructor had been talking about adverbs and how to use them: in small doses, Stavros gathered. The instructor claimed the real skill lay in picking the right verb in the first place rather than in adjusting the meaning of one not so right with modifiers. Remembering some of his own papers, he decided the notion sounded reasonable. He wondered what Andrea would think of it.

"I'm back," he called as he opened the door to his rooms.

No one answered. His dark brows drew together. He and Andrea did not spend all their nights together, but she'd been there when he left, and he hadn't known she was going anywhere. He stepped toward the computer, wondering if she'd left a message.

He stumbled over a shoe and almost fell. That forced him to notice what a mess the place was. Stavros was not a neat housekeeper. Few men had occasion to learn such skills on New Thessaly. But nearly drowning in junk made him pay some attention to keeping things tidy, and his desire to keep Andrea happy had done more.

Leaving the place in such disarray was not like her, but Stavros did not think anything of it until he saw that his icons were missing. He had brought the hand-painted images of Christ, the Virgin, and John the Baptist with him from home. Though he was no longer devoutly Orthodox, the icons still served to remind him of New Thessaly: he felt good every time he glanced over at them. Now they were gone.

They were not the best work New Thessaly had to offer, but on Hyperion, where their like was rare, they were worth a fair amount. Stavros swore and dashed into the bedroom. He kept the rest of his valuables in a drawer under the bed.

Andrea's body sprawled across the mattress. For a moment, not understanding, Stavros thought she was asleep. Then he saw the blood under her head. He moaned, something he had heard of but never remembered doing.

The drawer under the bed was open. So was the little strongbox inside. Stavros noted all that peripherally, though later his recall of it would be perfect: disaster has a way of printing tiny details forever on the brain.

He stumbled forward to take Andrea's wrist, thinking there might be some hope she still lived. Her flesh was cool; it had begun to stiffen. He knew what death felt like. He staggered into the bathroom and was sick.

Mechanically, he rinsed his mouth. Tears streamed down his face. He did not realize he was crying until he went to pick up the phone and found he could not read the buttons.

The phone was next to the computer, where Andrea must have put it after her last useless call to the newsies. Stavros recalled the number for the police and had punched in the first three digits before he paused, scowling, and put the handset down again.

What had happened in his room bore every sign of being a random break-in and killing. But then, Professor Fogelman's death had looked the same way. Stavros turned on his computer. He could not access any of his files. They were not there to access—they were gone. If he hadn't made a habit of carrying the original data card with the report on Bilbeis IV around with him, it would have been lost too.

He had not thought he could be more afraid. Now he discovered he was wrong. A random burglar would not have lobotomized his computer. Someone from the Survey Service would. Van Shui Pong knew what to worry about.

Stavros started to call the police again and stopped for a second time. He suspected they might be more interested in him as a murderer than as the victim of a crime. He knew logically that he could prove his whereabouts when Andrea had been killed. Something old and watchful in him, though, warned that the police might not be thinking logically, not if the Service put enough quiet pressure on them. He thought the Service might do just that. After the *Clark County*, he could not afford to think otherwise.

He did not call the police. He packed a tote instead, the kind that looked as though it might be full of anything. He slung it over his shoulder and locked the door behind him. With luck, he had a couple of days to do whatever needed doing. Without it, he'd be scooped up before daybreak, and his running away would not look good.

He headed for the library to kill the rest of the night; he had to fight down hysterical laughter when the phrase occurred to him. The university library held several thousand volumes and was easily the largest of the three or four on Hyperion. It was the main storehouse for works that reached the planet in hard copy format and had not yet been entered into the data retrieval system.

Several archeological journals arrived in hard copy; the librarians were used to Stavros's dashing in at any hour of the day or night. He managed only one-word replies to their greetings but hoped he managed to seem merely busy, not distraught. He must have succeeded; they went about their business without looking at him twice.

The cool silent isolation, the musty smell of old paper, the rows of study carrels took him back to the ancient days when all scholarship took place in rooms of this sort. He dug a couple of periodicals off the shelf, went to the most distant carrel, and pretended to start reading.

He could not keep up the pretense long. He buried his face in his hands. His shoulders shook, but he wept very quietly. No one came over to see if anything was wrong. The handful of other people in the library at that hour were all intent on their own concerns.

After a while, exhaustion and reaction combined to waylay Stavros. He fell asleep, still slumped over the desk. That did make the librarians notice him, but only with amusement: they were used to it.

The eastern sky brightened toward dawn.

In theory, seats in the Assembly gallery were first come, first served. In practice, if the Chairman of the Survey Service wanted a seat, she got one. Today she wanted one. She could have had a better, closer view of the appropriations vote from the terminal in her office, but it would not have been the same. Paulina Koch had worked too hard for the victory not to want to enjoy it in person.

To her annoyance, the diehard Purists insisted on a formal roll-call vote. Any dozen Assembly members could do that, but it was an archaic rule hardly invoked once a session. They must have spotted her, she thought, and decided either to make her leave before the vote was done or else keep her in the chamber for hours. She did not intend to give them the satisfaction of leaving or even of seeming discomfited. She did note their names for future reference. Maybe they did not realize how well she would be able to repay such scores after the vote was done. If they didn't, they would soon.

And before long, even the Purists must have realized they'd made a mistake. The steady litany of ayes showed how strong the Survey Service was, better than an impersonal display of green lights on the tally board ever could. Even some of the men and women who had demanded the roll call began to waver at the end. When Assemblyman Valleix abstained, Paulina Koch needed all her self-control to keep from laughing.

After the last vote was cast and the appropriation overwhelmingly secured, the Chairman allowed herself to think of other things. These days Bilbeis IV was never far from her mind. She knew the silence she had imposed was only a temporary solution. Eventually calls for a new examination of the planet would come. She wondered if she could quell them. She did not think so; there had been enough quelling already. Yes, it had worked, but one reason it had was that it did not call too much attention to itself. More along the same lines would.

What then? The next best thing to no report on Bilbeis IV—maybe even better than no report on Bilbeis IV, now that she thought of it—would be a report that minimized the results of cultural interference there. That would give the Purists something to beat their breasts about without raising their paranoid suspicions the way a clean bill of health would. If she could not put together a tame Survey Service team that would see things her way, she did not deserve to be Chairman.

Thinking of tameness reminded her of Roupen Hovannis. The External Affairs Director was not nearly tame enough to suit her. Unfortunately, however, he was too useful to dispense with. So long as his interest and hers ran in the same direction, he was no problem. The tricky part would be keeping their interests aligned without giving him the idea that he could make her dance to his tune.

She had been a manager for a lot of years. The precise nature of the problem Hovannis posed was new to her, but it was not altogether different from others she had faced before. Again, if she couldn't handle it, what was she Chairman for?

Hovannis's henchmen were something else again. That

discreet individual on Hyperion, for instance, was really too effective to suit her. No, that wasn't quite right. The trouble was, he had been used too often. Anyone with the talent he obviously owned would draw the proper conclusions from his assignments. She did not like that.

The chatter of librarians changing shifts was low-voiced, but enough to wake Stavros. He groaned and stretched. His joints creaked, protesting the contorted position in which he'd slept.

The police had not nailed him yet. That was the only bit of cheer he could extract from the situation. He stood up and stretched again but still felt old and arthritic.

"Long night?" one of the new librarians asked sympathetically as Stavros shambled toward the exit.

"You have no idea."

The librarian laughed. Stavros did not.

His stomach growled. He started to head for a food machine, then stopped. He would have to go hungry a while longer. The more he used his credit card, the plainer the trail he'd leave. He'd need to use it one more time, but no help for that. He'd have to hope nobody had found Andrea by then.

The university was surrounded by a couple of kilometers of greenery on all sides. Shuttles into New Westwood ran regularly, but no one paid walking students any mind.

Once he was among the buildings, he had to wait; for reasons no one remembered, banks did not open till halfway through the morning. Stavros needed one of the two human tellers for what he wanted to do. "I'd like to turn my account to cash, sir."

The teller's eyebrows rose. "The entire sum?"

"Yes. I'm afraid there's an emergency in the family—"

The teller let out an audible sniff. People had been talking about phasing out cash since long before the Federacy began. It hadn't happened yet, and wouldn't any time soon. Anonymous money was too convenient to do away with. Yet if someone insisted on paying cash, the suspicion usually was that he had a good reason to.

Stavros had rarely handled cash before. Holding the crisp paper with its holographic designs sent an atavistic thrill through him, as if he were carrying gold coins. A credit card was mundane by comparison.

"Let me have your thumbprint and signature on the receipt, sir," the teller said sourly.

The discreet individual said a loud, indiscreet word. He had not been sure he would be able to monitor Monemvasios's bank account; banks were even more jealous of their privacy than newsnets, and worked harder to keep it. But for the moment, at least, his trapdoor program was working. He saw the account drop suddenly to zero.

He hadn't thought cashing out would occur to Stavros Monemvasios. In the phone calls he'd tapped, Monemvasios had seemed on the tentative side, while his woman friend had been brisk and forthright. Mistaking hesitance for stupidity, though, was evidently an error.

And now Monemvasios was going to be a real nuisance to keep track of. The discreet individual scratched his head. What would the wretch be up to?

He hadn't gone screaming to the police. The discreet individual would have known about that. He wasn't sure whether to be pleased or disappointed. Like Stavros, he thought there was a fair chance they wouldn't look past their noses. That would have dealt with that very nicely.

With a pocketful of cash, Monemvasios had to be on the run. Where would he go? All he knew of Hyperion was the university and its surroundings. He'd probably try to get off-planet, most likely to his home planet. Hyperion had two space ports, one of them halfway around the world. A stake-out of the local facility might prove productive.

The discreet individual gathered a few tools of his trade and headed for the spaceport. He left others behind with regret. The spaceport was too public for them. He would have to be more subtle than usual. That did not bother him for long. Minimalism was part of his art, too.

Stavros spent part of his wad at a small appliance store down the street from the bank. The clerk who took his money gave him a curious look with his change. "You don't seem to have much use for that," she said.

"It's for a friend," he answered. He was lying. He went into the restroom. When he came out a few minutes later, he was clean-shaven for the first time in a dozen years. His face felt naked. To his own eyes, he seemed quite different and five years younger. He hoped others would see as much change and not see *him*.

The next thing was to eat. The first place he happened into served the sort of bland, vaguely greasy fare that would annoy no one and excite no one very much either. At the moment, Stavros did not care. He wolfed it down. He gulped coffee, too; his fitful sleep in the library had not been nearly enough.

He never had learned to like the coffee they brewed on Hyperion—he found it a thin, bitter brew. New Thessaly coffee was almost strong enough to drink with a fork and was full of sugar and heavy cream. Now he did not even grimace at the stuff in the foam cup. He was drinking it for caffeine, not flavor.

He had never bothered—or needed—to notice whether the ground shuttle had a cash slot. If it didn't . . . He set his jaw. The spaceport was a dozen kilometers away, maybe more. Walking would take hours he might not have.

Nothing ventured, nothing gained. He waited on a street corner until the spaceport shuttle came by. The scanner spotted his upraised thumb. The shuttle pulled to a stop. The doors hissed open. He sprang onto the step and looked anxiously at the control panel.

He sagged in relief. To the right of the credit card opening was another, smaller one marked CURRENCY. He fed in a bill. His change returned a moment later.

As the shuttle purred toward the spaceport, Stavros did some hard thinking. Getting offplanet was one thing; deciding where to go, something else again. His first impulse had been to run for home. Now he wondered how good an idea that was. If the police were already looking for him, that outbound line would be one of the first areas they'd cover.

What to do, then? Random flight held no appeal—it was too much like giving up. His fist clenched. He wanted to hit back if he could find a way. But how? If he went to the capital to beard Paulina Koch in her den, he knew the fate he could expect. Fogelman and the *Clark County* and now Andrea had taught him the same lesson they'd given Van Shui Pong. Unlike the newsman, though, he was too stubborn to be scared off.

If the capital was hopeless, Stavros had to find an alternative. By the time he snapped his fingers in sudden decision, he could see grounded starships in the distance. The *Jêng Ho* had sent its report from a world called Topanga. Maybe, just maybe, some of the crew had talked with the locals about it before they set out on the doomed *Clark County*.

Stavros had no idea where Topanga was. There were too many worlds in the Federacy to keep track of, unless one was Isaac Fogelman. And a fat lot of good his gift had done him in the end, Stavros thought.

The shuttle sighed to a stop outside a big terminal building. Stavros shouldered his tote and descended to the concrete. The terminal doors opened for him and the other passengers.

He went to an information outlet, and tapped in the name Topanga. It was, he found without surprise, not far from Carson Planet. It had no direct connection with Hyperion, but ships from both worlds touched on Enkidu. Stavros was in luck; a ship outbound for Enkidu lifted off tomorrow. He checked the fare column. Yes, he could afford it.

He walked over to the ticket line. The clerk processing orders frowned a little at the sight of so much cash. "May I see some identification, Mr., ah"—she looked down at her screen for the name Stavros had plucked out of the air—"Mr. Mesropinian?"

Stavros went through his wallet with fingers suddenly frozen. Getting caught using an alias would lead to more questions, questions he could not answer. He shifted his feet and made ready to bolt.

And then he came upon his old ID from New Thessaly. It bore his picture and his name—but that, along with all the rest of the written information on the card, was in Greek. Affecting a nonchalance he did not feel, he put the card on the counter in front of the clerk.

Her frown deepened. "I'm sorry, sir, I can't read this."

"Is your ignorance my fault?" he said as cuttingly as he could.

He saw he'd angered her. "Let me have your luggage there, sir, for the contraband sniffer," she snapped. But the petty triumph faded from her face when he passed the tote to her without a word of protest. The sniffer's light went green, as Stavros had known it would. The only thing he was smuggling was information, the most deadly contraband of all but one without a smell.

The clerk looked as if she wanted to take things further, but the line was beginning to back up. "What's going on there?" someone called.

"*Is* anything wrong?" Stavros asked, softly this time.

"Well—" The clerk looked again at the all-clear light on the sniffer. "I suppose not." She punched keys with unnecessary violence and handed Stavros his ticket. But she could not resist a parting shot: "I do suggest, sir, that you obtain a more easily verifiable means of identifying yourself."

"I'll see to it," said Stavros, who had several, none of them, though, as valuable to him at this moment as that little incomprehensible piece of plastic.

The spaceport was studded with clocks, both FSY and local time. Twenty-nine hours to go, Stavros saw. He was not out of the woods yet. His main concern was staying inconspicuous; in a crowded spaceport, that shouldn't be too hard. All he needed to do was stake out a seat and look bored.

The discreet individual was wondering if he'd outsmarted himself. He had hooks into the spaceport information system, of course, but that was like saying he had a knitting needle lodged in a whale's fluke—he could not cope with the avalanche of data.

Restricting the incoming feed to travelers who paid cash helped some, but not enough. Too blasted many people came through the spaceport. Only a few of them, though, planned routes that would take them to New Thessaly or even the general direction of the planet. The discreet individual had his computer analyze the routing forms of cash customers going that way.

The conclusion became inescapable after awhile: none of those people was Stavros Monemvasios. Some were too old, others too female, and still others had papers an amateur could not fake on the spur of the moment.

All of which meant the discreet individual had miscalculated somewhere. He was still certain Monemvasios meant to get off Hyperion—what point to cashing out and then waiting around to be caught? And Monemvasios's home planet seemed the most logical place for him to go.

But logic and truth had at best a nodding acquaintance. The discreet individual always bore that in mind. He also had other things to do than worry about a student on the run. He decided to do some of them and come back to Monemvasios if inspiration struck.

As with peripheral vision, the mind is often sharper if it looks to one side of a problem. That evening, the discreet individual suddenly sat bolt upright. In guessing Monemvasios would head for New Thessaly, the discreet individual tacitly assumed his quarry would be trying to get away, nothing more.

What if that was wrong? What if Monemvasios was still in the mood to create problems? The discreet individual found that unlikely but believed in covering his bets. If it was so, where would Monemvasios go?

The discreet individual put the question another way— where offplanet could Monemvasios get backing for his claims? Not from the central bureaucracy of the Survey Service, that was for sure! Where had that miserable report come from? After a few minutes of searching through his files, he had the answer.

Then he had to reprogram his computer to examine cash customers en route to Topanga, or rather to Enkidu. When he found a certain S. Mesropinian, he smiled and picked up that attaché case. It was time to go back to the spaceport.

The preliminary screening gadgets at the terminal entrance never hiccuped as he walked through. The more sophisticated contraband sniffers that dealt with passengers' luggage would also have given his case a clean bill of health. Programmers, he thought smugly, did not know everything there was to know.

He queued up to use an information screen. The *Arminius*, the ship outbound for Enkidu, would be departing from subterminal seven—naturally, the one farthest from where he sat. He sighed and climbed onto the slidewalk that would take him there. All he'd need to do then would be to spot Monemvasios—Mesropinian and bump him a little. He'd have enough time for a getaway, but in a few minutes it would all be over.

Someone bumped *him* a little. "Beg your pardon," said a slim woman in business attire. She pushed past the discreet individual, adding her own walking speed to the steady roll of the slidewalk. He watched appreciatively; she had a nice backside.

Because she was so brisk, she soon put several people between herself and the discreet individual. Out of sight, out of mind, he thought as she disappeared. He went back to planning the credit-transfer scheme he could finally give full time to once Monemvasios was disposed of.

Waiting kept Stavros on edge. He migrated back and forth between the outgoing passengers' lounge and the cafeteria next to it. He was full to bursting by then, but each trip gave him an excuse for getting up and stretching his legs. That was easier than just sitting in one spot, headphones drowning out the world.

Or it would have been, except that every fifty-meter hike took him past the spaceport security guards. They ignored him, but each time he showed himself to them, he twisted with fear they wouldn't.

He was also, he noted ruefully, using the jakes a good deal.

The discreet individual glanced around the lounge. He saw no one who looked even a little like Monemvasios. Shrugging, he sat down to wait. The man he hunted could not be far away. He shivered. The air-conditioning was very high.

He stiffened. Was that skinny fellow walking out of the head the one? No, too short; no matter how desperate a man was, he could not shed ten centimeters.

There was Monemvasios, coming from the lunchroom! All he'd done was shave, but the discreet individual's first glance had slid right past him. Sometimes the least disguise was best.

The discreet individual got up, or started to. For some reason his legs did not want to work. He put his hands on the arms of his chair and pushed himself upright.

He shivered again. It's awfully cold in here, he thought. He took a step toward Monemvasios, staggered, caught himself. He took another step. This time he could not keep himself from sliding bonelessly to the floor.

His last conscious thought was that the woman who'd poisoned him really did have a fine behind. He never felt his head hit the ground.

Someone screamed. Security guards rushed into the lounge. Stavros almost jumped out of his skin. His body took two involuntary half-running steps before he realized he was not the target of the guards' attention.

They gathered instead around a man who had crumpled on

the thin carpeting. All Stavros could see of him was his shoes, for the guards screened his upper body from view. One guard was frantically massaging his chest, while another stooped to give mouth-to-mouth resuscitation.

The spaceport doctor came running in a couple of minutes later. She immediately pushed one of the security guards out of the way and got to work. Soon she rose again, her mouth twisted in a grimace of frustration.

Stavros reflexively crossed himself. At the doctor's direction, a couple of guards lifted the dead man and carried him away. The usual babble of the lounge was stilled. Background music, ignored a moment before, seemed loud and intrusive. Shivering as if he had taken a sudden chill, Stavros found a seat and waited for the *Arminius* to arrive.

The report was oblique, talking about a personnel transfer being satisfactorily expedited. Anyone who saw it on Paulina Koch's screen might have wondered why the Chairman had to deal with it herself but would have forgotten about it before he was out of her office.

The Chairman cleared the screen. Another loose end taken care of, and this time before any trouble resulted. Hovannis's discreet individual would never be anything but circumspect now. Better still, she had used her own contacts to arrange that, not going through the External Affairs Director. One day she might find it useful to have independent resources in that area.

She frowned, but only briefly. Bureaucratic language and patterns of thought made it easy for her to take an impersonal view of the operations she ordered carried out. She had trouble imagining people dead but could clearly see how her position and her agency had been protected by what she'd done.

And they had been protected. The appropriation was safe, the Purists discredited or ashamed of their own policies. The latest polls showed public approval of the Survey Service near an all-time high.

Now it was payback time. With her new power, she could make life very uncomfortable for the gadflies who'd been buzzing around the Service for years. Lately they'd thought they were vultures, come to pick her bones. It was time to remind them they were still small enough to swat.

What a delightful prospect, she thought.

* * *

Stavros had a bad moment boarding the *Arminius*. The steward who fed his ticket into the ships's computer nodded to him and said, "Glad to be aboard?"

"You'd better believe it!" he said fervently.

"Thought as much. You look like you're about three steps ahead of the executioner." The steward laughed at his own joke. Stavros managed a strained chuckle. The steward stepped aside and waved him into the ship.

Even after he was in his cabin, he did not feel altogether safe. The Hyperion police could still take him off the ship. If they came after him now, in fact, he could not even run. His stomach churned. He lay on the bunk and tried to relax. He couldn't. Pacing up and down in the narrow space between the bunk and the bulkhead helped more.

Because he was pacing, he never felt the *Arminius* lift off. He had to check his watch to realize he was in space. He had been running on nerves too long. As soon as he understood he was safe, at least for a while, he flopped to the bunk like a marionette whose puppeteer has dropped the strings.

"A chance," he said out loud. "A chance." Somewhere on Topanga, someone might have heard of the report on Bilbeis IV. And if someone had, he might yet call the Survey Service to account for Andrea—action had made him bottle up that hurt, but it came flooding back now full force—for Professor Fogelman, for the crew of the *Jêng Ho*, and for all the poor people who just happened to board the wrong starship at the wrong time.

The Service was huge and powerful, but it was not, must not be, beyond the reach of law. The Chairman had to be shown she and hers were not too big to swat.

What a delightful prospect, Stavros thought.

VIII

"Hello, Pandit," Magda said. "Let me guess—you've checked, and as far as Survey Service Central knows, you never sent in that report."

In the phone screen, the clerk's brown face grew even more troubled than it had been. "I am afraid that is correct. I tell you frankly, I have never seen another case like this. I don't know what to make of it. All the other documents I've processed have gone through flawlessly."

"It figures. Things have been going that way lately. As far as the credit system knows, I'm still dead, too. Something is screwed up in those computers, what's-his-name—Peters—says."

"I am sorry for your difficulties." Pandit actually sounded as though he meant it. Maybe he does, Magda thought; his orderly soul had to cringe for the chaos that had attached itself to her. He went on. "I suppose I can expect to see you again soon with our vanishing document?"

"No." Magda had decided to spread a little chaos herself. "I'm sick of this nonsense. I think I'm going to take the whole thing to the Noninterference Foundation and see what they make of it."

"You can't do that!" Pandit exclaimed in horror. Magda knew how he felt; giving information to the Noninterference Foundation was like going over to the enemy. The Foundation kept an eye on the way the Survey Service interacted with natives of pretechnological worlds. That would have been bad enough, but the private watchdog group got most of its support from the Purists, the people who thought the Service ought to keep off those worlds altogether.

Magda had about as much use for Purists as she did for cockroaches: to her they were two examples of pests the Federacy had never been able to eradicate. But that did not mean she thought the Survey Service ought to get away free when it made a mistake. Service personnel had interfered on Bilbeis IV, even if with the best of intentions, and the courses of billions of lives there had been changed as a result.

"Going through channels hasn't done me any good," she said. "I've told you before, Pandit—this report is important. One way or another, it has to get out."

"Yes, so you've said. All the same, do you feel like throwing away your career in a fit of pique over computer problems at Central? Think about the assignments you will draw when people know you collaborate with the Foundation."

Magda winced. What Pandit had suggested was illegal, of course. It was also very likely. For that matter, she wouldn't have wanted to ship with a known informer herself. "I've good reason to go," she said, but her voice sounded defensive even to her.

"Yes, so you've said," Pandit repeated. "I'm sure you believe it, but remember, it is a step you cannot take back. May I suggest something?"

"Go ahead," Magda said grudgingly.

"Why not try once more to transmit your report through the proper channels? If you fail after four attempts, I do not suppose anyone could blame you for doing something irregular."

"As far as I'm concerned, they couldn't blame me after three." But despite her tough talk, Magda was secretly glad to have a chance to put off the trip to the Foundation. "Oh, all right. I'll see you before long. It had better go through this time, though; that's all I can say."

She broke the connection, picked up the data card, and rode the elevator down to the lobby of the apartment complex. The nearest shuttle stop was only a short walk from the building.

A few minutes later, a slim, swarthy man somewhere close to her own age joined her at the stop. His clothes were on the faded side and he wore a backpack. He looked tired. After a casual glance that told her that much, Magda ignored him, or tried to.

He did not make it easy, though. He kept looking stealthily in her direction and jerking his head away when she caught him at it. They were not the sort of glances a man gives a female stranger he finds attractive; Magda would have thought nothing much of those one way or the other. It was almost, she thought, as if the fellow was wondering whether he knew her. With all the strange goings-on of late, she did not like that, because she was sure she had never set eyes on him before.

The shuttle came sighing up just as the man looked to have worked up the nerve to speak to her. With a feeling of relief, she fed Marie Roux's credit card into the slot by the door; she wanted nothing to do with him. Her leeriness only increased when she heard the fare apparatus suck up a bill—he had paid his way aboard with cash. People who used untraceable money generally had a reason for it, and rarely a good one.

From habit, Magda sat near the front of the shuttle. She was soon kicking herself for it. Once, when she yawned and stretched, she caught the stranger staring at her from behind, though again he quickly looked away when he saw she had noticed him. After that she did not look back, but she imagined she felt his gaze on the back of her neck. It made for an unpleasant ride; she was glad to get off.

That did not last long. The stranger scrambled down as the shuttle was on the point of pulling away; its doors, which had started to close, hissed open for him. He had been holding his backpack in his lap and paused to resling it before leaving.

A trifle faster than she might have otherwise, Magda walked toward the Survey Service office, fortunately no more than a block and a half from the shuttle stop. She scowled— the stranger was still following her. If he tries anything cute, she told herself, I'll make him regret it. Like anyone who did Survey Service fieldwork, she had been well trained in unarmed combat.

All of which, she thought, would do her no good at all if he had a projectile weapon. But if he planned on shooting her, he'd already had plenty of chances.

That reasoning was reassuring, but only until he came into the office after her. Then he made her feel like an idiot, because he headed straight for the director's room in the back. She supposed that having two people come from the same shuttle stop to the Survey Service office wasn't twisting coincidence's arm outrageously.

Pandit spotted her and saved whatever document he was working on. "My screen is clear," he declared. "We are ready for another try—a successful one this time, I hope."

"So do I," Magda said, taking the data card from her holdall, "but I'm not going to hold my breath. Central doesn't seem to want to know about Bilbeis IV."

She had forgotten the fellow who had been on the shuttle with her. He stopped in his tracks, turned, and walked back toward her. "You really are Magda Kodaly, aren't you?" he said.

"What if I am?" she said, her suspicion of him flaring again.

"I thought you were, but I didn't dare believe it. I thought you were dead."

"You aren't the only one," she muttered. He stared at her, not understanding. "Never mind. What do you want?"

"That's the report on Bilbeis IV you have there, the one from the *Jêng Ho*?"

"Yes. Who are you, anyway? How do you know about it? I've been trying for weeks to get it into Survey Service Central files, and I haven't had any luck yet. This is my fourth try."

Pandit had loaded the data card into his terminal and was about to hit the TRANSMIT button. *"Don't send it!"* the stranger exclaimed, so urgently that the clerk jerked his finger away in alarm. "Whatever you do, don't send it," the fellow repeated. He bent down, pushing Pandit aside, and took the card from the computer.

"Give me that back," Pandit said indignantly.

"No." The stranger stepped away from the terminal. He still had a tight grip on the data card. Magda tensed herself to grab it away from him. He noticed and handed it to her. "Here—it's yours. All I ask is that you don't transmit it until you've heard me out. You're in danger if it goes to Central— you may be in danger anyhow."

"Do you know," Magda said to nobody in particular, "I've had more melodrama in my life in the little while since we came back from Bilbeis IV than in all the time before that, and I don't like it one bit."

"I believe you," the stranger said with perfect seriousness. "So have I."

Magda studied him. He neither looked nor sounded like a madman . . . and things *had* been strange lately. "All right, talk," she said. "This had better be good."

"None of it is good," he said; again he seemed very tired. "I don't want to talk here, in front of Survey Service people."

Pandit let out an indignant sniff. The fellow said, "Nothing personal. Believe me, you're better off not knowing any of this."

"All right, we'll find a public terminal and see what you're so excited about," Magda decided. She pointed warningly at Pandit. "Don't go away. I may be back very soon." Then she turned back to the stranger. "Who are you, anyway?"

He waited until they were back on the sidewalk outside before he answered. "My name is Stavros Monemvasios. I am—I *was*—a grad student in anthropology at the University of Hyperion. My seminar group got assigned to summarize some newly arrived Survey Service reports."

Magda nodded; she'd had similar assignments herself before she escaped to fieldwork. She and Monemvasios walked into a bank. The terminals were next to the pay phones. "You haven't really told me anything yet, you know," Magda said as she stepped into a booth. It was on the crowded side for two.

"Yes, I do know. I want to show you instead." Stavros looked the terminal over and laughed ruefully. "You'll have to pay for it, though. This thing doesn't have a cash slot, and I cashed out my credit card to get off Hyperion without making myself conspicuous."

"Hmm." Magda gave him another hard look. Now he was practically admitting he'd done something shady on Hyperion. But she'd come this far . . . Clicking her tongue in exasperation, she shoved Marie Roux's credit card into the opening by the keyboard. The screen came on.

Stavros had been rummaging in his backpack. He pulled out a data card, fed it into the machine, and hit RECALL. The abstract of a document appeared.

"Where did you get that?" Magda was proud of herself. Instead of screaming the question, she let it out in a whispered hiss, but it was no less urgent for that.

"The report on Bilbeis IV , you mean? My prof gave it to me. I told you, it was my assignment. Go through it—make sure it's the same document the *Jêng Ho* submitted to Central."

Magda scrolled rapidly through the report, checking a page here, a page there. She was soon satisfied. "It's the same document." She was about to burst with questions and felt like reaching over to shake the answers out of Monemvasios.

"How did your prof get it? And why isn't he screaming his head off about it?"

"He got it because Survey Service records are—or are supposed to be—public documents. And he isn't screaming about it because he's dead." The flat statement brought Magda up short. Stavros also paused before he went on and seemed to have to bring out his words by main force. "So is a woman who was in my class—she and I were trying to make people notice what this report means. We were also falling in love with each other, but that's another story. And so is everybody who was on the *Clark County*. That includes the whole crew of the *Jêng Ho*, or I thought it did until I met you. Do I need to draw any more pictures for you?"

"You're saying the crash wasn't an accident." Magda's voice sounded far away in her own ears.

"If it was, it was a mighty *convenient* accident for the Survey Service. Not even the Assembly can subpoena dead people or ask them awkward questions about a report the Service calls a fraud from top to bottom."

"A what?" Magda clenched her fists until her nails bit into her palms. "The hell it is! We worked our tails off on that thing."

"I believe you," Stavros said soberly. "I daresay I know it better than anyone else who wasn't there, and it's a devastating piece of work—which only makes it more dangerous to the Service if it's true, because it shows just how serious the results of the interference on Bilbeis IV were. So they're denying everything—and with the *Jêng Ho*'s crew gone, who's to contradict them?"

Magda shook her head, but it was reflex fighting reason. What Monemvasios said made a horrid kind of sense. It certainly explained why she had not been able to get the report on Bilbeis IV into the files at Survey Service Central. She said so, adding, "No wonder they kept deleting it, if they can't admit it's real."

"No wonder at all," Stavros agreed. "Fogelman—my prof —must have accessed it just minutes after it came in the first time, before the Chairman decided she had to erase it."

"The Chairman?" Magda said, startled. She had never had much use for Paulina Koch, but there was a big difference between thinking her hidebound and the things Monemvasios was implying.

"Haven't you seen any news?"

"No, not much," Magda admitted. "This isn't my planet, so I don't really care about what's happening locally, and the locals don't pay any more attention to what's going on off-world than they have to. Besides, the one time I did turn it on, the big story was the crash of the *Clark County*. After that, I just felt like finding a hole and pulling it in after me."

"I can understand that," Stavros said. He made a wry face. "For all I know, the story never even got here—the Federacy is a big place, with a lot going on. I liked to think we were making an enormous splash, but how could we tell for sure? We did get the Chairman to deny everything about Bilbeis IV in a news conference, though, and in front of an Assembly subcommittee. I suppose that counts for something."

"I should say so!" Paulina Koch shunned publicity. If she stood up in front of people to tell lies, Monemvasios really had hit a nerve, or rather, the report had. And the Chairman never would have done it if she hadn't known the report had disappeared—Stavros was right about that, too. Magda said contritely, "I'll have to recall the old news shows. Somebody here must have mentioned this mess at least once."

"Never mind that now," Stavros said. "Just tell me one thing: What was the FSY date when the *Jêng Ho* got back to Topanga and filed that report?"

"I'd have to check; I've gotten used to local time here. It's at the front of the document, though—we sent the report in as soon as we landed. Let me look." Magda moved the cursor to the beginning of the report. "That's what I thought I remembered. It was FSY 2687:139."

Stavros smacked fist into palm in triumph. "I thought so! We have them, then, on that, too! When I checked on Hyperion, it was 157, and the Survey Service computer said the *Jêng Ho*'s report wasn't in yet—they'd erased it the first time, you see. But they still listed the scheduled arrival date of your ship as 139; the scheduling information must have gone on a different data base from the report itself. That 139 disappeared not long afterward, when they realized it was there, but —"

Magda followed him perfectly. "We can beat them over the head with their missing eighteen days," she finished.

"Exactly!" For a moment, excitement lit Stavros's thin, worn features. He soon grew grim again. "Assuming we live to do it, of course. The way things have gone, that's not the best bet in the world."

"No," Magda agreed, shivering. "It's just accident that I wasn't on the *Clark County*." Even more quickly than she had with Pandit, she explained why she hadn't been.

Stavros nodded. "I have the feeling I got off Hyperion maybe one step ahead of the bastards who killed Fogelman and Andrea. I was the next logical target, even if the Hyperion police didn't try to hold me for Andrea's death. After everything else that's gone on, I was afraid the Survey Service had enough clout to make the constabulary think that way."

"I don't blame you," Magda said. "No wonder you've been using cash, come to that. Nobody can trace you that way."

"That's right. You're lucky yourself, even if it's a grisly kind of luck, having your roommate's credit card to use. You don't draw any attention to yourself with it. Even the coordinator at the local Service office thinks you're dead."

"Does she? She's an idiot, then. I've worked with her clerk since the *Clark County* crashed."

"She doesn't know about it. When I got to Topanga, I was just hoping to meet somebody who'd talked with the *Jêng Ho*'s crew, somebody who could help me show this report was genuine. The director gave me the address of what I gather is your apartment complex because several crewpeople had been staying there. 'Had been,' she said; she had no idea anybody was still there." Stavros stopped and looked alarmed. "Wait a minute. Have you tried sending the report on Bilbeis IV since the *Clark County* went down? I thought I stopped you."

"You did this time, but I'd already transmitted it once before that. I thought it was the last thing I could do for the *Jêng Ho*. What difference does it—" It was Magda's turn to break off abruptly. "You think they're going to come after me?"

"How can they afford not to? After everything they've done by now, they won't just lose their jobs if the truth comes out. They'll face rehab." Stavros and Magda both flinched at that.

"You're right, worse luck," Magda said. "Well, that tears it. Save your document there; I need to get a directory listing from the computer."

Stavros obeyed. "What are you going to do?"

"What I almost did earlier this morning: I'm going to take the whole miserable, stinking mess over to the Noninterference Foundation."

"Good!" Stavros exclaimed. "I wish Andrea and I had done that right from the start instead of going to the newsnets ourselves. We need somebody on our side big enough to stand up to the Survey Service."

"Big enough to step on us, too, maybe," Magda said. "I don't like the Foundation very much. They can talk about being disinterested till they're blue in the face, but everybody knows the Purists bankroll them."

"Purists." Stavros's voice showed his distaste. No one who wanted to do fieldwork on pretechnological planets thought well of the Purists. If the Purists had their way, they would get rid of the Survey Service altogether. A vocal minority of public opinion agreed with them.

"I know how you feel," Magda said. "I feel the same way, only more so, believe me. That's why I let Pandit talk me out of seeing the Foundation before. But the best shield I can think of against an assassin is publicity, and the Noninterference Foundation can give us that. They're good at it."

"And we don't have any better choices," Stavros said.

"That we don't." Magda stood up. "Let's go."

The local headquarters of the Noninterference Foundation was across town from the Survey Service office—not a good place for a watchdog, Magda thought sourly as she and Stavros took the long shuttle ride. She realized that was unfair; the real monitoring went on at Survey Service Central and outside the Federacy. She could not help being annoyed anyway.

To make things worse, the trip got interrupted when a horde of emergency vehicles, sirens screaming, tore across the shuttle's path. That did a splendid job of fouling up the traffic pattern.

Seeing Magda fidget, Stavros said, "The computer will fix things soon."

"Fat lot of good that does us now," she answered, but snapping at him did no more to relieve her concern than worrying about where the Foundation office was.

That office, when Magda and Stavros finally arrived, proved a good deal more luxurious than the one out of which the Survey Service operated. Looking around, Magda found herself with mixed feelings. A private organization needed to be affluent to take on a well-entrenched bureaucracy. On the other hand, these self-appointed advocates of poor, deprived people plainly had no experience of either poverty or deprivation themselves.

"What can I do for you people today?" asked a chunky bronze-skinned woman who, coming out of her office, saw the two newcomers standing irresolutely just inside the door. Neither of them replied at once. The woman repeated, "Can I help you? I'm Teresa Calderon; I'm a senior analyst here."

"This is about the recent report on Bilbeis IV," Stavros began. "I don't know if you've heard about it—"

"Oh, yes, aside from the Foundation's own bulletins, it's been in the news here," Teresa Calderon replied at once.

Magda wanted to kick herself. She asked carefully, "What is the position of the Noninterference Foundation on Bilbeis IV?"

"Frustration would probably be the best word for it; the Chairman has consistently denied the report's authenticity, and no one has been able to disprove what she says. After the *Clark County*, I don't expect anyone will. Speaking only for myself and not for the Foundation, it almost makes me believe some of the wilder claims that have been made in the affair."

"Believe them," Stavros said. Magda nodded.

Teresa Calderon's polite smile wavered. "Excuse me, but may I ask who you are?"

They told her.

The smile went out, to be replaced by incredulity. "One of you is dead, the other one wanted for murder," Calderon blurted.

"I'm getting tired of being told I'm dead," Magda said. At the same time, Stavros was exclaiming, "What did I tell you?"

When some measure of calm finally returned, Magda produced her own credit card, saying, "I can't spend money with this, but viewing it ought to convince you that I'm me." Teresa Calderon fed the card into a terminal. She looked from the picture on the screen to Magda, back again, and slowly nodded.

Stavros said, "I'm too many light-years from Hyperion to prove anything, but I was in a class when Andrea was killed. I don't know whether anyone went to the trouble of erasing that

computer record, but people will remember if somebody
bothers to ask them instead of jumping to conclusions."

By then, Teresa Calderon was almost beside herself with
excitement. "This is the opening we've been after for years!
We can finally show how the Survey Service has been deceit-
fully concealing its blunders and how its meddling has resulted in the exploitation of a whole planetful of innocent
people for over a thousand years."

"That's not the word I'd use," Magda said sharply. She was
reminded of why she mistrusted Noninterference Foundation
people. The Federacy hadn't exploited Bilbeis IV; no one had
been there at all between FSY 1186 and the visit of the *Jêng
Ho*. That didn't mean the early interference had been right,
but it had not been malicious.

The concealment afterward, of course, was something else
again.

Stavros broke her train of thought—and probably fore-
stalled a good, snarling argument—by yawning enormously.
"I'm sorry," he said. "I haven't done a whole lot of sleeping
since I got to Topanga—actually, Magda, what I have been
doing is looking for you, but I didn't know it. I told you about
that before. Anyway, I don't have a place to stay."

"Come back to my building, then," Magda said. "It's
cheap—"

"It had better be!"

"—and I know there are vacant rooms. Ms. Calderon, you
don't need us any more today, do you?" Magda looked at her
watch. "It's later than I thought. You can get things rolling
without us, I'm sure. For better or worse, we're allies for a
while, it seems."

"So we are." Teresa Calderon sounded very little more
pleased at the prospect than Magda was. That did not keep her
from diving for a phone even before Magda and Stavros had
left the office.

"Exploitation," Stavros muttered as they boarded the cross-
town shuttle. He made it into a swear word.

"You caught that too, did you? Good. You might as well
get used to it. We're going to be the Purists' little darlings for
a while. That's not what I had in mind when I joined the
Survey Service."

"I don't suppose you had murder in mind, either," Stavros
said, and to that Magda had to shake her head. They rode in

uneasy silence for some time after that and changed shuttles the same way.

"Wait a minute—we're not supposed to go down this street!" Magda exclaimed when the shuttle that usually went past her apartment complex took an unexpected turn.

Stavros pointed to the screen at the front of the passenger compartment. ROUTE CHANGED DUE TO TRAFFIC EMERGENCY AHEAD, it read. He and Magda looked at each other in alarm, both visualizing a Survey Service hijacking. The Service could probably foul up a shuttle route if it wanted to badly enough. No, scratch probably, Magda thought—the Service *could*.

She stabbed at the STOP AT NEXT CORNER button with her finger. Fearful sweat made it skid off the smooth plastic. She punched again, harder. Stavros was pressing the matching button on the arm of his seat. By the look in his eye, he didn't expect it to do any good either.

But the shuttle slid smoothly to a stop. The doors opened. Magda and Stavros scrambled down to the sidewalk with almost unseemly haste. They spun around, sure enemies would be lurking somewhere in the twilight. The shuttle disappeared down the street. Groundcars and lorries hissed by. No one paid the slightest attention to them.

Magda started to laugh and found she could not stop. Stavros finally had to hold her up. When the seizure was over at last, she stepped free of the arm he had around her shoulder. "Thanks," she said, wiping her eyes and rubbing at the pit of her stomach, which hurt. She told him, "If you ever had any doubts about whether I believed you, forget 'em. It's only taken me the afternoon to get as paranoid as you are."

"You're not paranoid when they're really after you," Stavros said grimly. "It's just as well you distracted me for a minute there; otherwise I expect I'd need a fresh pair of breeches." He did not sound as if he were joking.

"Let's get back to my complex," Magda said. She took a step and almost fell over; relief had left her giddy. She caught Stavros's arm, and he straightened her again. He was stronger than his skinny build would have made her think. "Thanks. We're just a couple of blocks away. Come on."

As they rounded the next to last corner, Magda stopped in her tracks. This was the route the shuttle should have taken, and she could see why it had been diverted. Police and people in emergency gear were everywhere. Something fell with a rending crash. An ambulance screamed past.

"Here, you can't come any farther," a harried-looking police-woman said, holding up a hand to stop Magda and Stavros.

"But I live down this way," Magda protested.

"What address?"

"It's the apartments at 141 Surf."

The policewoman's face changed. "I'm sorry," she said, but she made no move to let them by. Instead, she pointed down a side street. "Emergency shelter arrangements are that way."

"Emergency—" Magda left the word hanging.

"Honey, you can count yourself lucky you weren't home this afternoon. That building blew up; a lot of people are still trapped. They'll arrange temporary housing for you down that way"—the policewoman pointed again—"and see that you have a bed and a hot meal tonight."

Magda still tried to press ahead. "Isn't there any chance I could salvage some of my stuff from the ruins?"

"Honey, if you lived at 141, you don't have much to salvage. Now just go on, will you?" And stop making me trouble, Magda read between the lines. The policewoman went on, not unkindly, "Survivors will have a chance to search for their effects after we make sure things are stable. You'll be informed, I promise."

"Thanks." Numbly, Magda went in the direction the policewoman had pointed out.

"You see," Stavros said, following.

"Oh yes, I see." Magda's tone was still flat, stunned. Somehow that made her sound more menacing, not less. "I'm not the only one who will, either."

"I said that too, and look how well I've done," Stavros told her. "Now you know what you're up against—they're playing for keeps."

"So am I."

IX

"Thank you for coming here today," Paulina Koch said,
looking out over the rostrum at the horde of video cameras.
They peered back like so many long-nosed cyclopean beasts,
and seemed more the masters than the servants of the people
accompanying them. People and cameras alike were preda-
tors, she knew, and the blood they sought today was hers. The
solid timber of the rostrum felt like a shield, holding them at
bay.

"Chairman, do you have an opening statement?" called one
of the reporters.

"No, I do not. I am here to respond to questions, and that
is what I will do," Paulina Koch replied. She found no point
to handing her foes free ammunition. Anything they wanted
from her, they would have to earn. She pointed to one of the
many upraised hands. "Yes, Mr. Karakoyunlu?"

The newsnet man was so surprised and excited at being
called first that he forgot his carefully prepared question and
blurted, "What about Bilbeis IV?"

Paulina Koch resisted—as many would not have—the
temptation to reply, "Well, what about it?" Her answer was as
painstaking as if the question had been a good one. "Bilbeis
IV is a pretechnological world outside the Federacy. It was
first visited by a Survey Service team in FSY 1186, at which
time its civilization was early Bronze Age–equivalent."

"No!" Karakoyunlu was hopping up and down in frustration. "What about the *interference* on Bilbeis IV?" he shouted,
hoping to make himself clear.

Again the Chairman chose to take him literally. "You are
quite correct, of course. The anthropologist on that first expedition did interfere, contrary to all Survey Service policies and
regulations, which even then were both clear and stringent.
Upon his return to the Federacy, the individual in question

129

could offer no acceptable defense for his actions and was quite deservedly cashiered." She chose another reporter. "Ms. Zedong?"

"What about the results of that anthropologist's interference on Bilbeis IV? Aren't they reflected in the recent report from the Survey Service ship *Jêng Ho*, and don't they show the interference caused a profound change in the planet's development, a change of exactly the sort the Survey Service is pledged to prevent?"

"Is that all one question?" Paulina Koch asked, raising some polite mirth. She grew serious at once, though, both because that was far more in her nature than frivolity and because she knew she could not seem to be evading the issue that had prompted the news conference. She said, "I presume, Ms. Zedong, you are referring to the report bearing the FSY date 2687:139."

"Of course, Chairman Koch. This is the report that first surfaced on Hyperion and is now vouched for by the Noninterference Foundation and by the one surviving crewmember of the *Jêng Ho*—"

"I'm sorry to disappoint you, but the Survey Service's position on that report has not changed since it—what was the word you used?—surfaced. Yes, that is apt. The person who brought it forward then is at the moment a fugitive from justice—a fugitive from a murder indictment, I might add. He hardly seems a trustworthy source."

"He denies it," three people said at once.

"Wouldn't you?" Paulina Koch retorted. She had strong doubts that this Monemvasios was guilty of anything—far more likely that was one of Roupen Hovannis's acquaintances —but she also knew she had told the precise truth: Monemvasios *had* run, and he *was* charged.

"Well, what about—" Zedong looked down to check her reminder screen. "—Magda Kodaly? She, after all, was present on Bilbeis IV and is the source of much of the critical data in the report."

"Certainly Magda Kodaly was a crewmember aboard the *Jêng Ho*. Whether the person using that name today has any right to it is another matter, however. Note that Magda Kodaly was reliably reported to have been killed in the tragic crash of the *Clark County*, and her credit card was recovered from the wreckage. Note also that the woman currently employing Kodaly's name has been using on Topanga the credit card of a certain Marie Roux. Nor did this alleged Kodaly respond to the recent subpoena sent to Topanga on behalf of the Assembly Subcommittee on Non-Federacy Contacts."

"Yes, but how much of an effort was made to serve that subpoena, Chairman Koch? After all, by then the *Clark County* had already gone down."

"So it had. As for what went into serving the subpoena, you would have to inquire at the Assembly. I am certainly not in a position to comment on the diligence of its employees." The small bit of sarcasm went down well; the newsnet people were avid for dirt on any segment of the Federacy government, not just the Survey Service. "You do understand, however, that I am not yet in a position to acknowledge that the person claiming to be Magda Kodaly is in fact she. If anything, her association with Monemvasios would tend to make me think otherwise . . . Mr. Salaam?"

"Isn't it a fact, Chairman Koch, that Kodaly's association with the Noninterference Foundation is what prejudices you against her?"

"Certainly not. The Noninterference Foundation is a public-spirited body with the highest ideals, many of which I share. The Survey Service has nothing to hide or to fear."

Salaam's eyes twinkled as he asked his follow-up question. "Chairman Koch, isn't it a fact that you wouldn't believe it if the Noninterference Foundation told you the sun was shining?"

"I would look outside, Mr. Salaam." Paulina Koch had not intended the reply to be funny and was taken aback by the laugh she got. She did not show it; she had schooled herself not to show anything. When the chuckles subsided, she nodded to another reporter. "Mr. Mir?"

"Hasn't Magda Kodaly taken steps to reestablish credit in her own name, and don't the physiological data she has submitted match those of the person who previously held credit under that name?"

"There you have the advantage of me, Mr. Mir. I would have to check on that." Again the Chairman spoke the truth, but not all of it. One of Hovannis's better computer people was still trying to change Magda Kodaly's credit system records. So far she had had no luck; the credit system's safeguards were the toughest in the Federacy. It was a losing bat-

tle, anyway. Sooner or later, Kodaly would be able to estab-
lish her bona fides.

Mir shrugged but was not through. "There is also the matter of the eighteen missing days, Chairman Koch."

Paulina Koch's expression of polite interest did not change.
"To what eighteen days are you referring, Mr. Mir?"

"You and the Survey Service have insisted the report on
Bilbeis IV is not genuine. It is, however, dated 2687:139. On
2687:157, on Hyperion, your computer reported to Hyperion
Newsnet that the *Jêng Ho* had not yet come back from its
mission to make a report. When asked when the ship would
return, though, it gave a date of 2687:139. You stated at the
time that this was computer error, yet Magda Kodaly insists
that 139 is in fact the correct date of the *Jêng Ho*'s return.
Your comments?"

Only that it appears you're able to add two and two, the
Chairman thought. She tried to picture what the newsnet
man's face would look like if she said that out loud. Too late if
she intended to stay in the post she'd held so long—too late if
she intended to stay free, for that matter. "I have seen nothing
to make me change my mind, Mr. Mir, and you already know
my reaction to the person claiming to be Magda Kodaly. It is
remotely possible, however, I suppose, that an error has been
made that is not accountable to computer malfunction. Ac-
cordingly, I have ordered Dr. Cornelia Toger, Survey Service
Internal Affairs Director, to conduct a full investigation of any
possible wrongdoing in this matter—which I stress I do not
find likely—and to cooperate fully with any outside agencies
conducting similar inquiries."

The newspeople sat up straighter—that was something
they didn't know. They scribbled notes and muttered into recorders. Paulina Koch went on. "Dr. Toger will respond to
your questions as to the nature of the inquiry now. I assure you
that she is fully familiar with all aspects of the situation." She
stepped away from the podium and beckoned Dr. Toger forward.

Dr. Toger did not know anything, did not suspect anything,
and would not be allowed to find out anything. She fielded
questions as best she could. She was earnest and sincere but
very much out of her depth.

Paulina Koch listened to her luckless aide flounder. She
realized she herself had had no questions about the immortal

Queen Sabium. Down deep, she suspected, the reporters had trouble believing in the existence of a woman fifteen hundred years old, no matter what the report on Bilbeis IV said. She understood that. She had trouble believing it herself, and she knew only too well the report was real. Sabium would have been so much more . . . convenient as a legend.

When the conference was finally over, she went back to her office, where Hovannis waited. "What do you think, Roupen?"

He shrugged. "We're down, but we're not out. In a way, having the Noninterference Foundation weigh in against us does us a good turn. People know they hate us—it'll be easier to tar everything Kodaly says with their brush."

"Sensible plan." The Chairman nodded. "She's Survey Service herself, too, you know, even now. I wonder how much she cares for her new friends."

The talk-show host was suave without being oily, smooth without being facile. He had every hair perfectly in place. "Thank you for being with us, Ms. Kodaly," he said. "I'm sure you must be relieved to have formal use of your own name again."

"Yes, I certainly am, Mr. Vaughan." Magda's ears were full of the applause the audience had given her; she was still not used to being a celebrity. "Now that I've proved who I am, I can do a better job of proving just how accurate my colleagues' report on Bilbeis IV is."

"Of course." Vaughan nodded. "And of course you must agree with Dr. O'Brien that this kind of meddling on primitive planets can never be allowed to happen again."

Magda glanced toward the man sitting to the right of her on the couch. Peter O'Brien was the Foundation's head on Topanga, and fit the part: he was closing in on fifty and looked more like a well-fed executive than an activist. He was directing the media campaign against the Survey Service; he had pulled the strings to get Magda into the studio.

She did not resent O'Brien for appearing with her. The Noninterference Foundation was backing Stavros and her to make political capital for itself; she understood that. But she had no more intention of turning into a Foundation puppet than she'd had of turning a blind eye to what the Survey Service had done on Bilbeis IV.

She said, "I do agree with Dr. O'Brien on that, Mr. Vaughan, but—"

"Call me Owen, please," the emcee broke in. "Sorry to interrupt. But what, Magda? Tell us, please."

"But I don't necessarily feel the remedies he proposes are the right ones."

Beside her, O'Brien shifted in annoyance. Vaughan's eyes lit up. Magda had no idea what his politics were, but a good argument would liven up his show. "Why is that, Magda?"

"They're too drastic. The Survey Service monitors thousands of planets, almost every one of them with no trouble at all—in spite of what happened on Bilbeis IV—hell, partly *because* of what happened on Bilbeis IV back in FSY 1186. The Service takes the rule of interference very seriously. Disbanding it would be like cutting off your leg because you've an ingrown toenail."

"Dr. O'Brien, what do you think of—"

O'Brien did not need Vaughan to prompt him. "Magda's views reflect her training, naturally. I'd hoped the frantic concealment effort the Survey Service is making here would have opened her eyes to the cynicism inherent in all its policies."

"I don't see that." Magda was beginning to get angry; there was a difference between political capital and bullshit.

"Don't you?" O'Brien might look like a businessman and even act like one most of the time, but underneath that veneer he was still passionately convinced of the righteousness of his cause. "I'm referring to the cynical pretense that Survey Service fieldwork has no influence on planets where it occurs," he growled.

"It doesn't, and you know it perfectly well," Magda said. "You're acting as if you don't know a damned thing about the training we go through—"

"'We'?" O'Brien said icily. "I'm sure Paulina Koch would be pleased to hear you say that."

"Well, up yours, too. She's wrong, but that doesn't make you right, you sanctimonious know-nothing son of a bitch."

Owen Vaughan sat back, steepled his fingers, and kept his mouth shut. His sponsors had been complaining that nothing really juicy had happened on his show since the night the actress got drunk and threw a glass of brandy in the mullah's face. They'd have nothing to grumble about tonight.

"Doesn't it?" O'Brien shot back. "Why do we have any

right to meddle in the affairs of people whose only crime is
being culturally younger than we are? Let them develop their
own way, I say, instead of corrupting them by our presence. I
thought you would agree with me: you're the one who
brought to the attention of the whole Federacy the sorry spectacle of millions of deluded people on Bilbeis IV following
their false religion because of what the Survey Service did
long ago."

"With Queen Sabium as she is, they have a lot better reason for believing what they believe than most worshipers I
know." But even Magda backed away from that one in a
hurry—she needed to swing people to her way of thinking,
not alienate them. "Besides, you're making it sound as if all
the primitive planets the Service visits are more Bilbeis
IVs—"

"They are, just waiting to happen."

"They are *not*!" Magda slammed her fist down on the arm
of her couch. "For one thing, Survey Service procedures are
different from what they used to be: we've already talked
about that. For another, there just aren't that many Sabiums
around, or key situations where interference really affects a
world's development."

"Where's your evidence for that?"

"Where's yours?" Magda retorted. "If interference were as
widespread a problem as you claim, we'd see cases like Bilbeis IV every other year. And we don't. We don't. Most of the
time, the Survey Service does a good job. But when it
doesn't, it has to be called to account. That's why I'm here
tonight. That's supposed to be the purpose of the Noninterference Foundation, too, as I recall, not wrecking the Service
altogether."

"That is what we are for," O'Brien said, giving ground
before her vehemence and also remembering she was valuable
to him. "Where you and I differ is in judging how likely
interference is. There's no doubt, though, that Bilbeis IV is a
particularly flagrant case."

Magda nodded; she too was recalling that they had interests
in common. "The worst of it, though, is the way Survey Service Central has done its best to sweep the report under the rug
after the *Jêng Ho* submitted it. All my crewmates are dead,
and so is the professor who first accessed it from public
files . . . which it isn't in anymore."

"There's such a thing as too much coincidence," O'Brien agreed. He did not say any more than that, not when he had no proof linking any deaths to Survey Service Central.

Owen Vaughan sighed imperceptibly. He had been hoping they would come to blows—*that* would have sent ratings through the roof on half the planets in the Federacy. But Vaughan was a practical man who took what he could get and knew how to cut things short when the heat went out of them. "Let's take a short break for these words from our sponsors," he said, "and we'll be right back."

Magda pounded on Stavros's door. They were staying in side-by-side furnished apartments in a building owned by a prominent contributor to the Noninterference Foundation. Both apartments still kept the air of sterility that such places have when uninhabited: neither Stavros nor Magda had enough in the way of belongings to dissipate it.

He took his time answering the door. Undoubtedly, Magda thought, he was checking the security camera first. She didn't blame him. She was cultivating the same habit herself.

"How did it go?" he asked. "You still have your makeup on."

"Yes, I know. I haven't even been in my own place yet—I'm too disgusted to sit by myself. You're in this same miserable boat with me; if anybody would understand, you're the one." She threw herself into a chair. Except for being blue instead of green, it was identical to the one in her apartment, right down to the scratchy upholstery.

"That bad, was it?"

"Worse. Let me put it like this: if this O'Brien person had Paulina Koch's job, we'd be in the exact same mess we are now. Well, maybe not, on second thought—Koch can keep her mouth shut and deny everything with a straight face. That's not O'Brien's style. He likes to hear himself talk, so he gives away more than she would. The other delightful thing is that he's a damned Purist and hardly bothers to hide it."

"I got that feeling, too, when I met him," Stavros said. "So much for the impartiality the Noninterference Foundation is supposed to show. Trouble is, we need him."

"I know, I know, I know. Otherwise I'd have loosened a few of his teeth for him. I still wish I had. He left a bad taste in my mouth."

Stavros got up. "Want to clean it out with a drink?"

"That's the first sensible idea I've heard since I got on camera." Magda held up a hand. "Wait a second, though— you don't like the sweet slop they drink here, do you?" Topangan taste in spirits ran heavily to liqueurs and creams, all of which Magda found cloying.

"Is vodka over ice all right?"

"Sure; that's fine."

Stavros went into the kitchen. Magda heard ice rattle in glasses. He brought the drinks back, handed Magda hers, and shook a few drops from a small bottle into his. It turned milky. "What's that?" Magda asked, intrigued.

"Anise extract," he answered. "It turns the stuff into poor man's ouzo. Everybody drinks ouzo on New Thessaly."

"I know what you mean. We're the same way with plum brandy on Kadar, where I come from." She held out her glass. "Let me try some." He gave her drink the same treatment he had given his. Knocking back a good-sized swallow, she felt her eyes water. She tried not to cough, and almost succeeded.

"Are you all right?" Stavros asked anxiously.

"Takes getting used to," she said. She drank again, more cautiously. "Not bad, I suppose, but it must be a lethal hangover mix."

"Retsina—resinated wine—is worse."

Magda's stomach lurched at the very idea. The things some allegedly civilized people drank—

She glanced over to the screen above the apartment terminal. She had noticed it was on when she came in but had been too full of irritation to pay any attention to what Stavros was looking at. It was a sequence from the report on Bilbeis IV. She tried to recall whether it came from Irfan Kawar's ring camera or the one she had worn on the shattering day when they found the locals' undying goddess was in fact Queen Sabium of Helmand.

Stavros followed Magda's eye. "I don't know how many times I've been through that part of the report," he said. "I keep trying to get a feel for what it must be like to have lived so long and to have been the focus of a whole planet's devotion for—how long?—fifty or sixty generations."

"I know what you mean. I've been trying to do the same thing myself, ever since I met her. The other thing to keep in mind is that the tape can't convey more than a fraction of the presence she has. It really is as if she can see into your heart."

"I believe it," Stavros said. "There can't be much she hasn't seen, dealing with century after century of priests and courtiers and petitioners. There's nothing anywhere to compare her to: she's been the keystone of that planet's culture for almost as long as its had civilization."

"There's more to it, though." Magda was glad for the chance to talk about Sabium. The flap over Central's suppression of the report on Bilbeis IV had pushed the queen herself into the background, even in Magda's own mind, and Sabium was too remarkable for that. Stavros made a good audience, too; he had studied the report enough to be as familiar with Bilbeis IV as anyone outside the *Jêng Ho*'s crew could be. As familiar as anyone alive, Magda realized, was another good way to put it.

But he had not stood before Sabium's throne, had never felt the crashing awe that came with meeting the queen who had become divine. Magda struggled to put that into words. "It's not only the length of life Sabium's had. Even more of it, I think, is the person she was before we tinkered with her immune responses."

Stavros frowned. "I'm not sure I understand."

"I'm not sure I do, either. But even back in her mortal days, Sabium was a good queen. She cared about her people and about bettering the way they lived. The first Survey Service crew saw that—it's the main reason their anthropologist decided to cure her cancer. I suppose it's why he managed to talk the rest of them into it. And look at the mess he left behind."

"He didn't know—"

"No, he didn't." Magda cut off Stavros's beginning protest. "That's why you don't interfere—you don't know. I've sometimes shuddered, thinking how much worse things might have been if Sabium hadn't really been the able, kindly queen the first expedition thought she was."

"That hadn't occurred to me," Stavros said in a low voice. By his expression, he was going through the same set of appalling possibilities Magda had already imagined.

She said, "Here's something else to worry about: you're about the same age I am, aren't you—around thirty standard years?" She waited for him to nod and went on. "Did you ever have the feeling you're more distinctly *yourself* these days than you were, say, eight or ten years ago?"

Stavros nodded again. "Sure. The older I get, the more experience and knowledge I have to judge things by. My tastes are more settled, too: I like this kind of music and that kind of food. I expect I'll keep adding things as long as I live, but in the context of the structure I already have."

"That's exactly it—that's clearer than I ever thought it through, as a matter of fact," Magda said in surprised admiration. Because she was doing fieldwork while he was still a grad student, she automatically thought of herself as being more mature. His answer made her wonder. She continued more carefully, trying now to make each word count. "You and I have been growing into ourselves as adults for those eight or ten years. Sabium's been doing it more than a hundred times as long. As much as anything else, I think that's what makes her so intimidating—she's uniquely herself, uniquely an individual, in a way that no one who hasn't lived so long ever could be."

Stavros raised his glass in salute. It was nearly empty. "Well put," he said. "That's part of what I was looking for when I booted up the report tonight." He downed the rest of his drink and muttered something under his breath.

"I'm sorry, I didn't hear that," Magda said.

Stavros's swarthiness could not quite hide his flush. He hesitated, plainly of two minds about repeating himself, then blurted, "I wonder what she's like in bed."

Magda burst out laughing. "Well, there's one I hadn't thought of." She looked at the screen again. Sabium appeared no different from the way she had at the time of the first Survey Service visit to Bilbeis IV, fifteen centuries before: a handsome woman in the first years of middle age. Her gray-pink skin, blue hair, and the light down that grew on her cheeks were only exotic details. They might even make her more attractive to a man, not less, Magda thought. "She'd be interesting, I expect," she said.

"Even with the chance, I don't know if I would," Stavros said, "or could, for that matter. I can't imagine anything more inhibiting than thinking of how much experience I'd be measured against." He shivered in mock fright at the very idea.

"Don't worry about it," Magda advised. "It's not as if it's something that's likely to come up."

"I thought I just said that."

Magda snorted. She held out her glass. "Fix me another one, will you? I'll pass on the anise this time, though."

She was not surprised to end up sharing Stavros's bed that night. Alcohol had little to do with it; that the two of them were trapped in the the same precarious situation counted for much more. She and Irfan Kawar had slept together when Sabium's priests conveyed them across the main continent of Bilbeis IV to meet the undying goddess. It had brought comfort to them both, and did again, until Magda thought of Kawar's dying on the *Clark County* with the rest of the *Jêng Ho*'s crew.

She did not want to remind herself of that, not again, not tonight. She turned to Stavros and touched his shoulder. "I don't think Sabium would complain." She was not exaggerating much; her knees felt pleasantly unstrung. He hardly seemed to notice the compliment, though. She wondered if she had pleased him. "What's wrong?" she asked.

He brought himself back to the here and now with a visible effort. Magda recalled she was not the only one with dark memories. "Sorry," Stavros said. "It's nothing to do with you, not really."

Any reassurance he'd meant to give collapsed with that two-word afterthought. He realized it at once and made an annoyed noise deep in his throat. Magda lay beside him, waiting till he was ready to go on. After a little while, he did. "I'm sorry, Magda. It's just that this reminds me too much of the way Andrea and I ended up making love with each other not so long ago."

"Oh." It was Magda's turn to be silent and thoughtful. She finally said, "You told me once—I think it was the first time we met, after we came out of the Survey Service office—that you were falling in love with her."

"Yes, I think so." Stavros's eyes went first distant, then furious. He sat up and slammed his fist into the mattress so hard that he and Magda both bounced. "And not only did those bastards kill her, they landed the blame for it on me."

"You ought to talk with the Foundation people about that. There's bound to be a branch on Hyperion. Heaven knows I don't love them, but they have the money to dig out whatever they need to prove you were innocent—and once that's done, people are bound to start wondering just who did kill your Andrea, and why."

"You're right!" Stavros bounded out of bed. "Fogelman belonged to the Foundation. In fact, I think he was one of the higher-ups. And he was murdered, too, and all his data banks scrubbed. What burglar would bother? Andrea and I tried to bring that up on Hyperion, but no one took it seriously—until the *Clark County* crashed, and then all it did was scare people. Now, though—" His lips drawn back in a predatory grin, he started for the phone.

Magda coughed dryly. "Probably a good idea to put some clothes on first."

"Hmm? Oh!" Stavros clutched at himself.

"No need to hide from me, not now. Just pick up your pants." Watching while Stavros dressed, Magda saw she was forgotten for the moment. Now that he was reminded of his Andrea, she wondered whether he would have any more interest in her. If nothing else, life would be less lonely if he did.

She rolled onto the wet spot on the bed, swore, and then laughed. That was realism on the most basic level. Very few men, she thought, turned down the chance when it was there. That was realism, too. She got out of bed and went into the bathroom to clean up.

"It is always a privilege to meet with you, of course, Mr. Prime Minister," Paulina Koch said, smoothing an imaginary wrinkle on the sleeve of her gray smock, "but may I ask the reason for which you invited me to Government Mansion?"

Amadeo Croce matched her formality. "It is this Bilbeis IV matter, Madam Chairman." He tried to sound stern, and did not succeed well. Administrations came and went, but senior bureaucrats held the real, the lasting power in the Federacy. He and Paulina Koch both knew it.

"In what connection, sir?" the Chairman asked, deferential as protocol required. She would not flout his nominal authority, not now, not when the Survey Service needed every scrap of political help it could get.

Croce frowned a little. The expression did odd things to the lines on his face, which years of smiling at cameras had set in a mold of permanent affability. He said, "I feel the Service is, uh, unduly dilatory in dealing with the accusations of mishandling that have so persistently wrapped themselves around the situation relating to that planet."

"To which accusations are you referring?" Paulina Koch asked coolly. "The ones that allege Survey Service personnel guilty of everything from sabotage to murder to who knows what else? If you believe those, sir, I can only wonder why you called me here and not to the Office of Rehabilitation."

"No, no, of course not," Croce said, to Paulina Koch's well-hidden relief. One power the prime minister did have was control over the constabulary. It was a more brutal sort of power than the clashes of influence that formed the usual government shake-ups, but it was there. The Chairman had never had to fear it before. Now she did. She was the only one who knew it, but it still weakened her.

Her musings made her miss the prime minister's next sentence, which was also unlike her. "I beg your pardon, sir?" She had no great regard for Croce, but the apology was genuine; she did not like to slip.

"I was just saying that as far as I can see, no convincing evidence for anything past happenstance has surfaced concerning those charges. But the ones touching on Survey Service Central's handling of the report on Bilbeis IV itself do concern me."

"Given the nature of the people making those charges, sir, I must confess to wondering why. The Noninterference Foundation has been sniping at the Survey Service for several hundred years now—"

"I wasn't referring to the Foundation," Croce interrupted. "I meant the principals themselves, this Monemvasios person and the anthropologist off the *Jêng Ho* itself. If they are to be believed, Bilbeis IV has encountered interference in its development, interference caused by Survey Service personnel, and the report documenting that interference is genuine. And I have to tell you, the more they talk, the more credible they sound."

"It does appear that the person who claims to be Magda Kodaly may in fact be she," Paulina Koch admitted grudgingly. "As for the other one, though—"

The prime minister broke in again. "I know what you are going to say. I have information, however, that the authorities on Hyperion are dropping all charges against him: he definitely was in a classroom when his girlfriend's murder took place."

"Really?" Paulina Koch's eyebrows arched in surprise, but she had known that bit of news for a day and a half. Croce's interrupting her twice worried her more. Attuned as she was to the nuances of bureaucratic maneuvering, she read there the warning that he no longer felt as much need to conciliate her as he once had.

"Yes, it is true. And if this Monemvasios individual is to be believed, and if the woman Magda Kodaly was in fact aboard the *Jêng Ho*, I hope you will not be offended by my repeating that their view of the report on Bilbeis IV is also enhanced."

"Sir, I take no offense, but I respectfully have to disagree with you."

Croce raised an eyebrow. "You must tell me why."

"Even if Kodaly was in fact on Bilbeis IV, that says nothing about the accuracy of the document submitted as a report on the mission of the *Jêng Ho*. Kodaly was, if you recall, one of the two main actors in the wilder claims that the text of the document makes, and the interpretation of events going into those claims is almost exclusively hers. To put it as mildly as possible, her objectivity is suspect. If she were well-disposed to the Service, would she be associating with the Noninterference Foundation?"

"An interesting question," the prime minister said. Paulina Koch studied him with sudden sharp attention, thinking she scented irony, but his politician's face was proof against her scrutiny. He continued, "A pity we lack the remaining members of the *Jêng Ho*'s crew to give her the lie, is it not?"

"A great pity, and a great tragedy." Paulina Koch reminded herself that she still did not *know* exactly what had happened to the *Clark County*. She did not remind herself that she had not tried to find out. Ignorance felt more comfortable, to say nothing of safer.

"That being the case, however, I suppose you are going to accede to the Noninterference Foundation's request that they conduct a new investigation of the situation on Bilbeis IV, to ascertain precisely what that situation is."

Only the Chairman's wariness and experience let her evade the trap. She was sure her meeting with Croce was being recorded; a panicky shout of "No!" could be plenty to sink her, while a "yes" was even more unthinkable. Her voice came out steady as she replied, "I have several reasons for believing that to be inadvisable." Down deep where it did not show, she was proud of her sangfroid.

"Let me hear them." If the prime minister felt disappointment, he was also a dab hand at not showing it.

Many sessions of testifying before the Assembly without notes had given Paulina Koch the knack of quickly organizing her thoughts. "First, of course, is the question of impartiality. The Noninterference Foundation's ties to the Purists are notorious, and have been only too evident throughout the present affair."

"That statement is self-serving, you realize."

"Yes." Paulina Koch was always ready to yield a small point to gain a large one. "That does not make it any less true."

Croce chuckled. "Well, maybe so. Go on."

"Thank you, sir. I also must remind you that for the Noninterference Foundation to undertake such a mission is in itself a contradiction in terms. Are the Foundation's people so steeped in moral purity that they can avoid causing the very kind of interference they claim to reject?"

"Were you to ask them, I am certain they would tell you so," the prime minister said. He had been in his profession far too long to have escaped cynicism.

"Yes, no doubt," Paulina Koch agreed as sardonically. "I was, however, asking you. I would also ask you to consider that while they spend so much of their time complaining about what we do, they lack the training for survey missions of the type we do routinely, let alone for one as delicate as this."

"I begin to see your drift."

Croce did not sound happy with it. Paulina Koch played her trump card. "Finally, think about whether you would be happy at the precedent set for a private organization's usurping here the function of a government bureau. Are you willing to have that happen whenever a publicity campaign whips people into a frenzy, deserved or not?"

The prime minister stiffened. That, thought the Chairman with the first real optimism she had felt during the meeting, had hit him where he lived. No official, elected or appointed, could warm to the notion of having authority taken out of his hands. "What do you suggest, then?" Croce asked.

"I suppose that in light of the hue and cry over Bilbeis IV, regular procedures must be set aside." The distaste in Paulina Koch's voice was twofold. Setting aside regular procedure was unpleasant to her in and of itself. And when doing so also involved having to retreat to a fallback position, that only made things worse. She did her best to maintain a bold front. "Any new survey team that visits the planet will have to be extraordinarily discreet. Survey Service personnel are the only logical choice for the mission."

She already had most of the crewmembers in mind—loyal, pliable souls one and all, people who would see only what did the Service the most good. Fallback positions were stronger when prepared in advance.

"I had thought you might say that." Amadeo Croce took a deep breath. "I must tell you that in the view of this administration, what you have suggested is not adequate. I shall so state on the floor of the Assembly. I would sooner have the Noninterference Foundation conduct the inquiry. The Survey Service is too deeply compromised to be the sole arbiter of its own affairs."

Behind her unrevealing features, Paulina Koch's mind raced. This was what Croce had summoned her here to tell her. Normally, the administration backed its bureau chiefs to the hilt; they were the ones who carried out the policies the politicians set. And Croce was no Purist, nor were the members of his cabinet. He had no strong ideological commitment to going after the Survey Service. He had simply scented weakness and decided to get clear of it.

"What plan do you have in mind, then, sir?" the Chairman asked, tasting gall.

"I shall propose a solution that would make Solomon proud," the prime minister answered. Seeing that the allusion meant nothing to Paulina Koch, he explained, "You are right in one way, Madam Chairman—we have to send a new mission to Bilbeis IV. I think you also make good sense when you advise against putting the expedition in the hands of the Noninterference Foundation. One of your people will retain overall command. But I will urge that the mission be made up half of Service personnel, half of individuals chosen by an independent agency, and for that role the Foundation seems the obvious choice."

The solution struck the Chairman as contrived; whoever this Solomon had been, he hadn't had much upstairs. On the other hand . . . she nodded slowly. A divided expedition could be counted on to produce an ambiguous report. At the moment, she—and the Survey Service—could hope for nothing better. A couple of other possibilities also occurred to her.

"Very well, sir," she said.

The prime minister had opened his mouth to argue her down. He shut it again in glad surprise.

"They're not going to get away with that!" Stavros exclaimed, staring at the formal hard-copy message he had just opened.

Magda read it over his shoulder. "You bet your life they're not." Her voice was full of the same furious disbelief that filled his.

Stavros took her cliché literally. "Yes, I have, and so have you. Is this the gratitude we get for it?" He read in a singsong voice: "'Thank you for your interest in participating in the renewed investigation of the planet Bilbeis IV. Unfortunately, these positions require more experienced individuals.'"

"There are no people more experienced with Bilbeis IV than the two of us," Magda said. "Me directly—hell, now I'm the only person in the Federacy who's ever been there—and you because you've been through our report until you probably know it better than I do. And so—" She took her anger out on the phone buttons.

A well-scrubbed young man's face appeared on the screen. "Noninterference Foundation."

"We're Kodaly and Monemvasios. Put us through to Dr. O'Brien right now. If he doesn't feel like talking to us—and he probably won't—tell him his other choice is listening to us on the newsnets later, and that he'll like that even less."

"Remind me not to let you get angry at me," Stavros whispered when the screen went momentarily black. "I think I'd sooner just stand in front of a shuttle and get everything over with at once."

Magda managed a grim chuckle. "I'll take that for a compliment. You know what we're going to hit him with?"

"A hammer, by choice," Stavros growled. His temper was not as quick as Magda's, but she had already found he was impossible to move from a position once he dug in his heels. He squeezed her hand, saying, "I think so. I'm with you all the way. I—"

He broke off abruptly, because Peter O'Brien's image replaced that of the Foundation underling. O'Brien eyed Magda with a singular lack of warmth. "What's this all about?" he demanded.

"I think you know," Magda said. She smiled a little when Stavros wordlessly held up the form letter; sure enough, he knew what she was up to.

"I am sorry." O'Brien did not sound sorry. "You must understand that we have to involve only the most qualified people on a project of the importance of this one. There is nothing personal involved."

"For one thing, I don't believe you. For another, where will you find anybody else who's met Queen Sabium, the undying goddess a whole planet worships? For a third, where would you be without Stavros and me? You owe us slots, and you will pay off, or I'm sure the newsnet people—and the whole Federacy—will be fascinated to hear how the high and mighty Noninterference Foundation shoved us to one side the minute we weren't useful to you anymore."

"Do you think you can blackmail me?" O'Brien snapped.

"Damn right I do," Magda said gleefully. "Fix it and fix it now, or we'll have other calls to make. Remember, the more you look like Purists, the less reason people will have to believe your side of the story. And kicking us off your crew will make you look an awful lot like a Purist to an awful lot of people. Me, I'm one of 'em."

"I'm another," Stavros added.

"Now," Magda said with a sweet smile, "shall we ring off and start getting hold of the newsnets?"

"I can't permit that," O'Brien said. "It would be—"

"Can't?" Stavros broke in. "Can't? How do you propose stopping us? The same way the Survey Service stopped Professor Fogelman and Andrea and the *Jêng Ho*'s crew? Do we ask for protection from you next?"

"No, of course not." O'Brien made a pushing-away gesture, as if to put distance between himself and Stavros's suggestion. For the first time, he seemed flustered. "We would never do, never think of such a thing. Of course you are free to do as you wish. It would hurt your cause as well as ours, though. Please think of that, please don't do anything you might come to regret—"

"You know what we want," Magda said implacably.

"Let me get back to you," O'Brien pleaded. "This is too big a decision for me to make on my own."

"We'll wait until tonight, no longer," Stavros told him.

"Tonight?" Now O'Brien looked horrified. "That's much too soon. Some of the people with whom I have to consult are offplanet, and—"

"Tonight." Stavros switched off the phone in the middle of O'Brien's protest. When it chimed again a moment later, he hit the REFUSE button. The noise cut off. He grinned a small-boy grin at Magda.

She hugged him. "You couldn't have backed me better! Nothing makes the Foundation angrier than being compared to the Service."

"I meant it." Stavros was still serious. "The minute any power group sees an edge, it grabs, and anybody in the way had better look out. And we aren't the kind of friends Purists feel comfortable with. That show you did with O'Brien must have made him sure of that."

"I don't want any Purists feeling comfortable with me," Magda snorted. "All they want to do is set every social science there is back a couple of thousand years. And speaking of setting back, you just cost the Foundation a nice tidy sum there."

"Yes, I know. If O'Brien does have to confer offworld— and he probably does—he'll need to use the FTL links, and those aren't cheap. But I figured that setting a deadline he'll have to scramble to meet would show him we weren't fooling."

"Smart." Magda was still discovering just how good an ally Stavros made. He was unprepossessing, especially at the moment—he was regrowing the beard he'd shaved off when he escaped from Hyperion. Unlike her, he was given to hesitating before taking something on. But once he committed himself, he did not back away, and the rein he held on his temper let him keep getting in telling shots after she was reduced to outraged incoherence.

His single-mindedness could also be irritating. Once O'Brien was no longer an immediate concern, he went back to what he had been doing when the Foundation's letter arrived: poring over the report on Bilbeis IV. Magda draped herself against his back. "Shall we kill some time until they call us again?"

Without looking away from the screen, Stavros said, "Let's wait until we know whether we have anything to celebrate." She angrily strode away and had very little to say to him the rest of the afternoon. She would have got more satisfaction from her silence had he noticed it.

But they both dashed for the phone when O'Brien called back not long before sunset. "You win," he growled, and switched off himself.

"Probably making sure you didn't beat him to the—" Magda began.

Stavros found a very effective way to interrupt her. She never did finish the sentence. Sometimes, she thought a good deal later, single-mindedness was an advantage.

Survey Service crews normally departed with no more fan-fare than anyone else going off to do a job. The takeoff of the *Hanno* was different. It drew Assemblymen, Noninterference Foundation bigwigs, the Chairman of the Survey Service, and enough newsnet people to fill a luxury liner past takeoff weight.

Magda preferred the usual way. Everybody wanted to make a speech, and everybody's speech was running long. The only thing she was grateful for was that the crew got to sit down. A camerawoman, on her feet for hours, had already passed out.

A black Assemblyman named Valleix was just finishing putting five minutes' worth of idea into a twenty-minute speech. Listening with one ear, Magda gathered that he was against the Survey Service and everything it stood for; he did not seem clear on what that was. The Foundation honchos up on the platform with him applauded lustily. Gritting her teeth at having to work with such people, Magda only wished he would shut up and go away.

Stavros might have been reading her mind. He leaned over and whispered, "I'd sooner be meeting interesting people in-stead of going through all this nonsense."

"Me, too." The crew of the *Hanno*, at least the half of the contingent that the Noninterference Foundation had chosen, was a high-powered group. Magda knew several members' work.

Paulina Koch was coming to the podium. Magda's feelings about the Chairman were still mixed; it was hard to think of her longtime boss, the head of the organization in which she had wanted to spend her whole career, as the enemy. At least Paulina Koch was not long-winded. She would say what she had to say and then quit. Magda turned and said as much to Stavros.

"A subtracter is also nice and straightforward," Stavros said. "All it does is kill you."

"What's a subtracter?"

"A big poisonous worm-type creature we have at home."

"We have something like that on Kadar, too. We call the thing an adder, after the Terran snake."

"I suppose one of our early settlers decided that didn't make much sense," Stavros said, "considering what it does. Greeks are very logical people." He grinned. "We also love to play with words."

The byplay had made Magda miss Paulina Koch's opening remarks. The Chairman was saying, "It is our hope that this mission will succeed in bringing back an unbiased account of conditions on Bilbeis IV, so that we can, if necessary, evolve new techniques for making contact with pretechnological cultures even more effective yet discreet than is the case at this point in time."

"'If necessary'!" Stavros snarled. He was no friend of the Chairman's and never would be.

"In all candor, we initially doubted the necessity for a new visit to Bilbeis IV," Paulina Koch continued, "but we are now convinced that valuable data may be gleaned from it. It will also serve as a model of cooperation between our agency and organizations which hitherto have not always been in accord with us. From it we may learn to go forward in harmony."

"And I may learn to go into stardrive without a ship," Magda muttered. She had been in the Survey Service too long to believe the Service and the Noninterference Foundation were ever going to get along. She did not believe Paulina Koch thought so, either. The hypocrisy in the speech made her grimace; it reminded her all too much of the political games she had had to play herself lately.

Paulina Koch stepped down. Somebody else stepped up. More rhetoric spewed out for the cameras. Magda endured it, dose after dose. Finally it was done.

"At last, the point of the exercise," Stavros said as the crew of the *Hanno* followed their commander to the ship. As was customary, the commander paused at the top of the boarding ramp to greet the people with whom he would be traveling.

He was a dark, broad-shouldered man who looked more like an engine tech or a stevedore than any sort of leader. That was Magda's first impression of him, at any rate. She changed her mind when she saw his eyes, which were shrewd and opaque. He wore Survey Service coveralls.

"Captain Hovannis," she said, holding out her hand.

He did not take it. "Ms. Kodaly," he said. His voice was deep and rough. He did not shake Stavros's hand, either, and ignored the glare he got.

Stavros was still fuming as he got ready for lift-off. "Cold-blooded bastard," he complained over the intercom.

"Screw him," Magda said. "He's Service, and he doesn't have any reason to like us. The angrier we let him make us, the happier he'll be. If I do get angry at him, I want it to be for my reasons, not his. Make sense?"

"Yes," Stavros said reluctantly.

"Relax, then. We're on our way."

"We are?"

Magda waved at her outside viewscreen. It showed the black of space.

Stavros laughed at himself. "I keep missing takeoffs."

"You're here, and that's what counts."

"No," he said. "What counts is when we get there."

Magda thought about it. "You're right."

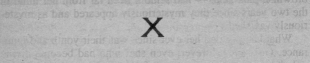

X

"The disputed orchards, I find, do in law lie under the jurisdiction of the town of Khonsu. Yet because the representative of Shirik has shown that its townspeople have used these orchards for two generations without protest from Khonsu till now, they may still harvest up to one hundred *tals* of fruit per year there at no cost to themselves. Above that, they shall pay Khonsu at the market rate."

The spokesmen—actually, one was a woman— of the two towns bowed low before the glittering throne. "We thank the eternal goddess," they intoned. The words were ritual, but the goddess heard no great dissatisfaction in them. She had been able to give both sides something, which went a long way toward stifling resentment.

The claimants bowed again and walked out of the audience chamber side by side. No, there would be no further trouble there for a man's lifetime or two, the goddess thought. She turned to her majordomo. "They were the last for today?"

"Yes, goddess." Though the priest had served in the Holy City since before his beard sprouted, his voice was as full of awe as those of the petitioners from distant Khonsu and Shirik, who were seeing the goddess for the first and almost surely last time in their lives. He asked, "Will you return to your chambers now?"

"Not just yet, Bagadat. I will sit for a moment first." The goddess leaned back and smoothed a wrinkle in the fine white fabric of her robe. Suddenly the weight of the gold circlet on her brow seemed heavy and oppressive, though she could not remember the last time she had noticed it . . . perhaps not even since the days when she had been known as Sabium.

She needed all the discipline a millennium and a half had granted to keep from her face the complex concerns that thought evoked. The last meeting with the representatives of the higher gods, the ones who had given her eternal life, had been oddly inconclusive. The bronze-haired woman and bald-crowned man—strange, alien features only accented by their brownish-pink skins—had seldom been far from her mind in the two years since they mysteriously appeared and as mysteriously vanished.

What had puzzled her ever since was their youth and ignorance. Gods lived forever; even she, who had become divine only by the grace of more powerful deities, enjoyed that boon. Surely the same had to be true of divine messengers as well. Yet these claimed no more than a man's span of years and, by every subtle sign she had learned, were speaking the truth.

Moreover, she was convinced her own immortality had surprised and shocked them, though they knew of the events that had created it. She did not have many mysteries in her life; people had become transparent to her after so many years of observing them, guiding them. She worried away at the riddle of the messengers as at a piece of meat stuck between the teeth.

And as with a piece of meat, she was confident the mystery eventually would yield. The patience to wait for the fullness of time before acting was no small part of what had won Sabium dominion over most of her continent and a good portion of the smaller one to the east. Her rivals, being mere mortals, always moved too soon.

Behind her mask of calm, a wry smile stirred. Now she had no choice but to wait. She accepted that with the same resolution she had used long ago to face her own death. She rose from the throne. "I'm sorry, Bagadat; I've changed my mind. You may escort me after all."

The majordomo bowed very low. "Of course, goddess."

Paulina Koch ruled an empire older and vaster than Sabium's. Indeed, were it not for the Survey Service, Sabium's empire would never have come into being. Bureaucracies, too, have something of immortality about them and distill wisdom from the years. Had Paulina Koch been a person who framed mottoes and hung them on her wall, pride of place would have gone to the one that read, "When in doubt, do nothing."

The Chairman was not that sort of person. She loathed display in any form; all she wanted was to do her job, do it well, and be left alone. Most of the time she got her wish.

Even after the mess about Bilbeis IV had blown up, she had guided the Service's appropriation through a hostile Assembly with her usual sharp skill.

But waiting would not always serve, and while the Survey Service might go on forever, Paulina Koch knew only too well her own tenure as Chairman—to say nothing of her freedom —would not last ten minutes past final confirmation of just how she had covered her tracks. It behooved her, then, to make sure those data stayed buried.

Cornelia Toger's report, which she had just reviewed, was no threat. The Internal Affairs Director hadn't been able to find anything wrong at Survey Service Central. Paulina Koch had not expected her to; the only reason Toger headed the internal investigation was her inability to see past her nose.

The Chairman almost laughed at her suggestion that the problem really lay on Topanga. Then she stopped, thoughtful. Pinning a piece of the blame there might not be a bad idea after all.

Getting Roupen Hovannis offplanet was a more certain insurance policy, though, she thought. For one thing, he would help keep a lid on this new investigation of Bilbeis IV. Self-interest was a perfect lever there: Hovannis knew his neck was on the line, too.

For another, now that he was gone, Paulina Koch had a better chance of teasing out of the computer whatever incriminating evidence he had on her. She knew it was in the system. Hovannis would have been a fool not to keep that kind of file, and Paulina Koch tolerated no fools in the Survey Service.

But data processing had been the key to her own rapid rise through the ranks. Hovannis was very good at hiding information. With no false modesty, she thought she was better at digging it out.

The trouble was, she had so much to go through. No one, and no army either, could hope to keep up with all the information the Federacy generated. And as External Affairs Director, Hovannis had access to almost all the veiling techniques the Survey Service had ever had to devise. If he wanted to conceal dirt in six-hundred-year-old committee meeting minutes against future need, he could change those documents without leaving any sign that their ancient obscurity had been disturbed.

Or so he thought. Still, there were ways. Like any safety-

conscious administrator, Paulina Koch held a few tricks in
reserve about which her subordinates knew nothing. Some,
unfortunately, left traces behind—otherwise the Chairman
would have been using them all along instead of having to
wait until Hovannis was away from the scene.

Until she began her search project, she had had only an
intellectual feel for the sheer size of the bureau she ran.
Watching the computer spin its metaphorical wheels as it
ground through enormous chaffheaps of data, though, gave
her an emotional grasp as well, one she would just as soon not
have had. Someone else might have given way to despair—
what she was looking for might be *anyplace*.

Paulina Koch did not give way. In what free time she had
from the day-to-day problems of running the Service, she refined a couple of search routines to make them harder to de-
tect and, more important, faster.

Unlike Sabium, she knew she did not have all the time she
needed.

Magda slammed her hand down on the table in disgust. "I
don't know why I bother talking to you, Pierre," she snapped.
"You're only using half the data we have, and the less important half, too."

Pierre Bochy gestured defensively. "You will forgive me,
but I see no reason not to rely on language tapes, records of
diet and dress, and the like. But I find a woman more than
half as old as the Federacy much harder to take seriously."

"Survey Service hack," Stavros said, flipping his head
back in a way that combined contempt and an effort to get a
lock of hair away from his eyes.

Bochy rose, bowed with grace surprising in a man so
portly, and stalked out of the small study compartment.

Magda sighed. "That's not going to help, Stavros." Ever
since boarding the *Hanno*, she had worked to keep her temper
under control. The *Hanno* was tense enough already. The Survey Service personnel looked on their counterparts from the
Noninterference Foundation as a pack of meddling amateurs
along only because of political pressure, while the Foundation
contingent viewed the Survey Service team as, at best, hidebound button pushers and, at worst, wanton despoilers and
murderers. No one seemed shy about saying so, either.

As Bilbeis IV neared, Magda found her good intentions

fraying. Though she and Stavros were nominally part of the group from the Noninterference Foundation, they had few friends there. Most of the Foundation people were Purists, and mistrusted anyone who was not all for destroying the Survey Service. Magda's years with the Service only made her doubly suspicious to them.

Yet to the Survey Service staffers, she was a traitor for having gone over to the Foundation and, though no one would say so out loud, for airing dirty Service laundry in public. That bothered her less than she'd expected, and she took a long time to figure out why.

Stavros's rude crack summed it up as well as anything. The Survey Service people on the *Hanno* were . . . almost second-rate. If Magda had to guess, she would have said they were chosen much more for adherence to accepted views than for brilliance. Bochy was a case in point. He was competent enough, but his mind moved in preselected tracks.

Caught in her reverie, Magda did not notice the measuring stare Stavros sent toward her. Though they were allies in this, though she had given him no reason for it, he also worried about her coming from the Survey Service, worried that in the end her quarrel with the Service turned more on information suppressed than on lives suppressed.

He knew that was a paranoid thought; Magda had lost more people close to her than he had. But seeing the whole Service as an enemy, as he did, sometimes made him have trouble separating her from it. And thinking like a paranoid had kept him alive more than once lately.

Enough, he told himself firmly; he knew he was vaporing like a fool. Next he'd start hearing voices, and the ship's officers would fill him so full of happy pills he wouldn't care what day of the week it was, let alone anything else.

He touched Magda's arm, wanting to make amends the best way he knew how for thinking ill of her, even if she had no idea he'd done so. "Shall we go back to my cubicle?"

She glanced at the clock on the wall. "I'm supposed to be here another fifteen minutes, but why not?" she said sourly. "I don't know why they even bothered scheduling these briefing sessions in the first place."

"Well, thanks to their killing off everyone else who's ever been to Bilbeis IV, your opinions do have a certain value."

She laughed, but the mirth washed out before she was

through. "You're getting as cynical as I am. Are you sure you want me to come along with you?"

"Yes." Stavros realized they were lovers more on account of the events that had thrown them together than for any more solid reason, but the pleasure and moments of forgetfulness they shared were no less desirable because of that.

"All right. Like I said, no one here pays any attention to me anyway. The Service people have their chunk that they can handle, and the Foundation people have theirs, and nobody wants to look any farther. Screw 'em all."

"No thank you," Stavros declared solemnly.

This time, Magda's laugh stayed happy. She took Stavros's hand and pulled him up from his seat. "Come on. Doesn't it make you feel like you're ditching a class?"

"I can't think of a better incentive," he said, smelling the clean fresh scent of Magda's hair. But though he bantered with her as they walked the *Hanno*'s corridors, some of the happiness had leached from him. Once or twice, back on Hyperion, he had cut class to sport with Andrea . . . who would still be alive had he not gotten that copy of the report on Bilbeis IV and recognized it for what it was.

His mood darkened further when he and Magda turned a corner and almost ran into Roupen Hovannis. The captain of the *Hanno* scowled his dark-browed scowl at them, then pointedly checked his watch. "Why aren't you at your assigned station?" he growled at Magda. It was only the second or third time he had spoken to her since the flight began. Stavros, as usual, he ignored altogether.

That suited Stavros fine. He distrusted Hovannis on general principles as being a creature of Paulina Koch's. But even without connection to the Chairman, the captain would have frightened him. There was no give anywhere to Hovannis. He even walked with his hard, stocky body leaning slightly forward, as if to bull obstructions out of his path.

No attitude could have been better calculated to get Magda's back up. She retorted, "Anyone who wants me that badly can call me in my cubicle. Sitting in that study chamber wastes its space and my time."

"I'll log your disobedience," Hovannis said stonily.

"Go ahead. While you're at it, log that a grand total of three people showed up in the last week and that none of them had any idea what questions to ask."

Shaking his head, Hovannis stamped away. Magda glared at his broad back, then surprised Stavros by chuckling under her breath. He said, "As far as I can see, that one's about as funny as a funeral."

"Nowhere near. I was just thinking, good luck to anybody who tries to call me in my cubicle, seeing as I'll be in yours."

Suddenly that prospect looked very good to Stavros again. "Let's go, then."

Afterward, Magda said with malicious glee, "We'll be landing in a couple of days. Then all the people who stayed away will wish they hadn't."

The phone chimed. "Usually that happens in the middle of things." Stavros got out of bed to pick it up. He answered the call, then, abruptly quite serious, turned to Magda. "It's for you: the Foundation's comparative theologian. She was surprised when she got me—thought she was punching for your cubicle."

"Then how in blazes did her call end up here? Our extensions aren't even close to being—" Magda paused as her brain caught up with her mouth. "Hovannis," she said slowly.

Her brows knit in a frown. She'd been thinking of the captain as someone with more muscle than brains. Now she saw that was judging him only by the impression his appearance gave. He had to have been the one who diddled with the call-forwarding system; undoubtedly he *had* been hoping she and Stavros would get interrupted. Hovannis was smarter than he seemed. That was worth remembering. He also had a mean streak. That was worth remembering, too.

As she did every so often, the goddess sifted through reports of prodigies that came to the Holy City. She did not believe, as she once had, that such things foretold the future; she had seen too much future unfold for that. But such fears and hopes still lurked in the hearts of her people. A soothing proclamation every so often, when something particularly strange happened, did no harm and some good.

Strange to mortals, at any rate, the goddess who had been Sabium amended mentally. After fifteen hundred years, the cries of alarm over misshapen animals and men and over such perfectly predictable matters as eclipses and transits all sounded very much alike. Sometimes she thought she would reward the reporter of a new kind of prodigy in the same way she did inventors. The drain on the treasury would be much smaller, that was certain.

Having thought that—not for the first time, nor for the hundredth—the goddess found herself only a short while later tugging in bemusement at the fine down on her cheeks. Several herders northwest of the Holy City had reported a great shape in the night sky, visible only because it blotted stars from view as it moved.

At first she thought a group of drovers had gone too deep into the ale pot. Then she noted that the reports had been turned in to priests in villages a fair distance apart. Those from villages farther east noted the prodigy in the western sky, while the westerly ones claimed it was in the east.

She tugged again, searching for a memory. Something of the same sort had come to her notice a couple of years before. She'd paid scant attention then, being still in a turmoil over the visit of the divine messengers. She stiffened. Could there be a connection? She was positive she'd seen nothing else like these messages, not in all her time on the throne.

She wondered if, around the time she had become immortal, similar news had come to the town that had been Helmand and was now the Holy City. She did not recall it offhand, but that meant little, given the span of years involved. She summoned Bagadat and told him to have a search made of the most ancient records. He hurried away, puzzled but as always obedient.

She was disappointed when no such report turned up, but not overwhelmingly so. Record-keeping had been catch as catch can in the early times; not only that, but in those days, with far fewer people about, drovers did not have to take their flocks so far into the northern desert. If something obscured the stars with no one there to see it, how would she ever find out?

She summoned Bagadat again. "Send word to the priests of Charsadda, Pauzatish, Izala—" She named several more northern hamlets; Bagadat's stylus scratched across wax as he scribbled notes. "Tell them visitors such as we last had two years gone by may soon come among us again, and bid them send on to me any strangers they reckon may be such."

"Yes, goddess." Bagadat's face was worried. He had never seen his divine mistress disturbed until the strangely colored foreigners appeared before her; he would have given much never to see her so again. All across the world, people loved and worshiped the goddess, but he was one of the lucky handful privileged to serve her person. He had never thought he might want more distance from her so he would not need to know she could be troubled.

Sabium—(she thought of herself more that way since the divine messengers had reappeared than she had for centuries)—sensed that and spoke quickly to reassure her chamberlain. "Have no fear, Bagadat. This meeting will find me better prepared than the last, I promise you."

Bagadat dipped his head in acquiescence. "Of course, goddess. I shall ready the dispatches at once." His back was straight as he left Sabium's presence; at bottom, like all those who worshiped her, he had confidence in her ability to meet any challenge. Over the generations, she had given them every reason for that confidence.

She felt less of it herself. Coming face to face with those who knew of her most ancient past had reminded her of how vulnerable she once was. Against her own folk, that was true no longer. The gods, she alone recalled, though, did what they would with mortals and could grant like powers to their messengers.

She was no longer a mortal, but she did not know where the balance of power lay. She would take what precautions she could.

Roupen Hovannis drained yet another cup of coffee. His eyelids still wanted to sag. He muttered something under his breath, dry-swallowed a wake-up pill, leaned back in his chair until the pill kicked in, then went back to studying.

He had thought the outward trip in the *Hanno* would be like a vacation: after the Byzantine machinations of running the Service's External Affairs Bureau, keeping track of a couple of dozen scientists had to be a piece of cake.

That much, at least, was true. But it dawned on him only gradually that he might have to do more than keep track of them once they got to Bilbeis IV. With things as they were down there, he might have to get his feet muddy himself. And if he was going to do that, he had to conform as closely as he could to all the niggling Survey Service rules, or else blow the mission by bringing even the tame Service people down on his head. He had already learned more about the local unwashed barbarians and their language of clicks, coughs, and grunts than he ever wanted to know. All the same, he kept at it; as a security man, he had long ago learned that one could never tell beforehand which piece of data was the important one.

He had another reason, too. The more people saw him operating inside the rules, the less it would occur to them that he could step outside any time he chose.

The desert air seared the inside of Stavros's nostrils. He felt his eyeballs start to dry out. He blinked. In moments, the savage sun baked the moisture away again. Sweat sprang from every pore of his body. "Whew!" he said, wiping his forehead with the back of his hand. "I've been shipboard too long; I'm not used to real weather anymore."

"You have to be born to this to be used to it," Magda answered. "Even then, the locals like to sleep for a couple of hours around noon." She dabbed at her face with a kerchief and looked down to examine the cloth. "This bloody makeup had better be as sweatproof as they promised; it's going to get a workout here. Not only that, my false cheek whiskers itch like hell. How can you stand that beard of yours?"

"It's not glued on, which helps, I suppose. I'm not used to the green tint in it, though." Nor was Stavros used to the grayish-pink skin dye, though he trusted it further than she did: if it had not come off in the shower, it would probably survive Bilbeis IV. He found her fuzzy cheeks more disconcerting—the last hairy face he had kissed had been his grandfather's.

The natives were humanoid enough that under most circumstances the crew of the *Hanno* could have gone without disguise, passing themselves off as travelers from a distant land. But nothing was normal about Bilbeis IV. With Sabium's priesthood alert to bring Terran-type humans to their goddess, more than usual discretion was called for. Even Hovannis wore makeup, though nothing could make his dour, craggy features much resemble anything Bilbeis IV produced.

For the moment, Stavros was content merely to forget the captain rather than worrying about him as he usually did. Doing fieldwork for the first time, getting sand in his boots from a world outside the Federacy, was exciting enough to make him unusually charitable. He said as much out loud.

"I know what you mean." Magda nodded. "I was so

thrilled to be loose on my first planet that I almost killed myself out of sheer stupidity. I swaggered into a tavern and ordered the wrong kind of drink—like an idiot, I'd managed to forget the locals got high on methanol as well as ethanol. I'm just lucky the veteran I was with stumbled against me accidentally on purpose and knocked the mug out of my hand before I swallowed any."

That thrill never wore off, not completely, not if you were meant to be a Survey Service person. But experience tempered it for Magda. So did caution, here. No matter how big a technological advantage she had on Sabium, she did not feel safe matching wits with the goddess. Sabium's edge in wisdom, Magda was uncomfortably aware, was just as great.

She said, "I only hope we're far enough into the desert to let us practice being native without any real natives spotting us. If the locals see people walking into and out of a small mesa, then we might as well not have bothered turning on the *Hanno*'s camouflage screens."

Stavros glanced back at the ship. It looked like an outcropping of the yellow sandstone that underlay the dunes and emaciated plants thereabouts. "I think I trust the sensors that far."

"They're only as good as the people monitoring them." Magda rubbed a couple of new bites; whatever the sensors managed to pick up, they weren't worth a damn against flying pests. She scrubbed at her dyed skin with a wet finger. When she stayed gray-pink, she grunted in dubious satisfaction. "I am glad this stuff has a sunscreen in it; otherwise I'd be about ready to take out of the oven and eat."

Being darker under the makeup, Stavros was less concerned about sunburn. Still, the feeling of being stuck in a blast furnace had begun to outweigh his delight at working on a primitive planet. "I wouldn't mind some ice water."

"Or cold beer," Magda said. "Enjoy it while you can. Beer isn't the same at blood temperature." The memory of six months of such beer on the way to the Holy City made her shudder.

She gave a luxurious sigh at returning to cool, conditioned air, then sneezed several times in a row. She wiped her nose and scowled. She didn't like to be reminded of any little drawbacks of technology, not when she had just been counting on it as her big edge on Sabium.

As usual, an argument was going on in the lounge. Pierre

Bochy, Magda thought, did not look good made up as a native of Bilbeis IV, not even in Survey Service coveralls. The dye turned his plump features the color of stewed pork. Which was also what the anthropologist was using for brains, Magda observed; he was blithering on again about how the local matriarchy was really no different from a good many others. "Take the Shadofa culture on Wasf II, for instance: quite similar in a large number of their beliefs and customs."

"How about historical development?" Magda broke in with a sweet, carnivorous smile. "The Shadofa hadn't made a new invention in two thousand years, never ruled more than part of one small island, and were losing ground there the last time the Service visited. Besides which, you'll forgive me for reminding you, their goddess isn't real."

"Not relevant," Bochy said blandly. "They believe in Acca without reservation; she has the same force in their lives that the eternal goddess does here." He would not speak Sabium's name.

His effrontery left Magda momentarily speechless, something not easy to accomplish. But Justin Olmstead, his opposite number from the Noninterference Foundation, returned to the attack he had been making when Magda came into the lounge. "I've urged you before, Pierre, don't refuse to face facts merely because you are a member of the organization responsible for the problem."

Olmstead's voice was deep, smooth, and mellow, his gray hair—now dyed gray-blue—perfectly in place. Even made up, he looked as though he would be more in place in front of a holo camera than in the field. From what Magda had seen of his professional work, in front of a camera was where he belonged. He was an excellent popularizer, though. More people knew his data cards and books than those of any three dozen serious researchers.

The Foundation had insisted on adding him to its contingent along with Magda and Stavros. Magda grinned to herself; she was getting to enjoy being considered unreliable. Still, she had to admit Olmstead was a shrewd choice. He would make a good talking head once the *Hanno* got back to the Federacy, always assuming he didn't get himself killed trying to be an anthropologist instead of just looking like one.

He did not overawe Bochy, however. "What are the facts?" The Survey Service man shrugged. "At the moment, they are

in dispute; otherwise we would not be here. Have you so
made up your mind that it is closed to anything new we may
find?" Bochy was tenacious, Magda thought as she saw Olmstead frown; she would have reckoned him pigheaded had he
come back at her that way.

Stavros broke in harshly, "How many people have died to
keep these nonfacts of yours from ever coming to light? Isn't
it a fact that your precious Service has been busy trying to
bury the truth and the people who know it?"

Bochy shrugged again. "I know nothing of that. I was on a
pre-Federacy world myself when the *Jêng Ho* was last here."

"Yes, I understand that," Stavros said, and surprised
Magda by adding, "I apologize." After a moment he went on,
"But doesn't it matter to you whether that's so?"

"Of course it matters to me. As I said, though, I had nothing to do with it." Bochy seemed to think he had made a
complete answer. He turned away from Stavros; he was as
eager to claw pieces out of the rich and famous Olmstead as
the latter was to attack the minion of the corrupt Service.
Stavros doubted that either saw the other as a human being.
He wondered if Bochy saw anyone as a human being.

When, later, he said that to Magda, she shook her head.
"I'm sure he's normal enough with his family and friends. But
if he didn't see a Service screwup with his own eyes, it's not
real for him. There was some phrase I ran across in an ancient
lit class that puzzled me for years, until I joined the Service
and saw the thing it pointed at. Bochy fits the type."

The ancient literature Stavros had read was mostly classical
Greek. Doubting that Sophocles had been talking about Pierre
Bochy, he raised a questioning eyebrow.

"'Good German,'" Magda told him.

The investigator was very young, very neat, and very self-
assured. "Surely, Madam Chairman, you remember more
about the day the report on Bilbeis IV reached Survey Service
Central than is yet on the record," she said. "That was FSY
2687:139, if the precise date will help you."

"I doubt it," Paulina Koch said indifferently. The investigator had done her homework if she could pull the date out of
the air like that, but the Chairman refused to let such a parlor
trick rattle her. She went on, "If I'd thought the day somehow
special, perhaps I would have taken more care to fix it in my

mind. All I can say for certain is that I was busy. I usually am. For details, you will have to refer to the printout of the log I have submitted."

The investigator nodded and fought back a sigh. Sitting across the table in her trademark gray, Paulina Koch remained sweatless and elusive. She was taking exactly the right line, instead of falling into the trap that would have snared so many detail-oriented people: that of recalling far too much about a day supposedly ordinary.

No one, though, the investigator told herself firmly, was invulnerable. She tried to act as if she believed it. "About that printout, and others we have received from your staff," she resumed. "Analysis shows the paper on which they were printed is from a lot procured from a new supplier, one not yet sending shipments to Central on the dates the documents were produced."

"Let me check," the Chairman said. She tapped at the keyboard of the terminal beside her. "Ah, here we are."

The investigator came around the table to see. There on the screen was a requisition ordering a small trial shipment of the new paper. It showed the blasted stuff had been in use at Central on the days in question.

"Is there anything more?" the Chairman asked politely.

The investigator tried a different set of questions. Paulina Koch relaxed as much as she let herself relax these days. This line was not dangerous. The last one had been. Had she not happened to hold a couple of memos—an old one and a new one—side by side, she never would have noticed that they were printed on sheets of slightly different color and thought to insert that false requisition into the files. It would not stand up to close scrutiny, of course, but with luck it would not get any. Just having it in place should do the job.

That was a loose end tied up. She wondered how many were still around, lying there for her to trip over. Enough earnest young hatchetpeople like the one in front of her were out looking for them. She knew they were trying to penetrate her own private computer records, but so far—she thought—they'd had no luck at that. She had enough false trails there to bewilder the most resolute snoop.

She knew, though, that her precautions were not what kept her safe, not anymore. The most important thing in her favor was a collective will to disbelieve that any bureaucracy could get out of hand to the extent of plotting murder. Concealment of faults, yes; any agency would do that without thinking twice. But such determined mayhem—

She could hardly blame the investigative team. Not so long ago, she would not have believed what she had done and ordered, either.

The woman pestering her gradually realized her latest line of questions was going nowhere. Paulina Koch almost felt tempted to laugh. Being asked about things of which she was actually innocent made for a pleasant novelty.

At last the investigator said, "Thank you for your time," and left. Paulina Koch went back to her office. Before she did anything there, she ran a scanner over herself to make sure the investigator hadn't managed to plant a bug on her. That was no baseless worry; it had happened more than once. She was clean this time, though.

Once satisfied of that, she rushed through the Service business that had piled up on her desk while she was away. She felt guilty at giving it such short shrift, but there was no help for it now. If she was going to go on guiding the Service, she had more important things to tend to.

The most important of those was penetrating Roupen Hovannis's files. She knew where they were now, or thought she did, but she was having no more luck accessing them than the outside investigators were with hers. Sure enough, he had his own undocumented entry codes.

Under other circumstances, Paulina Koch thought, she would have fired him for that.

The meeting broke up. Magda's head ached. She stayed in the conference chamber after most people had filed out. "I need a drink," she declared to anyone who would listen, which meant, in essence, to Stavros. She punched the refreshment panel and ordered anise-flavored vodka over ice.

He smiled when he saw the cloudy white liquid. "I'm corrupting you."

"Don't use that word, not when this whole mission smells like dead fish." Magda tossed down the drink at a gulp and threw the glass in a wastebasket. Being plastic, it denied her the satisfaction of shattering. She snarled and began ticking off points on her fingers. "Geology? The *Jêng Ho* did a first-rate job; everybody says so. Linguistics? Fine. Architecture?

No problems. Biology? Good. There I won't argue; Atanasio Pedroza, may he rest in peace, was a bastard but a damned capable bastard. Then they get around to the anthro stuff, and all of a sudden dead fish is perfume by comparison."

"That's not quite true." Stavros knew Magda required careful handling when she was in one of these fits of temper. "They're ready enough to accept anything that doesn't touch too closely on Sabium."

"That doesn't leave bloody much, not on Bilbeis IV." She somehow contrived to look plump as she did a wicked imitation of Pierre Bochy, intoning, "'Further study and examination of this anomaly will be required before a final determination can be completed.' What really frosts me is Olmstead agreeing with him. Those two can't agree on which direction the sun comes up from, and now this." She felt—and sounded—betrayed.

Thinking that, Stavros got a handle on what had perplexed him as much as her. "If Olmstead agrees your data are valid, then what's he doing here? Confirming a Survey Service report? How much good would that do his career?"

Magda slowly nodded as she saw where Stavros was going. "Olmstead'd sooner be castrated with a microtome than admit the Service can do anything right. Whereas if *he* were to make the astounding discovery of an immortal goddess..." She let her voice trail away.

"With the tapes and books he churns out, he'd live fat for the rest of his life," Stavros finished for her.

"So he would. Yes, that fits very well." Magda nodded again. "And so off we'll all go, on pilgrimage to Canterbury."

"To where?"

"Never mind. More clutter from that class of mine; I must have it on the brain. I even thought about majoring in ancient lit once or twice, till I realized I'd have to teach for a living and that I liked fieldwork better." With the almost-ouzo warm in her, Magda tried to be optimistic. "One more band of pilgrims shouldn't be conspicuous, not with us in disguise and not with the number of people who go to the Holy City every year. It shouldn't be," she repeated, and tried to make herself believe it.

The goddess frowned, wondering whether the orders she'd passed to her priesthood had been too vague. She was not

often guilty of overreacting, not after gaining perspective for
so many years, but even she had scant experience to guide her
when it came to dealing with the strange beings who had made
her what she was.

Winnowing grain from chaff was the problem. Now more
alert than ever to the presence of unusual strangers, some
priests were sending her reports of anyone they spied who was
even slightly out of the ordinary. Sabium had not realized so
many of her subjects possessed large moles, lacked a digit or
two, or had curiously stained teeth. A glance sufficed to con-
sign most such sightings to the rubbish heap.

Some were harder to evaluate; even with instructions to
send information as detailed as possible, all too many priests
were maddeningly unclear. That problem seemed worse in the
first messages now reaching her from the eastern continent,
where her rule was newer and less firm. Before long, she
decided to ignore news from the eastern land. Divine messengers, she reasoned, could come closer than that.

Had she not just reached that conclusion, she might have
paid scant attention to another of the endless stream of reports.
The people of whom it spoke, after all, had gray-pink skins
and greenish or bluish hair like everyone else, not the exotic
coloration of previous visitors. But they had arrived on foot at
Mawsil, only a day's journey west of the Holy City, and no
other pilgrims there remembered seeing them at any earlier
stops in the Margush valley.

Sabium made a note to commend the priest who had written her; this woman, unlike so many others, had her wits
about her. She had not just listened to travelers' gossip. Before sending word to the goddess, she had checked with the
priesthood back in Rai, the town just west of Mawsil. On
learning that no one there recalled this new band of pilgrims,
she had observed them more closely.

They spoke with an odd accent—and the priest empha-
sized that she was familiar with most of the ways the dominant tongue of Sabium's realm could be flavored. More
interesting still, they seemed to have more money than they
knew what to do with. Yet they were walking, not riding on
beastback or traveling in carriages or sedan chairs. They also
seemed, the priest wrote, curiously unworn for people who
must have come from far away.

The more Sabium studied the parchment, the more it intrigued her, especially when she remembered that the moving patch that obscured the stars had been seen fairly close to Mawsil. She wondered if the herders had seen the messengers' conveyance descending from the sky. That would have to be investigated.

A servant stood nearby. Servants were always at hand, except when the goddess chose privacy for herself. She turned to the woman and said, "Bring me Bagadat, please." The servant hurried away.

By the time the majordomo arrived, Sabium had the orders she would give clear in her own mind. She could see he was unhappy with them. But when he said, "Goddess, it shall be done," she knew he was telling the truth. Few mortals tried to lie to her; fewer still succeeded.

Mawsil, Stavros thought, was a tawdry town. Gateway to the Holy City, it was anything but holy itself. Its chief industry seemed to be separating pilgrims from cash. What really embarrassed him was how the people from the *Hanno* threw themselves into the spirit of the place. "Everyone's acting like a bunch of tourists," he complained to Magda, "running around buying everything in sight and gaping at all the fancy buildings. It's disgraceful."

This time she refused to take his side. "That's what you're supposed to do in Mawsil. If we weren't gathering great armloads of overpriced trinkets, the locals would be muttering behind their hands and wondering what was wrong with us. As is, we're effectively invisible."

"I suppose so," he said grudgingly. "It just doesn't seem very—"

"Scientific?" Magda suggested, grinning. "There's no law that says you can't have fun doing fieldwork, only one that says you can't make a spectacle of yourself. Someplace else, that might mean being quiet and contemplative. Here it means buying trash and oohing and ahhing over the sacred spot where Sabium—excuse me, the goddess—assumed the kingship of Mawsil. And since that last happened something like fourteen hundred years ago, it's worth a few oohs and ahhs."

"I suppose so." Now Stavros sounded more as if he meant it. "Tomorrow's the anniversary of that, by the way; there's a reenactment or some such ceremony planned."

"I suppose we ought to be there, then." Magda grinned

again. "I wouldn't put it past the Mawsuli to hold an 'anniversary' once a month, to fleece each new crop of visitors. No, I take it back: Sabium would hear about that and put an end to it. But if they could get away with it, they would."

The entire contingent from the *Hanno* went to the plaza to watch the reenactment. It had something to interest anthropologists, historians, linguists, comparative theologians, and literary specialists. Also, they were supposed to be pilgrims, and that was the kind of thing pilgrims did.

Stavros whistled when he saw the rich display in the square and the large numbers of priests who joined the laity in celebrating the festival. "I owe the Mawsuli an apology, don't I? They must take this much of their faith seriously, anyhow."

"Maybe because it involves them," Magda suggested. "I have to admit I'm impressed. I didn't get to see this the last time I was here; the season was wrong. They have spent some money, haven't they?"

The plaza was gaudy with banners, streamers, placards, flags, fragrant branches. Behind them, Magda knew, the buildings were mud brick, as they had been when the *Leeuwenhoek* visited Bilbeis IV long ago. Nor were they much different to look at from those early structures. None of that surprised Magda. Hot-climate river-valley cultures built the same way almost everywhere; if something worked, people would find it.

But despite outward similarities, so much had changed. Iron, the alphabet, the very idea of progress. . . . Bilbeis IV had risen far and fast, thanks to Sabium.

Horns brayed, distracting Magda. A fat man came out onto the platform at one end of the square. He bawled something to the crowd through a megaphone. Thunderous, rapturous applause interrupted him. Magda and Stavros turned to each other. "What was that?" they said at the same time, each having caught perhaps one word in five.

"And now, ladies and gentlemen, our feature for the day," Magda guessed.

The robe, Magda saw, was much like the ones kings had actually worn when the *Leeuwenhoek* was here. Most cultures at this stage of development would have dressed the actor in contemporary clothes, having forgotten any other styles were ever worn. Sabium again, Magda thought. Not only was she pushing Bilbeis IV ahead, she also remained a link that gave it perspective on its past.

The horns blared out a fanfare, a theme that had once been the anthem of the kings of Helmand and now belonged to the goddess. "Nice touch," Stavros remarked, "though I suspect only Sabium gets the whole point anymore."

The fanfare rang out again. The actor playing the king of Mawsil fell to his knees. The crowd gasped and murmured excitedly as the native playing Queen Sabium made her appearance. She was wearing a robe as antique as the king's, but her simple, direct style contrasted curiously with his florid overacting. It might almost have been . . .

Observing the locals' reactions, Olmstead spoke in pontifical tones. "See the superstitious fervor with which they respond even to a representation of their living deity. The Survey Service has much to answer for, its machinations having propelled such primitives to a technological level far beyond their mental sophistication."

"Oh, shut up, you pompous fool," Magda snapped.

Olmstead glanced at her with what looked like scorn poorly masked by kindliness. "Even after exposing one of them, are you still blind to the fact that the Service makes such heinous blunders?"

"No, and I'm not blind to the fact that that's really Sabium up there either, the way you seem to be. Which gives the locals some excuse for being a little less restrained than usual, wouldn't you say?"

Olmstead, for once, said nothing at all, though his mouth silently opened and closed several times. The rest of the group from the *Hanno* made up for him; as they exclaimed and pointed, they were suddenly noisier than the natives around them.

Stavros had been paying more attention to the crowd than to what was going on up on the platform. Nowhere in any of the data on Bilbeis IV had he seen mention of a ceremony where so many priests mingled with the laity. He had been wondering why they were there until Magda's words made him stand on tiptoe and stare toward the platform again. He had never heard of the goddess's coming out of the Holy City, either. The priests had to be guards, to make sure nothing went wrong.

Someone took him by the right elbow: a priest, he saw as

he turned in surprise. "What are you doing?" he asked. He had a moment of pleasure and pride: he got his grammar straight, and his voice did not squeak.

"You will come with us, please," the priest replied. To emphasize her words, another priest, this one a man, seized Stavros's other arm. He tried to shake free and could not.

As he struggled, he saw that all the Terrans had been netted with similar efficiency. No one else had been disturbed. No wonder Sabium's clergy were out in such force, he thought as the priests hustled him along. Finding out why too late seemed worse than never learning at all.

Magda, he saw, was going along quietly and without resistance. He remembered she had been taken by the clergy before. He managed to steer his way close to her and muttered his aphorism.

"Finding out too late, eh?" she echoed with a sardonic grin. "If you could come up with a better epigram for this whole bloody planet, I don't know what it'd be."

XI

Paulina Koch punched EXECUTE. She would not have
minded implementing the command on the investigators who
still peered at the Service like so many scavengers making
sure the carcass they were going to eat was really dead. Hit-
ting a computer button seemed a poor second best.

If this program runs, though, she thought, it may combine
the literal and symbolic. She had thought that before, more
than once, and been disappointed each time. Roupen Hovannis was even better than she had figured at covering his
tracks.

The Chairman waited. Every time she had tried it before,
her only reward had been a blank screen. Seconds stretched,
but whether in the computer's circuits or only in her own mind
she did not know. No matter how she armored herself against
them, she was not immune to anticipation or hope.

Surely now, she told herself, things were taking longer to
develop than they had before. . . . The screen lit. Paulina Koch
nodded once in satisfaction. Hovannis had been clever, but not
clever enough. Now that she had access to one of his files, the
rest would yield more easily.

Then she began to examine what the External Affairs Director had stowed away for stormy times. Her pleasure gave
way to cold anger. A copy of the *Jêng Ho*'s report on Bilbeis
IV, complete with the original, damning FSY date—Hovannis
hadn't wasted any time taking his own precautions, had he?
Recordings of several conversations between the two of them.
She listened to a few moments of each of them and frowned.
Taken all together, they were even more damning than she
remembered. Others were not in this file and had to be stored
elsewhere.

She began the process of scrubbing the file—carefully,
carefully, so that no trace it had ever existed was left behind.

At last she knew she had done a proper job. And even while she was deleting that first dangerous chunk of information, her program, like a killer fish scenting blood in the water, had latched on to another. That one, she saw when she could look up from what she was doing, lurked in a completely different index. Clever, Roupen, she thought, but not clever enough.

She wondered how Hovannis was doing in the field. Now that his little data collection was being neutralized, an unfortunate accident might be much the tidiest thing that could happen to him. Had she been certain of breaking his codes, she would have arranged for one.

She still had hope. Hovannis was ruthless and able but, like herself, had risen though the Survey Service central bureaucracy. He had never been out on his own on a primitive planet. Any small mistake, Paulina Koch thought, could easily be his last.

"We apologize for the indignity to your persons," one of the priests told the people from the *Hanno*. She had said it at least a dozen times. She even sounded sincere.

"Give us back our clothes and gear, then," Pierre Bochy shouted. Other Terran voices echoed him. Once inside the temple, the priests had stripped the study team and confiscated everything they were carrying. A few people fought back and got lumps for their troubles. As Magda had already found out, the priesthood of the eternal goddess knew some decidedly unprimitive combat tricks.

A couple of male priests came in with armloads of robes. "Here, you may don these for the time being," the woman said as they began to pass them out. "They are finer than the ones you were wearing. As I have said already, your own garments and goods will be returned to you, along with a goodly reward to salve your tempers."

"Believe her; she's telling the truth." Magda had repeated that almost as often as the priestess had made her apology, and with almost as little effect. Whatever Sabium's priesthood was, Magda felt confident it was not vicious. As with so much on Bilbeis IV, that reflected the character of the goddess.

Stavros, at least, had followed Magda's lead and offered no resistance. He glanced down at himself as he belted the new robe, which was indeed of better quality than the one that had been taken from him. "I'm just glad we were thorough with the dye job."

She chuckled. "Yes, that would have been embarrassing, wouldn't it? I wonder what they'd have thought if they'd found us two different colors apiece, and that the hair hither didn't match the hair yon."

The priests had not gone so far as stripping off the Terrans' rings and bracelets, perhaps to help reassure their uninvited guests and perhaps, Magda thought, simply because it never occurred to them that such trinkets could be anything but what they appeared. The people of Bilbeis IV had gotten sophisticated quickly, but they were not to the point of looking for recorders and video cameras disguised as jewelry. Several men and women from the *Hanno* moved their arms and turned this way and that to capture their surroundings on tape.

A plump functionary stood in the doorway and clapped his hands for attention. Magda grew alert. This fellow had been at Sabium's court before; if he was here now, Sabium could not be far behind. A moment later, his words confirmed her thought: "Bow, all of you, bow before the eternal goddess!" Despite his best efforts, his voice was shaky.

"I'm glad he's nervous, too," Stavros muttered as he bent from the waist.

When he straightened, Sabium had taken her chamberlain's place. She was silently studying the group from the *Hanno*. Stavros had to work to keep from dropping his eyes when her gaze fell on him—and he was prepared for the moment, which Magda had not been when the *Jêng Ho* arrived. Tapes offered only the faintest suggestion of the calm majesty Sabium projected. She was, he thought, used to being worshiped, and used to deserving worship, too.

Once she released him by looking away, he found he was not the only Terran to have fallen under her influence. Nearly everyone seemed as awestruck as he was himself. The effect, he saw with ironic pleasure, was particularly strong among the Survey Service personnel, who had perhaps thought themselves immune. Pierre Bochy, for one, looked almost ready to go down on his knees.

"Serves the obfuscating bastard right," Magda answered when he whispered that to her.

She felt uneasy herself; Sabium's glance kept returning to

her. "We have met before," Sabium said. It was not a question.

So much for disguise, Magda thought. "Yes, goddess."

"Is this your true seeming, or do you wear it merely to appear less noticeable among my people?"

"The latter, not that it seems to have worked any too well."

Magda's candor made Sabium smile, but the expression slowly faded as the goddess continued to look around the chamber. She turned back to Magda. "I fail to see your former companion, even in the guise you choose to wear now. Irfan was what he called himself, was it not?"

"Yes, goddess, that was his name." Magda felt sadness wash over her, sadness and rage at what had happened to Irfan Kawar. "I fear you will not see him again, goddess. He is dead."

The word hung in the air. Sabium recoiled, almost as if against physical attack. "Dead?" she whispered, sounding for once not the least bit queenly. "How can that be?"

Her priests glowered at Magda; seeing their goddess upset rocked their world. She suspected she understood better than they what the trouble was. Sabium must have assumed all her long, long life that people from the Federacy were at the very least messengers from the old gods she alone remembered. Learning they were mortal after all had to come as a shock. Next thing you knew, Magda thought, she might even wonder if they were fallible.

On the record, people from the Federacy looked quite a bit more fallible than Sabium had been for centuries. Fortunately, the goddess would still be a while realizing that.

Watching Sabium adjust to an idea that looked to change a millennium and a half of assumptions only made Magda admire her more. Had she been that old, she suspected she would have rejected out of hand anything that did not fit her view of how the world worked. The goddess showed no signs of that. Maybe, Magda thought, the continuing changes that sprang from her incentive-for-inventions scheme had helped keep her mind flexible. And maybe, too, she was simply an extraordinary individual, and not just for her length of years, either.

On second thought, that last was too obvious to need a "maybe" in front of it.

Sabium turned to her priests. "I will speak more with these

strangers later. Feed and house them as you would yourselves, but do not let them leave." She looked at the group from the *Hanno* again and rubbed her chin. "Take their ornaments from them, and sequester those with their other belongings. Who but they can say where their power resides?" She left the chamber.

Magda swore under her breath as the priests confiscated her bracelets, which held a video link, and her earrings, which were just jewelry. The little transceiver implanted behind her ear still gave her an audio link with the *Hanno*, but a lot of data was going to go down the drain.

Stavros's trinkets, like everyone else's, were also a mixture of the technological and the innocuous. After he surrendered them, he said to Magda, "She doesn't miss much, does she?"

"Wouldn't do to count on it," Magda agreed soberly. She'd thought the jar of wine she and Irfan had planted between the guards they'd stunned when escaping from the Holy City would explain why those guards had fallen asleep at their post. Evidently not.

Pierre Bochy pushed his way through the crowd to Magda. His broad face was troubled. "I am beginning to think I may owe you an apology. If that is truly the Sabium from the days of the *Leeuwenhoek*—"

"If!" Magda's momentary pleasure vanished. She bristled. "What do you want, letters of fire across the sky?"

"Please." Bochy spread his hands placatingly. "Whoever she is, she is a most remarkable woman." With that, not even Magda could argue.

"It *is* Sabium, the one you mean." That was Nina Pertusi, the linguist from the Noninterference Foundation contingent. She sounded very sure of herself, and explained why a moment later: "I have—I mean, I had—a voiceprint comparator in my jewelry. There's a perfect match between this woman's voice and the old recordings of Sabium."

"Is there?" Bochy said.

Magda and Stavros could not resist a simultaneous triumphant, "You see?"

Servants soon fetched in food and drink. The meats and bread were strangely spiced but plainly well prepared and were served on silver. The beer was flat and the wine too sweet, but the locals liked them that way. Magda had tasted worse on some Federacy planets. She ate and drank her fill and used one of the chamber pots set against a wall without thinking twice about it.

Nina Pertusi approached her again. Magda was sure the linguist would have been scarlet without her makeup. "How can you do that so casually? I am almost ready to burst."

"Haven't you—" Magda began, and then reflected that maybe Nina hadn't. Linguists could get a lot done from tapes without going into the field. Magda patted her on the shoulder and said as kindly as she could, "Honey, when it's really a choice between bursting and going, you'll go, no matter who's around. The first time will be dreadful, the second one'll be mortifying, the third embarrassing, but after a while you won't think about it at all."

Nina made a small, wordless skeptical noise.

"It's true," Magda insisted. "Just remember, everyone else will be doing the same thing. That helps a lot. What they say about planets without soap is true—where everybody stinks, nobody stinks."

"I very much hope you are right," Nina said, "but I fear it will not come easily for me."

"Don't worry about it," Magda told her again. The whole Bilbeis IV affair, though, had taught the anthropologist not to say everything she thought. By the look of things, Nina Pertusi was liable to have plenty of time in Mawsil to learn to lose her inhibitions.

As a professional, Hovannis admired the efficiency with which the locals had scooped the party from the *Hanno* into captivity. He would have admired it even more if they had proceeded to send the survey team on to the next world with appropriately bloody rites. That would have made his job a lot simpler once the *Hanno* got back to civilization. From the reports he had reviewed, though, he gathered this Sabium creature didn't operate that way. Too bad.

Still, he felt like cheering when the goddess's minions confiscated everyone's data-gathering instruments. These scientists, he thought, wouldn't admit the sun had come up until they checked a recording of it. The less information they brought home, the better the Survey Service would end up looking.

But the more he monitored the tapes still coming in from the survey team's transceivers, the less happy he got. Nina

Pertusi's confirmation that Sabium was Sabium did not bother him. She was, after all, from the Foundation. What really did matter there was sticking to the story that Survey Service Central had never found out about what was going on on Bilbeis IV until just before the *Hanno* took off.

That was why Hovannis scowled when he heard Pierre Bochy sucking up to that Kodaly bitch. If things hadn't gone wrong with her too many times, the Service—and Hovannis—wouldn't have been in this mess. Didn't Bochy and the rest remember which side of their bread had the butter? Probably not, he thought, even if Paulina Koch had picked them for that.

He slapped his desk drawer. The stunner in there looked—and scanned—as nonlethal as any of the others allowed on the *Hanno*. That only proved Hovannis knew more tricks than the people who made scanners. The stunner's range was hardly more than arm's length now, but it would do the job.

No matter what the Survey Service scientists thought, he was *not* going to let this mission get out of control.

The investigator gave Paulina Koch a more-in-sorrow-than-in-anger look that he must, she thought, have practiced in front of a mirror. He said, "I truly resent the necessity of having had to obtain a court order to gain access to these codes."

You've made me work for a living, which is strange and unpleasant, the Chairman translated mentally. Out loud, she answered in the same formal language he had used: this was on the record. "The Survey Service has maintained the principle of privileged information since its inception. Despite the ruling of the court, I still maintain it and strongly protest this seizure."

"But you will comply?"

"Reluctantly, I will." She handed him the data card with the listings he needed.

"Thank you, Madam Chairman. Though my unit should have had these ten days ago, I am certain they will still prove invaluable to our inquiry."

She politely inclined her head. The investigator left, clutching his prize. Paulina Koch had not been lying when she defended the idea of confidentiality, but she had known the Service's court fight was foredoomed. As the investigator said, all it had done was waste time. The Service lawyers had told her the same thing, but they went out and fought for her anyway. That was what lawyers were for.

No matter how many codes he had, though, he could not find data no longer in the system. Now Paulina Koch was certain she had scrubbed away all of Hovannis's poison. Ten days ago, she had not been.

She did not show any outward signs of relief. Even if such had been her style, things were still too tight for that.

If these truly are divine messengers, Sabium thought, they are doing an excellent job of concealing it. They ate, they drank—they drank quite a lot—they produced full chamber pots as foul as anyone else's. Among themselves they spoke a language no one knew, but from the sound of things they mostly used it to quarrel. The priests had already broken up three or four fights before they got well under way. Divinities, by Sabium's lights, ought to act better than that. She certainly tried to herself.

Were it not for the curious objects the priests had confiscated from the strangers, she would have judged them mere men, foreigners from some distant land masquerading as subjects of hers. But those enigmatic objects were like nothing known in her dominions. Whatever they were made of, it was neither wood nor metal nor pottery nor bone. Some could be felt to quiver, almost as if alive, when held in the hand.

None of which would have made them any more than strange, but when an incautious priest pushed a button she should not have, the two people beside her and two more in the next room were rendered suddenly unconscious. Every one of the strangers carried a device like the one that produced that remarkable effect. None of Sabium's scholars and savants had any idea how it worked or how to make anything like it.

The discovery had not surprised Sabium, not after the way the last two of these—personages—vanished out of her palace. And how, if not divine, had the woman changed her coloring so completely? Its implications, though, worried her. With powers such as the strangers possessed, where in the world did they come from? Why hadn't her own folk found them long before, or they her empire? Even more to the point, why had they not come as conquerors? They were no normal people, that was certain.

And if they weren't people and weren't gods either, what did that leave? The only way to find out, Sabium told herself, was to ask. She had seen she could read the strangers almost as if they were her own subjects; they could not hide their bodies' involuntary responses to her questions.

When the goddess came to a conclusion, she wasted no time acting on it. "Fetch me the woman who was here before, the one who then had hair the color of copper," she told Bagadat. "Bring her new companion as well, the lean young man."

The majordomo gave a doleful nod. He resented the strangers for disrupting the smooth routine of the palace and even more for vexing his deity. "Do you wish guards, goddess?"

"No, no," Sabium said impatiently. "There is no danger in these—personages; that is another thing about them that puzzles me. Go now, if you please. I assure you, I will be safe."

"As you say, goddess." Bagadat had trouble disbelieving her, but did not sound convinced, either.

"Why does she want me, too?" Stavros asked for about the fifth time as priests hurried him and Magda through torchlit passageways toward the goddess. They were perfectly polite and made no move to touch the Terrans, but Stavros thought they would simply drag him if he faltered or balked. When Sabium bade them do something, they were not used to getting no for an answer.

Magda, on the other hand, was by then out of patience with the question. "How should I know why?" she snapped. "For all I can tell, she's divined what you said back on Topanga and intends to invite you into bed with her."

For a moment, Stavros waited for the priests to react in horror to her words. Then he realized that, unlike him, she had spoken in Federacy Basic. Some of her slips of temper, he thought, were very calculated things. Annoyed, he shot back, "Then it's you who ought to be asking what you're along for."

"Maybe just to give helpful advice," she said sweetly.

He refused to be drawn. "With the experience Sabium has, I doubt she needs it."

"I didn't mean her," Magda murmured.

Feeling his cheeks grow hot, Stavros gave up. The banter was making him nervous anyway. Wondering what bedding a woman fifty times his age might be like was one thing back on

Topanga: a topic of academic interest, so to speak. Even there, the prospect had been daunting. It was quite a bit more so when in the goddess's power.

Besides which, Sabium had shown about as much attraction for him as for one of the local draft animals, beasts that seemed to combine all the worst features of camels and zebras. In its own way, Stavros thought, that was reassuring.

Certainly the goddess's chamber was not set up for a seduction. Sabium waved the Terrans into chairs and seated herself in one facing them. A servant brought in wine and cakes, then silently departed.

"What would you do if I told you I had ordered you put to death?" the goddess asked without preamble.

Magda and Stavros exchanged appalled looks. Magda had been thinking for some time that Sabium was not showing the group from the *Hanno* the same deference Irfan Kawar and she had gotten, but there was a lot of difference between less deference and a death sentence.

"Are you telling us that, goddess?" she asked.

"Answer my question as I asked it." Sabium's face was an unrevealing mask; her words might have issued from one of the countless images of her that were reverenced over this whole continent.

"First I would ask why, then I would start trying to figure out how to evade your doom," Magda said.

Sabium's gaze swung to Stavros. "First I would ask if you are telling us that," he said after a moment's thought. That drive for precision was part of him, Magda thought, and a valuable part when he did not, as sometimes happened, let it run away from him. He got no reply from the goddess; seeing he would not, he sighed and resumed. "After that, I would do as Magda said, though in the opposite order."

Humanity returned to Sabium's features. "That is as good an answer as I could have hoped for," she said with a small, amused smile.

"Why are you trying to make us afraid, goddess?" Magda asked, sensing no trip to the headsman lay in the immediate future.

"To see what you are, of course." Secure for ages in her power, the goddess did not bother dissembling. "You and yours seek to hide your purposes from me, just as you hide your true appearance beneath colors that ape my people's."

Since that was exactly so, Magda kept her mouth shut.

"And you." Sabium returned to Stavros. "What do you really look like, without your false pigments?"

"Me? I am a dragon, goddess, about twice as tall as this temple," he said in a sober, reasonable voice. "I breathe fire."

She gaped at him, then burst out laughing. "Are you indeed? I must say, you hide it very well."

Seeing Sabium's mood softened, Magda dared ask, "What do you seek of us, then, goddess?"

"Still I do not know." Sabium frowned, as if she did not care to make that admission. "At times I feel in your folk the condescension a grown man might show watching children playing with toys. And yet at other times your comrades have in them more awe of me than my own people display. You would help me if you could explain how both these things can be true at once."

Magda knew she was treading on dangerous ground, even more so than in past conversations with the goddess. She picked her words with care. "For the first, I can only apologize; rude people are part of my nation, as they are of any other. For the second, well, your people know you, as they have for so long. Mine, on the other hand, have heard only travelers' tales. Those so often grow in the telling that the wonder is all the greater at finding them, this once, less than the truth."

"That is it precisely," Stavros agreed. He did not think he could have done such a smooth job of telling the literal truth without giving away the essential secrets behind it.

It did not do to count on too much in that regard, he discovered. Sabium's years let her fit together seemingly irrelevant bits of data as well as one of the mainframe computers back at the Federacy capital.

Her eyes measured Magda like a pair of locking calipers. "Yes, I know of travelers' tales. What I do not understand is where in the world they might have reached you. By the goods you carry, your people grasp the mechanic arts more deeply than my own, however hard we strive to learn. Yet we have found no land where that is so. Why have you not made yourselves known long before this?"

She no longer conceived of the Terrans as fellow gods, Magda noted; familiarity had bred contempt, at least that much. "We are a quiet, peace-loving people, goddess. We have little interest in other lands."

"Then why are you here?" Sabium's pounce was quick and deadly as a hunting cat's. "I think you have told me a lie. With the skills and devices you have"—the goddess was searching for the word "technology," which her language lacked—"you could not help gaining control over your neighbors without them, no matter how little you wanted to. I have listened to too many kings and princes proclaim how quiet and peace-loving they are, most of them just before they attacked me. No, those who have power will use it, and I do not see how you and yours could have gained your power anywhere in this world without brushing against my own folk more than you ever have."

Silence followed the goddess's words. Now neither Magda nor Stavros risked even a glance at the other; whatever they did or said could prove too disastrously wrong. For Sabium was right, of course: where technology existed, it would be used, and Bilbeis IV had no room for a technology—about which the goddess had only the slightest hints—to grow without impinging on her own state.

Magda wondered what that left. It left the existence of the Federacy, and precious little else she could see. She hoped Sabium's vision was not wide enough for her to make the same connection. It had not been when the *Jêng Ho* had been here.

No sooner had that thought passed through Magda's mind than the goddess said, "How much simpler to believe all you oddly colored people spring from another world. Then we would have no report of you save when you wish it, and then you might own all sorts of strange arts without anyone around you learning of them." Her tone was musing, but Magda was not taken in by that. Sabium's centuries had left her better than a polygraph at gauging reactions to what she said.

This time, Stavros's thoughts ran along a slightly different track. As far as he could tell, the game was up when Sabium used the word "simpler." The goddess might not know Occam's razor by that name, but she had to use it.

Neither Terran, then, for whatever reasons, felt much past a sense of inevitability on hearing Sabium's sudden sharp intake of breath. "And I had thought myself but making an idle jest," she whispered. "You will tell me at once how you accomplish this marvel. Is it a magic spell, or is there after all some means of flying my folk are as yet too ignorant to have come across?"

"Do not belittle your own people, goddess," Stavros said. "They have learned very much very quickly." He conceded otherworldly status but hoped his praise of Sabium's subjects would keep her from noticing he had not responded to her main question.

He should have known better. For the first time, he heard menace and chilly warning in her voice. "I am not a child, to be evaded by such small, silly ploys. Answer or learn of my displeasure." She sounded very much a goddess then, dreadful and remote. Stavros shivered. So did Magda, but she asked, "Are you sure that is truly your wish, Sabium?"

Again came that sudden indrawn breath, but on a rising note this time. Magda saw with relief that she had reached the person behind the divine facade. Only the Terrans—and Sabium herself—now recalled that name. Her subjects had forgotten it an age ago; to them, she was but the eternal goddess.

"I had thought it so," she replied slowly. "I take it you claim I am mistaken."

"Only that you may be." Magda fought for steadiness. "I would but remind you that what is given is often valued less than what is earned. Or have you not found it so?"

Sabium, who rarely hesitated, took a long time before saying, "You used the same argument when you were last here, or led me to find it myself. Perhaps it is so. I will think on it, then, before I demand your reply, and will also question others of your party." She nodded, as much to herself as to her guests. "Yes, that is what I shall do. Return now to the quarters my priests have assigned you."

By this time, much to Nina Pertusi's delight, the Terrans were out of the central hall and in individual cubicles. Magda's and Stavros's had that convenient invention so many races stumble upon, the connecting door. He threw himself on the bed in her chamber, while she, too restless to sit still, paced back and forth. "Wonderful!" she cried, throwing her hands in the air. "Not only is she immortal, she's figured out the bloody Federacy, too. Next thing you know, she'll be running for the Assembly."

"I'd vote for her," Stavros said at once. "Wouldn't you?"

"In a minute," Magda agreed. "She'd do wonders for us.

But picture the scene when the chaplain gives the invocation and she stands up and says, 'Thank you.'"

Stavros tried to, then gave up and laughed. After a while, he said, "It would never do. When was the last time you heard plain good sense in the Assembly?"

"The day they decided to go after Paulina Koch," Magda said, her voice suddenly savage.

But Stavros tossed his head in Greek disagreement. "They even botched that, or we wouldn't be here—they'd have accepted your last report and strung your dear Chairman up by the thumbs. Instead they sent out the *Hanno*, and this trip has done more to interfere with the development of Bilbeis IV than anything since the *Leeuwenhoek*. Before this, Sabium had no idea why she was the way she was or about anything off Bilbeis IV. Now she does, and—"

"—by the time some of the people we have with us are done jabbering at her, she'll know everything short of how to design a stardrive motor," Magda finished for him. She took off her sandals and hurled them against a wall. A guard knocked on the outer door and asked if everything was all right. Sighing, Magda reassured him. She turned back to Stavros. "I really feel like smashing this whole place up, but they'd probably break in the door and stop me. That wouldn't look good."

"No." Stavros rolled over onto his back. "Why don't you come here instead? With this leather strap arrangement underneath, the beds don't creak." He held out his arms.

"Well, why not?" Magda pulled her robe off over her head. "It's one way to work off my nerves." Hardly a romantic commitment, Stavros thought, but better than nothing. He had long since concluded he was not going to hear many words of romantic commitment from Magda. One day, back in the Federacy, with no one hot on his trail, he would worry about that. Not now.

Afterward, Magda leaned over and nipped him on the shoulder. He yelped. "What was that for?"

Her expression lay somewhere between mischief and malice. "I was just wondering if you still fantasized about having Sabium, now that you've met her."

He thought about it. After a moment, he tossed his head again. "Thank you, Magda, no. I only imagined I knew what intimidation was till I met her. I don't think I could manage it, even on divine command."

She snorted, a sound he had learned went with suppressed laughter. He poked her in the ribs. "'If it weren't for the honor of the thing, I'd rather walk,'" she quoted. He poked her again. He was getting tired of ancient literature.

"Good evening, sir. It was kind of you to invite me here again tonight. No, thank you, I don't care for anything to drink or smoke, but do by all means please yourself." Paulina Koch waited while the prime minister fixed himself a gin and tonic. Not even now, she knew, could she afford any relaxation from full alertness.

Amadeo Croce sipped, then set the drink down. "I appreciate your joining me on such short notice, madam Chairman. Really, I should have invited you to Government Mansion more often."

"In my years at the Survey Service, I've been here many times, sir." When Croce only nodded and did not respond to the veiled barb, the Chairman felt her confidence grow. The prime minister was as much weathervane as executive; he shifted with the winds of power. By his manner, Paulina Koch had gained strength since their last meeting. But she was too old a hand to ask how the investigation of the Survey Service fared. Instead she made small talk and waited; let Croce lose face by having to bring it up first.

At last he did. "I am glad to see that no evidence has been unearthed to connect you with the unfortunate turn of affairs we have witnessed in regard to Bilbeis IV."

Not "that you are innocent," she noted, admiring the careful phrasing. The prime minister owned more subtlety than she'd thought. "I'm glad too, sir, and I know the reason no such evidence has been unearthed is that it never existed. Undoubtedly the entire contretemps will in the end be discovered to have originated from some clerk's inadvertent deletion of the report on Bilbeis IV before proper corrective actions could be implemented."

"So it would seem," the prime minister said. It did not sound like agreement. It sounded more like, "Well, we haven't been able to pin this one on you; too bad." Considering the way things could have gone, that would do nicely.

* * *

"A remarkable woman, Sabium, truly a remarkable woman," Justin Olmstead declared, his rich baritone rising slightly to show just how impressed he was. More than ever, Magda chalked him up as a pompous ass. Neither she nor any of the other Terrans sitting around the table, though, could readily disagree with him.

The priestly guards in the big audience chamber looked bored. The group from the *Hanno* preferred Federacy Basic to the local language. Magda was relieved Sabium still let the Terrans gather together. Even if she no longer thought them divine, she still had to keep some lingering respect. It was, Magda suspected as she half listened to Olmstead pointlessly rambling along, more than they deserved.

She abruptly sat bolt upright, and she was not alone—several Survey Service people who had been enduring Olmstead's drone also seemed to wake up at the same instant. Her bellowed, "You did *what*?" was, however, the loudest of the chorus.

"I told her something of the working of the Federacy's parliamentary system when she asked," the other anthropologist replied, taken aback at the uproar he had caused. "She asked how we chose our kings, and when I told her we had none, she was interested in what we used instead. She grasped the principle very quickly."

"I'll bet she did." Magda spoke in loud, clear tones for the record being continuously taped on the *Hanno*. "I charge Justin Olmstead, a Noninterference Foundation appointee, with interfering in the cultural development of Bilbeis IV." When she turned back to Olmstead, she was snarling again. "You blundering booby, why didn't you teach her nuclear physics, too, as long as you were about it?"

"I'll thank you to keep a civil tongue in your head," he said, scowling at her. "And what is this nonsensical talk of interference? I merely answered a few of her questions, in quite abstract terms."

"Yes—questions about things she'd never thought of before, and wouldn't have, without you. Service personnel get warned about that somewhere around the second day of training. And abstract ideas—say, like religions"—she smiled nastily as she rubbed his nose in what was especially obvious on Bilbeis IV—"can change societies just as much as technology."

"Oh, but Magda, he's with the Noninterference Foundation, as you said, so how could his motives be anything but good and pure?"

She stared at Pierre Bochy in surprised admiration. The stateliness with which he delivered the sarcasm only made it more effective. She had not thought he had it in him.

"Fortunately," Stavros put in, "Sabium has better sense than Justin here and won't necessarily rush out to try everything he blabs on about."

It always came back to that in the end, Magda thought. Because Sabium had good sense, things ran well on Bilbeis IV. As long as she was here, things would . . . and she looked likely to be here about forever. After so many centuries, Bilbeis IV was unimaginable without her.

The longer Roupen Hovannis listened to the scientific crew sing paeans to Sabium, the longer his face grew. Paulina Koch would not be grateful when the *Hanno* came back and filed a report that made the Survey Service look even worse than the *Jêng Ho*'s did. And when Paulina Koch felt ungrateful, bad things had a way of happening. Having caused a good many of them, Hovannis did not relish the prospect of being on the receiving end.

He wondered what the Chairman would do were she there now. Of one thing he was certain: sitting quietly in the *Hanno*, kilometers away from the action, was not her style. But once she got to Mawsil, what then?

However tempting the notion was, Hovannis decided he could not take out the whole scientific contingent. The affair had already seen too many such tragic but convenient accidents. One more would draw too much notice. Too bad, he thought. Even the supposedly pliable Survey Service group was out of control. Dealing with a reasonably authentic goddess was more than they had been prepared to handle.

He wondered if he could arrange things through that chamberlain of Sabium's. That local—what was his name? Bagadat, that was it—plainly feared the Terrans for threatening whatever influence he had gained on his ruler. Reluctantly, Hovannis abandoned the idea. Sabium could read her people the way he read a printout. Knowing that, Bagadat would never even try to set up the job.

That moved Hovannis's thinking one step further down the line. What would Bilbeis IV look like, he wondered, without Sabium? She had lived an enormously long time; not many people back in the Federacy, his gut feeling told him, would be upset or, more to the point, suspicious if she happened to pass away. Down deep, people who hadn't seen her in action could not believe she was what she was.

And if she died, how would the locals take it? Only one image occurred to him: they would act like ants after somebody kicked in their hill. In that chaos, all sorts of interesting and profitable opportunities might arise. At the very least, Bilbeis IV would stop looking so outrageously abnormal.

What had Pierre Bochy said? Hovannis had it on tape somewhere—something to the effect that lots of peoples worshiped immortal goddesses. Only Bilbeis IV really had one, though, and if she suddenly became as legendary as all the rest of them—

That would fix a lot of problems, Hovannis thought. Paulina Koch couldn't have come up with a neater solution. He took out his modified stunner and tucked it into a pocket of his coveralls.

He drew a few odd looks when he checked out a flier in Bilbeis IV disguise but Federacy clothing. The only people who would have asked serious questions, though, were already in detention in Mawsil. None of the technicians and engineers did more than scratch his head when Hovannis skimmed silently off into the night.

Stavros rolled the wooden die, thumped his thigh with his fist as he saw a four turn up, and took Magda's last man. She said something rude. "That's fifty-five you owe me now." He grinned.

She stared at him. "The hell you say. I was up fifty, not down—you only owe me forty-five now." Putting five a pop on one of the local board games made it more interesting. They'd been playing since Magda had begged a set from a priest not long after they had taken enforced residence at the temple. They'd also, evidently, kept their running totals running in opposite directions.

"Come on, Magda," Stavros protested. "Remember that hot streak I had a couple of nights ago?"

"Sure I do," she retorted. "Without it, you couldn't have afforded to get back to the Federacy. Weren't you bitching that I was going to end up owning your grandmother?"

"You'd be welcome to her; then you could put up with listening to how nothing that's happened to her in the last eighty-odd years has been her fault." Stavros set his jaw. "But you have to win her fair and square. I'm not going to let you cheat me out of her."

Magda started to laugh, then stopped. "Damn it, I'm not cheating." As absurd arguments have a way of doing, this one was turning serious. She took a deep breath. "You really think you're up on me?"

"Yes, I do. In fact, I'll put another fifty on it."

"You're on." Glaring at him, close to being really angry now, she kneaded the transceiver behind her right ear. "I'll show you," she muttered.

"What are you doing?"

"Calling the ship. You get in on this, too, so you can't say I'm diddling with the count. We'll listen to the tapes of our game sessions and figure out who owes whom what."

"That will take hours," he protested.

"Do you have any urgent appointments?" she asked, and he had to chuckle as he denied it. "All right, then." She waited and swore. "God, are they all asleep over there? Where is everybody?"

At that moment, she and Stavros heard a voice in their heads. "Richards here." Magda told the first officer what they wanted. "Can't do it," he said, "not right away, anyhow. Captain Hovannis is out of the ship."

"So?" Magda's voice was dangerously quiet.

"So no traffic from the ship to you people without his authorization. Standing orders. Sorry." He did not sound sorry. He sounded bored. Magda had not had much to do with him aboard the *Hanno*, but did not think he worried about standing orders, except with regard to how he was going to carry them out. Usually that was a good trait in a first officer. Now it was only frustrating.

"Get him on the comm circuit," Magda said.

"No, wait," Stavros broke in. "Where is he? What's he doing?"

"I don't know," Richards said. Plainly, he had never thought to wonder.

"We're just fooling around here," Magda said, "but what if somebody needed something really important? It's a silly order, Richards. Get me Hovannis and get him now; I'll tell him so myself."

"Very well." There was a pause before Richards came back on the circuit. For the first time, his voice held a trace of uncertainty. "He's not answering."

Magda rolled her eyes, a piece of dramatics unfortunately wasted because the first officer had no vision screen in front of him. "That's good. That's really good. In his absence you're in charge, right? Countermand that stupid piece of nonsense and give us what we need."

She was so intent on what was directly in front of her—and on proving herself right—that she did not worry about anything else. Stavros, more suspicious of Survey Service people generally and of Hovannis in particular, interrupted again. "You didn't answer me, Richards. Where is Hovannis? The flier must have a tracer on it, in case it crashes or something."

"It does," Richards admitted. He went off-circuit again. A couple of minutes later he said, "The machine is grounded a couple of kilometers outside Mawsil. Sorry I took so long; the tracer seems to be inactive, and I had to home on engine emissions. Otherwise, the flier is mechanically sound. Still no response from Captain Hovannis. Odd." From Richards, the word spoke volumes.

"What *is* he doing?" This time Stavros was talking to himself.

"Coming into Mawsil, sounds like," Magda said. "But why is he sneaking in instead of just coming ahead?" She suddenly cut Richards out of the conversation and gestured for Stavros to do the same. He cut off the first officer in midquestion, as puzzled as Richards was himself.

"What the—" Stavros began.

Magda's frantic gesture reduced him to silence again. She opened the outer door and nodded to the pair of guard-priests outside. "Would one of you please fetch me a slate and a lump of chalk?" The woman of the pair nodded back and ambled away; Sabium had made clear that her guests were to have any reasonable requests met. The little while the guard was gone seemed like forever to Magda.

She shut the door in the guards' bemused faces and scrawled a note to Stavros: *Hovannis here for no good reason. Why else sneak?*

"You're right! You have to be. He—"

Stavros shut up again; Magda was scribbling, *Richards can still listen—everything gets recorded. Is he safe?*

"I don't think it matters," Stavros said. "If Hovannis is coming here for reasons of his own, this will all be decided before Richards can raise him. And if what he's doing is against the rules, he won't call back to the *Hanno* to advertise it. Am I right?"

Magda hesitated, then conceded. "Seems reasonable."

"All right, then. The next thing we have to do is think, and think hard. Otherwise we'll go rushing off and maybe give him the opening he needs. My first guess would be that he's after us, or maybe after the whole group here, now that the rest of them know about Sabium, too. It would fit everything the murdering bastards who run the Service have done so far: Fogelman, and Andrea, and the *Clark County*, and your apartment complex, too."

Magda started to jump up, then stopped. "You're right and you're wrong at the same time. What does the Survey Service need most from Bilbeis IV?"

"A clean bill of health, and they're not likely to get one."

"Too bloody right they're not. But they won't get one from a dead crew of scientists, either. That would probably be one too many coincidences for anyone to swallow, don't you think? The Service can't afford more bad publicity; for once, they have an interest in keeping us healthy."

It was Stavros's turn to consider. "Well, maybe so," he said grudgingly. "All right, then, maybe Hovannis isn't coming here to slaughter us in our beds. He's not on his way to give us a great big kiss, either. He wouldn't have to skulk in to do that. What does that leave?"

"Nothing." Magda did not like the answer. Roupen Hovannis was not coming into Mawsil—or was inside by now, she thought uneasily—for any good purpose; Stavros was dead right there. But she was still sure Hovannis would not, could not, move on them. A decimated *Hanno* returning to

Topanga would look even worse than a damning report. Magda balled her hands into fists. She felt as if her mind were running in a treadmill, a treadmill with no way off.

Then she saw there was one, after all. Stavros must have reached her conclusion at the very moment she did, for they both spoke the same word at the same time: "Sabium!"

They ran for the door together.

XII

Hovannis was sweating and swearing as he neared the city walls of Mawsi. He was also filthy; he had taken a couple of nasty falls walking in the darkness through fields and in a dirt roadway full of holes.

Though he did not realize it, he was lucky the town's gates were open. Most places locked themselves tight after nightfall. Had the eternal goddess not spent so much time in Mawsil, it would have done the same. But pilgrim traffic was beginning to shift away from the Holy City, and Mawsil had opened itself to accommodate the sudden—and profitable—influx.

All the same, the guard yawning in his sentry box cast a dubious eye on Hovannis as he trudged toward the town. "Why aren't you carrying a torch to light your way, fellow?" he called.

The true answer was that Hovannis had not thought of it; he had never had to worry about such things before. "It went out a ways back," he said lamely, adding, "When I fell in the last pothole."

The guard laughed. "A few potholes before that, by the look of you. What are you coming to Mawsil for?"

Despite Hovannis's bedraggled state, the question was strictly pro forma. The guard heard the same answer hundreds of times a day: "To see the goddess, of course." Had Hovannis taken a moment to consider, he would have realized that. But the topmost thing in his mind was that his mission had to stay secret. Not only that, he was offended that this native, this savage, dared question him. Thus his answer came out as a reflex snap: "None of your damned business!"

"No, eh?" The guard was suddenly alert. He hefted his spear. "Come along with me, then. We'll make it my captain's business instead. You keep your distance there, too," he warned as Hovannis took a couple of steps toward him. "By the goddess, I'll stick you if you come any closer."

"I don't need to come any closer." Hovannis twisted the doctored stunner on his belt so it pointed at the local and squeezed the firing stud. He hoped he was close enough for the weapon to work. He was. The guard toppled bonelessly. Hovannis eased him to the ground so his mail shirt would not clatter, checked to make sure he was not breathing, and then, feeling a bit like a primitive warrior himself, sauntered into Mawsil.

He soon decided the best thing anyone could do with the place was bomb it and start over. It stank of sewage and smoke and unwashed people. Hovannis heard scuttlings in the darkness around him. Some were vermin; others, he was sure, were vermin that walked on two legs. He wished his stunner had more range.

The people he could see disturbed him almost as much as the ones he could not. Disease and injury did not leave their mark so openly on civilized worlds. He had never seen a woman with an empty eye socket before; now he spied two in the space of a couple of blocks. Till now, he had never thought himself fastidious. He was finding his standards for comparison had been deficient.

Relief flowed through him as he spotted the mud-brick building—ugly pile, he thought—where Sabium was staying. He gave the stunner an affectionate slap. The sooner this job was done, the sooner he was back aboard the *Hanno*, the happier he would be.

"Harm me? Why should he wish to harm me?" Sabium stared at the two—whatever they were—as if they had begun to speak in a foreign language she did not quite understand. She wished they did not wear the seeming of her own people; their true, alien colors would have helped remind her how strange their thoughts were.

"It has to do with the politics of our, uh, homeland," replied the woman called Magda. The goddess sensed she was telling the truth. A wave of sadness swept over Sabium. No matter what she had thought, no matter what she still wished, these were truly no gods after all. Yet their kind had made her immortal. She would have to think long and hard on what that meant.

No time now. The young man with Magda—"Stafros" was the best Sabium could do with his name—said, "This man means more than harm, goddess; I think he will kill you if he can."

Sabium's servants gasped at the blasphemy. The goddess saw that, like his companion, this "Stafros" was speaking the truth as he saw it. As he saw it—there was the rub. She could also tell he hated and feared this "Hofannis." Maybe even he did not know how much that influenced his perceptions, and if he did not, how could she?

A priest came into the chamber and bowed before her. "Goddess, I pray your forgiveness for disturbing you," the woman said, "but outside the temple is one who would have speech with you."

"Yes, I know," Sabium replied calmly.

The priest accepted that with barely a blink; the goddess was the goddess and had her ways. The priest resumed, "A street vagabond, or even a magnate, we should of course have turned away to ask for a regularly scheduled audience, but this man wears the garb described in your Rituals of Search: the trousers and tunic all in one, and all over pockets. He is colored as we are, but—" She eyed the two strangers with Sabium.

"Yes, that matters less than formerly," the goddess agreed. She took a deep breath. "I will see him. Prepare the audience chamber in all ways."

She had to raise her voice to finish. Magda and "Stafros" were trying to interrupt with shouted objections. Her servants stared in open-mouthed horror; no one ever interrupted the goddess. None of her subjects would even have thought to. The strangers might not be divine, but they were very strange. Sabium had thought that before, often enough.

Now it was a nuisance. "Silence," she proclaimed, and was gratified to find that the tone of command worked on the strangers, though more slowly than on her own people.

The priest had already gone to do her bidding. She turned to Bagadat, faithful, fearful Bagadat. "Have these two escorted into the chamber after me. Make sure the escorts are large and powerful. I will not tolerate interference from them."

For some reason, that touched off hysterical laughter in the woman called Magda. Neither she nor Stavros resisted the soldier-priests who took their arms. Bagadat paced along beside them, trying to look strong and stern and not succeeding very well.

Sabium set her hands on the arms of the throne in the audience chamber. They did not feel quite right; she realized they were not worn to conform to her flesh through centuries of use. Neither, sadly, was the seat, and a goddess, she knew instinctively, must not squirm. She sighed instead.

"Fetch in the stranger," she said.

"Is she crazy? Does she want to die? Does she think we're kidding her?" Stavros said. He had lost track of how often he'd repeated that on the way to the audience chamber and now here inside it as they waited for Hovannis to arrive. His guards must have thought it some kind of prayer.

Magda had her own litany. "Goddam denim coveralls," she muttered over and over, which made little sense even to Stavros. But the Service's field costume had been standard so long that Sabium had seen it on the crew of the *Leeuwenhoek* . . . and she, above all others, had a special reason to remember it.

Set against that, comfort and practicality did not, for once, count for much. They should never have had the denims aboard the *Hanno*. Fine time to think of that now, she reflected bitterly, as the priests hustled her into the audience chamber.

Flanked by their keepers, she and Stavros were made to stand to the left of Sabium's throne. "Neither by word nor deed shall they meddle in the judgment of this man, for it is mine alone," the goddess warned their captors. She turned to the Terrans. "Know you shall answer to me if your accusations prove false."

A tide of despair washed over Magda. No matter how long Sabium had lived, she looked to be an innocent, after-all. A planetful of people loved her, and she could not conceive of anyone who did not.

"Goddam denim coveralls," Magda said again. It did not help, but nothing else did, either.

Following the local priest, Roupen Hovannis felt as though he floated upon a rising tide of confidence. Ever since he had knocked over that guard, everything had gone well. He'd more than half expected to be kept cooling his heels till morning. As things were, though, he'd likely be back in his own bed by then.

He gave his stunner another slap, liking the idea.

The native, who smelled overdue for a fumigation, threw wide a door. "The goddess awaits you," the fellow declared.

Hovannis strode in. His eyes darted around the room, as they did when he entered any unfamiliar place. He spared not even an instant for the play of light and darkness on the filigreework walls; he wanted to see where the people were, the better to work out his upcoming getaway.

He spotted Stavros and Magda in the crowd to the left of the raised chair near the far wall. They did not make him hesitate. Once Sabium unexpectedly expired, all the locals would rush to her. Then the traitor and her lover could meet misfortune, too. The stunner was silent. A couple of people falling down would attract no attention. If they didn't get up afterward, too bad—surely they had been trampled in the confusion.

Checking the place out took only moments. Then, at last, Hovannis looked toward Sabium. He was glad he had not glanced her way before, by accident; he surely would have revealed himself had he met her eyes unprepared. He found out what other Terrans had before: films just did not convey the awe she inspired. Perhaps part of it lay in the way she sat, as if she had all the time in the world. Why not? he thought— she did. Her gaze was the most arresting he had ever known, and he could never have told anyone why. But it was.

Still, he did not falter. He had kept secrets from Paulina Koch, and done it so well that she had never suspected. He had, in fact, kept secrets all his life; that was what an External Affairs Director, or even a security chief, got paid for. And did being an old primitive—or even an old, old primitive— make Sabium any less a primitive, or anything more than a primitive?

That he posed the question at all meant the answer was yes. He did not let it bother him. He had control over himself again. He did not think anyone else would notice he had lost it.

"What would you of me?" Sabium asked.

"Eternal goddess, I thank you for consenting to see me in such irregular fashion and at such an irregular time." He bowed and took a step forward. "I have traveled a great distance because of your glory." He bowed again, amused at actually telling the truth. He came another couple of steps closer to the throne. Soon, now. . .

Sabium was rarely puzzled, but these strangers had a gift for perplexing her. This one, by wearing clothes of his people's style rather than hers, set off further confusion in her, casting her memory back a millennium and a half to the pair whose cure for her illness had left her immortal.

Resolutely, she pushed that secondary confusion aside, for it only distracted her from the greater ambiguity surrounding this stranger: she could not read him. That was not because of his race; Magda and "Stafros" and the rest of them were no harder to gauge than her own people. But this one, this "Hofannis," drank in her examining glance and gave back nothing.

She sensed no violence in him. At first that reassured her and made her doubt the warnings the other two had given her. But the fellow did not seem particularly well-disposed to her, either. He was just—there. Her doubts returned.

"Why did you not come here at the same time as the rest of your countrymen?" she asked him.

"I had duties I could not set aside," he replied, slowly walking forward. "Still, knowing you are unique, I hurried through them so I could see you myself before we departed your land—with your gracious permission, of course."

Was he close enough now? Yes, probably, Hovannis thought. He took one more step, just to be sure. His hand drifted toward his stunner. No need to rush things now and spook Sabium. She would not know what a stunner was—not for long, anyway.

"What's he going to do, knock her out?" Magda whispered; she saw where Hovannis's hand was going. "He really has lost it—"

"It makes no sense," Stavros agreed, "unless that stunner isn't just a—" He stopped, appalled at where his mouth, without much intervention from conscious thought, had led him. He and Magda both opened their mouths to shout.

* * *

At last, as the stranger's hand approached the weapon that hung on his belt, Sabium read the tension in him and knew what it had to mean. She made a tiny gesture of her own.

The arrow that pierced the palm of Hovannis's right hand came as such a complete surprise that for a moment he only stared at it foolishly, as if wondering how it had come to lodge there. Then the pain reached him, and with it the realization he had been outguessed after all.

Another arrow struck him, this one in the right shoulder. The impact drove him back, away from Sabium. When he tried to use the arm, he found it was dead.

He snarled and tried to reach across his body with his left arm. But he was a long way from ambidextrous, and now the stunner's grip went away from his hand instead of fitting smoothly into it. That first hasty grab failed to pull the weapon free. He did not get another chance. The plump local who stood to one side of Sabium's throne jumped on him, hurling him to the floor. The native cursed and pummeled him.

The fellow was no warrior; with two good arms, Hovannis would have ruined him in seconds. Even wounded as he was, he took most of the local's punches on the top of his head and in other places that did him little damage. He drove a knee into his foe's soft middle, doubling him up with a grunt of pain. At last his hand closed on the stunner. He jerked it free and gave the local a full charge. The weight on top of him went limp.

Too late! Other natives were rushing up. Something—a foot or a club, Hovannis never knew which—exploded against the side of his head. The world spun into darkness.

When Magda and Stavros would have run forward to help bring down Hovannis, their guards restrained them, as if not trusting them not to take his side. "Let me go, you fools!" Magda shouted. She tried to break free. She failed, for Sabium's priests knew as many fighting tricks as she did.

Stavros, who did not, struggled less. Instead of writhing, then, he was watching as one of the priests bent by the fallen Hovannis to pick up his stunner. "Beware!" Stavros cried, urgently enough to pierce the din and chaos of the audience chamber and make the priest look his way. "Touch it wrongly and it may spit death."

"I think not," the priest said with a condescending smile. "We have made some study of these strange weapons you people carry. How you make them we have not learned, but we know they only cause sleep; they cannot slay."

"You stupid, trusting bastard," Magda yelled at him. She was still trying to get loose, but only by fits and starts. She was beginning to be convinced she couldn't.

Sabium spoke; at the sound of her voice, everyone else in the chamber fell silent. "See to poor Bagadat there beside that villain," she said. "If he but slumbers, you will be proved right. If he is dead, you shall add your thanks to mine, for then we shall both stand indebted to these strangers' warnings."

A few moments later, the priest said in a small voice, "He is dead, goddess." He put the stunner down very carefully, then bowed low to Stavros. "As the goddess says, I am in your debt."

That seemed to persuade the locals still holding Magda and Stavros that they could safely release them. "Goddess, where did the arrows come from?" Magda asked, her disposition improving quickly once she was free. "I thought you were doomed."

Sabium gestured at the filigree panels behind her throne. "Show yourselves," she commanded. Eyes appeared in several openings; arrows poked through others. "I am not unprotected," the goddess said. "I doubt if age or sickness may claim me, but I have never been so certain in the case of arms. The two of you having shown your concern, I took no chances."

Hovannis stirred and groaned, which served to recall the locals' attention to him. "He sought to kill the eternal goddess," one of them said, her eyes wide with horror at the thought. "For that he deserves death." A priest carrying a spear advanced on the downed Terran with deadly purpose.

"No," Sabium said. The priest halted, her spear poised above Hovannis. She obeyed her deity, but rebellion smoldered in her eyes. Then Sabium spoke again, and now her voice was that of the goddess passing sentence. "He wantonly slew my faithful majordomo Bagadat, who tried but to protect me. For *that* slaying, he deserves death."

The priest drove the spear home.

Magda almost cried out to protest the abrupt, unappealable sentence. Her mind was filled with thoughts of trials, of how Hovannis should be taken back to the Federacy to face justice there. But she could not speak of those things to Sabium, not without doing violence to the rule of noninterference. That rule had seen enough violence on Bilbeis IV. And so she hesitated for the bare instant between condemnation and execution, and then it was too late.

She did not feel very guilty. Hovannis's crime—and his attempted crime—were too blatant for that. Murder was foul enough in any case, but Sabium's death would have been a cataclysm to rock all of Bilbeis IV. And for what? For politics, she thought distastefully.

Stavros never had any impulse to cry out. As the spear went into Hovannis's vitals, he thought the External Affairs Director was getting exactly what he deserved. Then he watched, and listened to, and smelled, the man die. It took a long time and was worse than anything he had imagined. He had to look away. Hovannis's feet drummed and drummed in the ever-widening pool of blood that poured from his belly.

Finally he lay still. Only then did Sabium—who, unlike Stavros, watched to completion what she had ordained—turn her notice back to the two living Terrans in the audience chamber. She said, "I owe you a great debt for warning me this"—she nodded at the corpse—"was a miscreant. Had you not done so, I might have failed to take the precautions that saved me. Because you are who and what you are, I do not know with what gifts I might please you most. Therefore, I say to you, choose your own reward. If I may give it to you, I shall."

Magda and Stavros looked at each other. His mouth soundlessly shaped a word. She nodded; the same thought had been in her own mind. "Goddess," she said, "nothing would please us more than your having our belongings returned to us and our countrymen and letting us go home."

"It shall be done, of course," Sabium replied at once. "But is that all? Ask more of me than such a small thing."

"Goddess," Stavros said quietly, "freedom is never a small thing."

Sabium paused to consider that. "I think you may be right," she said at last.

*   *   *

Topanga's heat and sunshine reminded Magda of the vicious weather in the Margush valley but were less oppressive somehow: probably, she thought, because she could go into the cool indoors whenever she wanted. On Bilbeis IV, buildings were as hot inside as out and sometimes—especially at night—hotter.

Now she was out in the sun and reveling in it. She and Stavros stood outside the Survey Service field office while a swarm of holo cameras hummed and whirred around them. The data card she carried weighed no more than any other, but seemed heavier.

Someone called, "What do you think of what happened on Bilbeis IV?"

She'd answered that question a hundred times in the couple of days since the *Hanno* had come home. She had it down to half a dozen words now: "We were right the first time."

Stavros was willing to amplify that; media people were arriving on Topanga in a steady stream, and this poor woman might not have had a chance to ask anything before. "Even the scientists handpicked by the Survey Service acknowledge that serious interference, in technology and especially in religion and culture, did take place on Bilbeis IV," he said.

"Hard for them to get around it, when their own captain tried to get rid of the main evidence for that interference with a stunner he'd cooked up somehow into a deadly weapon," Magda agreed.

Peter O'Brien swung open the door to the office. "Here we are, back where it all began," the head of the local branch of the Noninterference Foundation said expansively. "Here the first true report on Bilbeis IV was delivered, and here we deliver the truth again. This time it will not be suppressed."

Magda wished he would shut up; for that matter, she wished he were not there at all. But the Foundation lost no chance to promote itself, and without it, she had to admit, the Service probably never would have felt enough pressure to send out the *Hanno*. In recognition of that, she decided not to step on O'Brien's foot as she and Stavros walked past him.

With as much good grace as she could muster, she endured more delay while the reporters jockeyed for position inside the small Survey Service office. She looked around. "Where's Pandit?" she demanded. "He's the clerk who took my report every time I sent it in to Central—only right he should do it again."

The coordinator in charge of the office looked embarrassed. The reporters looked delighted—here was something unrehearsed, while these formal events usually were stylized as *Noh* plays. The coordinator cleared her throat. "Ah," she got out, "intermediate clerk Pandit is in custody, charged with failing to properly transmit your report before. He was, it is alleged, a confederate of Roupen Hovannis."

"But that's absurd!" Magda said. "I saw him send it."

"Are you sure?" Stavros murmured. "Do you know what all the gadgetry back there does?"

She frowned. "It seemed simple enough."

The coordinator stepped forward and presented her better profile to the camera. "In any case, I will be pleased to handle the data transmission personally."

Reluctantly, Magda handed her the data card. She watched carefully as the coordinator fed the card into the machine and hit the TRANSMIT button. After a while, a light went from red to green. "The document has been acquired at Survey Service Central," the coordinator declared.

"She did the same damned thing Pandit did," Magda said mulishly.

"Have you an opening statement, Chairman Koch?" asked the reporter who was serving as moderator for the news conference.

"Yes, I do," Paulina Koch replied. A ripple of surprise ran through the Survey Service auditorium. Paulina Koch usually let reporters have at her as they would. Only a few veterans in the seats out there could remember the last time she'd broken that rule.

"Very well, then." The moderator stepped aside.

"I thank you, Mr. Mazyad." Paulina Koch took a deep breath and stepped up to the podium. This was it. If she got through this conference, she could ride out anything. If not . . . She built a wall around that thought. She would get through, because she had to.

She said, "To you, my friends"—if she was going to lie, might as well start early—"and through you to the people of the Federacy, I offer my apologies and pray your pardon. I, and through me you, have been betrayed. In all innocence, I told you that no deception was involved in the Survey Service's handling of the Bilbeis IV affair. It now appears I was in error.

"For reasons of their own, Roupen Hovannis and staff members of the External Affairs Division under his direction did attempt to destroy the report the survey ship *Jêng Ho* presented on Bilbeis IV. When their efforts began to come to light, they even engaged in acts of violence to hide their prior wrongdoing. Roupen Hovannis's death on Bilbeis IV itself came as a direct result of the last of those violent deeds.

"As Survey Service Chairman, I must of course take ultimate responsibility for the actions of all my subordinates. I stress, however, that I was unaware of Hovannis's machinations and was systematically lied to in my attempts to uncover the truth. The same applies to Dr. Cornelia Toger, whose investigative efforts were systematically hamstrung by Hovannis's henchmen."

Always a good idea to mix in a bit of truth, the Chairman thought. She went on. "Dr. Toger has offered me her resignation. I have not accepted it. She has done nothing wrong. Her next task, like mine, will be to restore effectiveness to the Survey Service and to restore public confidence in it. Now I will take questions."

"Have *you* offered to resign, Madam Chairman?" a woman called, springing up out of her seat in her eagerness to be recognized.

"No, Ms. Kluhan, I have not. I have confidence in my own innocence, and I feel I am still needed here. If Prime Minister Croce disagrees, I am sure he will make it known to me."

Actually, she was afraid Croce might have accepted a resignation. Requiring him to take the first step made things harder for him. No evidence focused on her. By now, she was sure she had done a good job of scrubbing the data banks.

"What are these mysterious 'reasons of their own,' Madam Chairman?" asked the next reporter at whom Paulina Koch pointed.

"Mr. Basualdo, I would not presume to act as speaker for the dead. Roupen Hovannis's motives, whatever they were, lie with him on Bilbeis IV. I would hope he acted out of a sense, however misguided, that he was serving the long-range best interests of the Survey Service. If so, he proved tragically in error. But let me say again, that is only my hope. We will never know."

That was all Paulina Koch had ever tried to do: serve the long-range best interests of the Survey Service. If she survived this, she might even have succeeded. She wondered for a moment how Sabium would have done, were their positions reversed. Then, brushing aside such a nonessential thought, she fielded another question: "Yes, Mr. Goldberg?"

"What about the eighteen missing days?"

The little man looked smug, thinking he had caught her out. Now she had an answer, though, and one that did not incriminate her. "I must assume, Mr. Goldberg, that when Van Shui Pong"—she prided herself on having the reporter's name ready to bring forth—"accessed the correct arrival date of the *Jêng Ho*, it called attention to the blunder Hovannis's henchmen had committed in not altering it prior to that point in time. The error was then rectified, but not before the discrepancy had been noted."

Goldberg sat down, deflated. Paulina Koch pointed. "Yes, Ms. Wakuzawa?"

"Damn her, she has all the answers," Magda said, watching the Chairman demolish another questioner.

Stavros made a disgusted noise deep in his throat. "Yes, but do you believe any of them?" When Magda did not answer at once, he looked at her sharply.

"I'd like to," she admitted at last. "I've been with the Service my whole professional life. I'd like to think we're clean at the top."

"What are the odds, though? How could anyone think that the things they've done somehow magically stopped one rung below Paulina Koch on the ladder, and that she never looked down to find out why there was a stink under her feet?"

"I don't suppose I do," Magda sighed. "I'd like to, that's all. And there are plenty of people who will, just because they can't see past their noses."

"Everything worked out so bloody well for her—"

"That's what you get for hanging around with me," Magda interrupted. "You're starting to talk the same way I do."

But Stavros refused to be sidetracked. "She's piling all the blame on Hovannis, and he's not around anymore to give her the lie. It couldn't have worked out better for her if she planned it herself."

"What did you think of the Survey Service Chairman's performance last night?" asked the woman whose desk at Hyperion Newsnet was next to Van Shui Pong's.

"Didn't watch it," he answered shortly. Since leaving —"fleeing," he told himself in harsher moments, was really the proper word—the investigation of the Bilbeis IV affair, he had not paid much attention to it. He wanted to think that sprang from simple prudence. More likely, it was guilt.

Shaking his head in annoyance, he started working his way through the morning mail. A lot of the data cards he got ended up erased so he could reuse them; what some people thought newsworthy never stopped amazing him. Today's run of the stuff that didn't come through regular channels seemed especially bad. Fortunately, telling when something was tripe usually took only a few seconds.

He blanked the card that was in his terminal, took it out, inserted the next one in the stack. A man's face looked out of the screen at him. The fellow seemed vaguely familiar. Whoever he was, he needed a shave.

Then Van's boredom and faint contempt fell away, for the image declared, "I am Roupen Hovannis, External Affairs Director, Survey Service. If you are viewing this, I will be dead. If I were alive, it would be none of your damned snooping business, I promise you that."

Hovannis's laugh was full of scorn. Van Shui Pong felt anger rise in him but made no move to kill the data card. Hovannis had hooked him, sure enough. His eyes narrowed at what he saw, then went wide.

The reports, the screaming headlines and lead stories, kept coming in from all around the Federacy. Paulina Koch declined any comment for as long as she could, and for a bit longer than that. Each morning, more camera crews appeared outside Survey Service Central. Each morning, she strode past them as if they did not exist and went in to do her job.

Roupen Hovannis had buried his bombshells to avenge himself on her if she played him false. She had thought he would and had rooted from the computer several "dead-man" routines designed to spill information on word of his demise. Either she had missed some after all, or Hovannis had given copies to people to throw in the mails. It did not matter much either way.

She even saw the irony of her predicament. The bombshells were going off without proper cause: surely Hovannis had not expected he would die at Sabium's hands instead of hers. That did not matter much anymore, either. What mattered was that everything was coming out, from the disposal of Isaac Fogelman to the destruction of the *Clark County* to the effort to change Magda Kodaly's credit records. And everything pointed straight back to her.

Still, she dared hope one day when she noticed a gap in the ranks of reporters in front of the Survey Service offices: were they getting tired of hounding her? Then she noticed the two men standing there, waiting for her to arrive. They wore the field-gray of the Rehabilitation Service. Not even reporters, the Chairman thought grimly, wanted to get close to rehab men.

She squared her shoulders. No point in hoping now. The only thing left was choosing how she went out. No point in whining either, not in public.

"May I make a statement?" she asked the taller man in gray.

She had the small satisfaction of seeing she had surprised him. She cherished it; she would get no more satisfaction for a very long time. After a moment, he politely dipped his head in assent. In public rehab men were always polite. He did not even tell her to keep it short.

She turned to face the cameras for the last time. "Citizens of the Federacy," she began, and almost stopped in despair. How could she get across what she had tried to accomplish by doing as she had done? Only the thought that she would never get another chance helped her go on.

"Citizens of the Federacy," she said again, this time more firmly, "for two decades I have had the privilege of serving you as Chairman of the Survey Service. Throughout that time, I have striven to make the Service function as effectively as possible in all areas of its operation. On the whole, I believe I have been successful in that undertaking.

"In administering so large an organization, I have been required to make large numbers of decisions and judgments. In making them, I have tried to follow the principle of seeking only what was best for the Survey Service. Inevitably, I fear, not all decisions and judgments I was called upon to make have proved correct. That appears to have been the case in the matter of Bilbeis IV.

"I regret any injuries that may have occurred as a result of my decisions concerning that matter. I would remind you, however, that those decisions and judgments were made in what I believed at the time to be the best interests of the Survey Service, and to protect it from those who would seek to curtail its activities where no good cause exists.

"I am to be Chairman no longer, but the Survey Service will remain, and will continue to perform its appointed tasks. I call on everyone, those who have supported me and those who did not, to put behind them the bitterness of the recent past and to support the organization I have been proud to lead for so long. That organization and its ideals must go forward, whatever becomes of me."

Her control held to the end. She had not been sure it would. She nodded to the rehab men. They moved in to take places on either side of her, two tall gray figures bracketing one short one, and led her away.

Stavros watched Paulina Koch disappear into the Rehabilitation Service groundcar. Then he ran the tape back to listen again to her parting statement. He shook his head wonderingly. "She's still talking her way around this whole thing. Some of her decisions weren't correct . . . injuries may have occurred. She ordered people dead. That's enough to create a little bitterness, wouldn't you say?"

"Yes," Magda said, but somehow the triumph she felt was muted. In stories, once the villains were gone, everyone proceeded to live happily ever after. Here and now, the trouble they had caused would go on being trouble. "The Purists are going to have just the kind of field day with the Service she started the stinking cover-up to prevent. The more she tried, the deeper she got."

"She should never have tried in the first place." Stavros thought for a moment. "Is 'hubris' a word in Basic, or just Greek?"

"Basic, too." On the screen, the rehab wagon purred away again. A commentator started making predictions about how the Survey Service would fare under the interim administration of Dr. Cornelia Toger. Magda switched him off. She could make her own predictions there. "The Service'll have a hell of a time. Toger's in way over her head. Maybe Sabium could straighten out this mess, but then, she'd have the time to do it."

"So she would." Stavros's eyes got a faraway look. "I wonder what Bilbeis IV will be like the next time the Survey Service checks it out."

"Now there's something to think about," Magda agreed, "but thinking won't take you far enough, I'm afraid. Sabium may still be around when the next survey team arrives, but you and I, my rather dear, won't be."

"Isn't that the truth!" Stavros chuckled. "'My rather dear,' eh? I rather like that." He gestured toward the screen. "Have you seen all you want of that?"

"Yes. We recorded it, so I can watch it again whenever I want."

"You have quite a taste for revenge, you know that? You'd make a good Greek; some of the feuds back in the mountains of New Thessaly got their start on Earth, or so the old men say."

"I like to be right, and when I am, I don't like anybody telling me I'm not. Speaking of which—" Magda went through the file of data cards and tapes she had brought off the *Hanno*. She ran one into a terminal, put on headphones, and started listening. Every so often, she made a tally mark.

"What are you doing?" Stavros asked. When she paid no attention, he pulled one earpiece away from her head and repeated the question.

She hit the PAUSE button. "What do you think? I'm going to find out who really owed fifty to whom. And if you owe me, by God, I'm going to collect!"

Sabium already had the desert scout's report nearly committed to memory, but she read it again all the same. A troop of scouts had gone north from Mawsil into the waste before the strangers departed the city. They shadowed them at the greatest possible distance, to learn what they could. Two did not return. The goddess had never learned to accept losses in her service easily. She made sure the scouts' families were provided for, but silver could not replace a man.

The rider whose words she was studying had not actually tried to stay close to the strangers at all. Instead, he'd almost killed his mount rushing far to the north, reasoning that the strangers, with their curious abilities, might be able to travel more quickly than they had shown. She made a note to reward him for his initiative.

He was soon proved right. They disappeared from their camp not long before dawn one night, with only briefly blotted stars to suggest something had swooped down from the air and carried them off. Most of the scouts came back then, baffled and afraid.

From a long way away, the one clever scout saw a flying sphere—"a ship, I would call it, not a creature," Sabium read, "for it had no wings—dash itself headlong into the side of a vertical bluff. But it did not tumble in ruins. Instead, it flew *into* the bluff, as if that were so much air."

Indeed, it might have been so; later, the scout saw people emerging from the rocks and then going back inside, with no sign of passageways or doors to explain how they did so. They did not spot him in turn; his mount was tethered behind an enormous boulder, while he himself moved only on all fours and wore the skin of a skulking desert predator across his back.

He waited the day away in the shade of a large bush. "Without it," he wrote matter-of-factly, "I would have died. But seeing that the strangers concealed the use of their powers under cover of darkness, I thought it best to wait for night to come."

His patience was rewarded, for about halfway through the first evening watch, the mesa he had been studying shimmered and vanished, to be replaced by a dark sphere many times vaster than the one the scout had seen before. Sabium tried to visualize the scene he described:

"By some art I cannot fathom, it rose silently into the air, as the smaller one had flown before. But it climbed straight up into the heavens rather than faring north or south, east or west. As it ascended, it appeared smaller and smaller, or so I judged by the stars it hid from sight. In the end I lost track of it; it must have grown too tiny to cover them anymore. You in your wisdom, goddess, may know its destination. As for me, I am but a simple soldier and would not presume to guess."

A disingenuous soldier, Sabium thought as she set down his report. She could only guess where the sky ship was going herself; the strangers who crewed it had been closed-mouthed, most of them. All her guesses, though, were full of marvels.

She wondered how long she would have to wait before the strangers came to call upon her land again. As long as the time between their first two visits? That would try even a goddess's patience.

She looked up to the roof, and in her mind's eye through it, to the dome of the sky above. Once more she tried to see a hugh sphere floating upward. She wondered how much her people would have to learn to build such a sphere for themselves.

She made herself a promise and spoke it aloud as if to seal it: "If they wait so long again, I shall go to visit them first."

She summoned her new majordomo and began to work to make the promise real.

ABOUT THE AUTHOR

HARRY TURTLEDOVE is that rarity, a lifelong southern Californian. He is married and has two young daughters. After flunking out of Caltech, he earned a degree in Byzantine history and has taught at UCLA and Cal State Fullerton. Academic jobs being few and precarious, however, his primary work since leaving school has been as a technical writer. He has had fantasy and science fiction published in *Isaac Asimov's*, *Amazing*, *Analog*, *Playboy*, and *Fantasy Book*. His hobbies include baseball, chess, and beer.